LAZAROS
ZIGOMANIS

MidnightSun

First published 2023 by MidnightSun Publishing Pty Ltd
PO Box 3647, Rundle Mall, SA 5000, Australia.
www.midnightsunpublishing.com

Cover design by Abby Stout
Internal design by Zena Shapter

Typeset in Palantino and Marydale.

Printed and bound in Australia by McPherson's Printing Group. The papers used by MidnightSun in the manufacture of this book are natural, recyclable products made from wood grown in well managed forests.

A catalogue record for this book is available from the National Library of Australia

MIX
Paper | Supporting responsible forestry
FSC® C001695

To the scared, confused kid in all of us crying out for understanding, crying out to be heard, and never knowing from where that solace will come.

AUTUMN

March–May 1989

1.

Mum's bawling comes in big, guffawing sobs. Dad's solemn – you couldn't tell what he's thinking; it might be about a horse race he's bet on. Steph, my older sister, is inscrutable, although she's like that a lot now. Uncles and aunts and cousins stand with heads bowed, some sobbing, others sniffling.

This is what Aunt Mena's life comes to. Her family will go home tonight, and things will be different. Her kids will never be able to go to her again. She'll never show up at our functions with that big, toothy smile and that laugh that trilled through every room.

She's gone, and all that's left is that emptiness wherever she used to be.

And the mourning.

And this funeral as a last goodbye.

Which prompts the question to jump into my head: *Who'll mourn for me?*

This isn't what a fifteen-year-old should be asking himself. My problems should be girls, school and keeping my parents happy. Not this. It doesn't even make sense. I have plenty of family. I have friends. Plenty of people would mourn me, wouldn't they? I tell myself they would but I can't shake the cold feeling that I might mean nothing, that I'm alone.

The priest is a stocky man with a big, square beard and little round spectacles. He finishes his benedictions, firing off rapid Greek – the same way he prattled on at the church service for an hour – that's indecipherable. We make the sign of the cross, then file in procession past the open grave.

As we pass it, we pick up a chunk of dirt and throw it in. I watch my clump hit the rosewood coffin and, for an instant, I see Aunt Mena lying in there, arms folded across her chest, eyes closed and now forever still. I think about myself in there and about my friends and family doing this for me.

The food comes out then, carried from the backs of station wagons – trays of flake, calamari, plates of chicken and bowls of salad, set up on picnic tables under the swaying willows that dot the cemetery. Eskies full of beer and soft drinks come next. The mood changes from funereal to picnic. Everybody mingles to talk about the nothings in life, except for my sister and me. We drift under one of the willows, like we're using the overhanging branches to shut ourselves away from everything.

Steph folds her arms across her chest. She's twenty-two, and while she might seem typically Greek – with her big, dark eyes, high cheekbones and dark hair drawn back – she does her best to hide it, or to at least try to deflect it into something exotic, like Italian.

'The only time we all get together nowadays are weddings and funerals,' she says.

'And birthdays,' I say.

'*Some* birthdays. That was the last time I saw Aunt Mena outside of the hospital – my twenty-first. She asked me when I was gonna get married.'

That's the eternal question when you're Greek. Life's about getting married and making a family.

'You never know when it's your time,' Steph says.

Aunt Mena had cancer – six months from diagnosis to her death. We saw her a couple of weeks ago in palliative care. She'd grown thin and the skin hung from her face. Although she was in pain, she'd come to accept she was dying. I don't get that. How do you just accept your life's over?

'You missing anything at school today?' Steph asks.

'Supposed to talk to the counsellor,' I say.

'The counsellor?'

This comes from my twenty-six-year-old cousin Jim, who's *bloated* over to us – bloated, not floated, because Jim's always been big and stocky, although hard work has turned it into muscle that could melt back into fat the moment he stops taking care of himself. His fiancée, Nicola, in a spotted black and white dress, hangs off his arm like a pair of fuzzy dice, while his teenage sister, Anthea, loiters behind him. Jim is the son of my Aunt Toula, Mum's younger sister. He's the family poster boy. He graduated high school with top marks, went to university to study medicine and is now interning at St Margaret's Hospital. Whenever Mum or Dad remind me, Steph, or both of us together, what the benchmarks in life are, Jim's trotted out. *Look at what Jim's doing.* But that's being Greek. You're always compared to somebody.

Well, somebody good, at least.

'You got problems?' Jim says, almost belligerently – not really at me, I think, but at the prospect that a counsellor should know your problems. More typical Greek. You never reveal problems to outsiders. You hide them so they don't cause embarrassment.

'It's about career's counselling,' I tell Jim.

'You're in what now? Year 11?'

'Year 10.'

Jim waves away Year 10 with a flick of his hand. Year 10's nothing. He has this big head, like a carved Halloween pumpkin that sits under a mop of curly black hair. He gets it from his dad. They should be in the line of heads on Easter Island.

'What're you going to do when you finish school?' he asks.

I shrug.

'You don't know?'

'I'm in Year 10.'

'Should have an idea.'

'He writes stories,' Steph says.

'Stories? What stories?'

'Just stories,' I say.

'What're they about?'

I shrug once more. This will be my blanket defence.

'You don't know?'

'Mostly, they're about this kid–'

'Kid? What kid?'

'This teenager, Jean Razor.'

'John Razor?'

'*Jean*.'

'It's a girl?'

'Jean is a boy's name.'

'So, he's French?'

'Yeah.'

'Why's he French?'

I think it's because *Star Trek: The Next Generation* started on TV not too long ago. The captain of the ship is Jean-Luc Picard. It sounded exotic and cool. But I can't explain that to Jim. Or that I like science fiction. He won't get any of it.

'The name sounded good,' I say.

'And what's he do?'

'He can travel through dimensions the–'

'Dimensions.' Jim waves it all away, annoyed, the way he might wave away a fly that keeps flying around in his face. '*Writing.* Where's that going to get you?'

'He's fifteen,' Steph says. 'Not everybody has it worked out so young.'

'I knew when I was fourteen.'

'Not everybody's as cluey as you, Jim.'

Jim tries to puzzle out if that's an insult or not – it *is*; Steph's telling him how full of himself he is. Steph doesn't care about this shit. *Posturing*, she calls it. And I can see that – a way to build yourself up through comparing. But Jim doesn't see it. He might be book-smart, but I don't think he's people-smart. He'll have terrible bedside manner. But he nods, deciding she's recognising how precocious he was.

'How's Furniture Warehouse going?' Nicola says. She flutters her long, curled eyelashes. There's a greasiness about her. I bet she's slimy to kiss, although kissing Jim would be like kissing a black hole. Even the way she asks the question is greasy, like it's meant to slide under Steph's defences.

'It's a job,' Steph says.

'A job,' Jim scoffs – Steph's story is legendary around our family circles. 'You got that fellowship prize in high school, that…what was it called?'

'The Boland Fellowship.'

'You graduated with better marks than *anybody–*'

Anybody includes Jim. But he's not going to point that out.

'–and then after two-and-a-half years at university, you dropped out,' Jim finishes. If he were a lawyer, he'd be preaching the defendant's guilt to the jury. 'And for what?'

'It wasn't for me.'

'Bet your parents went nuts,' Nicola says.

'They were okay,' Steph says.

They weren't. Everybody knows they weren't. Nicola's just point-scoring. Mum and Dad blew up. You'd have thought Steph had held up a bank. She should've. She would've gotten off easier. And a public defender in the process.

'I can't wait to get to university,' Anthea says.

Anthea's fortunate enough to miss the hereditary big head; she wears too much make-up and is always finding ways to be sultry – even now, in boots, tight black pants and sweater, and the sort of jacket that only buttons at the bottom and shows off that she's disproportionately big-boobed. She might've been dressing for a club, rather than to bury her aunt.

'I was thinking of studying law,' she says.

She won't. She's an idiot.

14

Jim grins, trying to inspire a familiarity between us that we've never had. 'You need to think about the future,' he tells me. He slides an arm around Nicola's waist and pulls her close. 'We should get going. But we'll see you at our wedding in December, huh?'

'Can't wait,' Steph says, with an eagerness you'd use for dental appointments.

Jim points at me as he leads Nicola and Anthea away. 'And I'm going to ask you again then – trust me!'

I force a smile and watch them pack into Jim's shiny new Ford.

2.

The only sound on the drive home comes from the tinny speakers of Dad's radio. Usually, he'd have it on the horse racing or the Greek station, but Steph changed it on the drive up. Dad lowers the volume. Bon Jovi's 'Born to Be My Baby' fades out and Melissa Etheridges's 'Like the Way I Do' starts.

I try to puzzle out my future – partly because of Jim and partly because I was meant to see the school counsellor today – but instead my mind goes straight back to my funeral. *Who'll mourn for me?* The thought nags at me.

I've been to other funerals: my maternal grandfather when I was five (heart-attack: I got to kiss his cold cheek, because it was an open coffin at the church service); my other grandfather when I was seven (cancer wasted him away, so there was no open coffin); and Uncle George (also a heart attack, at sixty-three) when I was ten. Last year, my grandmothers passed away within six months of one another. Now Aunt Mena.

'Did you see your cousin Jim?' Mum asks.

So it begins. You won't get the full effect. Mum and Dad *only* speak Greek to Steph and me. I'm not going to remind you of that all the time. I will tell you that what they say loses something in the translation. You don't get tone,

16

either. Greek condemnations should be acted on stage as some great tragedy, even when the things you're talking about aren't that tragic. Also, this is coming from people who left Greece in the 1950s, got menial jobs because they couldn't speak English and worked tirelessly to build lives for their kids, so every word comes from this fountain of sacrifice that you bathe in every day until you reek of the guilt.

'He's going to have a good job,' Mum goes on. 'He's going to be married.'

Steph glowers out the window.

'He's going to be a doctor,' Dad says.

'A doctor!' Mum says. 'Do you know what people think of me when they see you, when they find out you dropped out of school?'

'Mum, they don't care–' Steph says.

'I'm embarrassed to be seen,' Mum says. 'Even at your poor Aunt Mena's funeral, I know that they're thinking of her and looking down on me.'

'They're not looking down on you, Mum.'

Mum's sigh is overdone. Everything about her is sad: her eyes, her face, the way she slumps, the air she exhales, the seat she sits in. A tear slides down Steph's cheek. But it's not sadness; Steph's happy with who she is. It's anger. She doesn't want to be made to feel this way, like all she's ever doing is letting them down.

'Mum, can you please–?' Steph says.

'You don't shout at your mother!' Dad says, glancing back at her.

His own anger gets the better of him as he remonstrates.

The car swerves – not a lot, but enough that it's a momentary fright.

'You watch your driving!' Mum says.

This is how things unfold. Nobody's ever safe during these times. Dad tries to support Mum and then *he* gets it. It's not that they hate each other – this is the way they communicate.

Dad flicks the radio back to his Greek station. I don't know the song that plays – they all sound the same. I hope it'll mellow Mum and Dad, but I know that some new recrimination is building.

Mum pats her chest, like she's trying to soothe a pain in her heart. 'It's all right,' she says. 'We came here to give you a better life. And now…'

Steph's jaw clenches.

'You take the opportunities we give you and you throw them,' Mum says. 'You throw them away.'

Mum goes on. None of it's malicious. Every parent wants their kids to do better than they have, but with Greek parents it's rocket-fuelled. And whatever we achieve, I always feel like it'll never be enough.

When we get home, Steph flees into the bungalow Dad and the uncles built for her in the backyard, right by our lemon tree. Steph was always complaining about privacy, about the way Mum and Dad would storm into her bedroom without knocking, about the way their shouting disturbed her when she was studying, so this is what she got: this bungalow. Six months later, she dropped out of university.

I follow Mum and Dad up the stairs to the back door. A fence – narrow side passages to either side – separates our house from the neighbours'. Their yard is manicured, the grass so neat and bright because they water every night. Rows of tomato and corn fill their garden. You could get lost in there.

The screen door at the back of their garage swings open and Olivia, Steph's best friend, comes out and heads up the stairs. Olivia's the same age as Steph, but worldly. Steph hasn't left the state. But when Olivia graduated high school, she backpacked over Europe for a year, sending Steph postcards. Now she works as a hairdresser. She's tall and athletic and always dragging Steph to stuff like yoga and pilates at the gym. Her dark hair is cropped short.

I lift my hand to wave, then stop myself, because waving would make me look like a dork. I've just started noticing Olivia. I mean, we've lived next door to one another for eight years, but she was always *just* Olivia. Now, she's *Olivia*. I want to be cool. But that's when Mum chimes in.

'Hello, Olivia, love,' she says.

'How're you?' Olivia stops at the back door to her house. 'Steph told me she was going to a funeral.'

'Our cousin.' Mum clutches her chest. 'Cancer.'

'Oh, that's horrible.'

'It was very painful.'

Mum's English is fluent, but I'm unsure how much she really understands. She knows what to say and when and where to nod, but I don't get the sense she's taking anything in. Or maybe she's just not listening.

'I'm so sorry,' Olivia says.

'Thank you, love.'

As Mum goes on, I burst into the house and retreat to my bedroom.

As far as bedrooms go, mine's simple – the single bed (with its new gold doona) sits by the curtained window, adjacent to a wall closet. Opposite it is my desk, flanked by a set of drawers on one side, and a narrow bookcase angled against the corner in the other. There's nothing on the walls – not like my friend Riley, who has pictures of Madonna, Kim Wilde, and Samantha Fox topless; or my best friend Ash, who has pictures of Guns'n'Roses, Metallica, and his footy team. Mum wouldn't want to spoil the room that way.

I change into a T-shirt and a pair of shorts, then sit on the bed, trying to figure out what I should do. Whatever happened at the funeral still buzzes through my body as a weird sense of restlessness. I check my clock radio: *2.22*. I'd catch up with Ash and Riley, but they'd still be in school.

I grab my folder from my school bag and flick through it. I've done my book report on *I Am the Cheese* for Mr Baker's English class, the report for Mr Tan's computer class and the legal quiz for Mrs Grady's Legal class.

That leaves *my* writing.

Three orange A5 exercise books sit at the top of my bookshelf. I've gone through four exercise books – Steph's reading the other one – writing short stories about Jean Razor. I grab the top exercise book, find a pen, lay down on my bed, and flick to where I left off.

The Soulless Lords have cornered Jean Razor at the top of the Temporal Tower, by one of the Mirror Portals. I reread the last paragraph. My handwriting is a scrawl – sometimes, even I have trouble reading it.

I force my pen down onto the page. The ideas come slowly at first, but I focus on Jean Razor getting through the Mirror Portal. A new world opens to him – and me. And with the new world comes a new story. Now, my writing grows quicker – and uglier. The Soulless Lords have minions – the Grave Shadows. They're dispatched to catch Jean Razor. Jean Razor escapes to the Forest of Volcanoes.

I keep writing, until my hand cramps up over an hour later. I've written six pages – a lot, even for me. Most of it is a mess, but it feels good to spill the story out onto the page. I was even able to forget about what happened at the funeral. But the moment I think that, it's there again – faint, but unsettling.

I storm from my bedroom and open the kitchen door. 'Mum–!' *I'm going to Ash's.* That's the plan. But Mum's lying on the couch. If she were a volcano, she'd spew sadness and pain over the neighbourhood. Now, it smothers not only what I was going to say, but even the intention of going to see Ash. On the chair to the right of the couch, Dad studies the form guide as he drinks a beer.

'Get me one of my pills,' Mum says.

Mum's pills: she keeps two sets in a sugar canister where she stores her knickknacks – one pill is a tiny, round blue thing, the other a small, flat oval with a pink cast. She's been taking either (and sometimes both) for as long as I remember – I'm not sure why. I asked Steph once. Her answer: 'For her nerves.'

'Which one?' I ask Mum.

'The blue one.'

I grab a blue pill, a glass of water, deliver it to Mum, then get out of there, sliding the kitchen door quietly closed behind me.

Dad bought a pool table when I was a kid and set it

up in the garage – that's where I go now. Usually, I can play alone for hours, finding creativity in the way I can get balls in, but now I can't help but think of Mum. For all her bluster, the funeral has shaken her. I don't want to go see Ash now because I know Mum will worry once I'm out.

One day, she'll be gone. Steph and I will bury her.

Then, it'll be Steph.

Then me.

Unless I go first.

The thought jags into my head so I deflect it by thinking about what it'd be like to kiss Olivia. I've kissed three girls in my life: Justina Marino in Year 7 behind the school portables (she tasted like cherry gum); Mary Hatchet several times throughout Year 8 when we were like boyfriend-girlfriend (she was an awesome kisser, and I was shattered when she dumped me for Ethan May, the captain of the school soccer team); and Penny Coates at a Year 8 dance (a very wet kisser, like she was slurping on me – that didn't last). Olivia would kiss with the confidence of a woman – not that I know what a woman kisses like.

But, for now, I can lose myself in the fantasy.

3.

In the morning, I get up around 7.30 and stumble into the kitchen. Steph's showering. Mum and Dad are already at work – they would've left at 5.00 to get to the office buildings they clean. I make and eat breakfast, then jump in the bathroom after Steph comes out to make her breakfast. I get dressed – no uniform for school; they encourage us to express our individuality (within reason) – and come back into the kitchen just as Steph's putting away dishes. We always finish about the same time. Steph will offer me a lift to school, but I only accept when it's raining.

Usually, I'll meet Ash at the corner of Manning Street (my street) and Arbuckle Avenue (where he lives). Sometimes he's first, other times it's me. A handful of times we miss each other, but that's not often.

Ash isn't much different to me in height (about normal for our age), but he's bigger across the shoulders and chest and so plain-faced he's unremarkable. He has three younger brothers and his parents are prone to big arguments – not like mine, who shout because that's the way they talk. Sometimes, Ash can be quiet, like something's wrong, so I wonder if his parents do more than argue. He doesn't say much about them.

'I miss anything?' I ask him, when I meet him at the corner.

'Some stupid Legal homework from Ms Grady,' Ash says. 'She was bitchy yesterday. Kept Riley all through recess because he was talking in class. He wasn't happy.'

Riley's not often happy, though. He makes trouble and can never understand when the teachers pull him up on it.

'What about the counsellor?' I say.

'Asked me what I wanted to do when I left school – like I know,' he says. 'She also brought up the Boland Fellowship – said I should go for it.'

The Boland Fellowship is awarded to one Year 10 student from schools in our area for academic excellence. Later in the year, they'll announce a longlist of the students who've been selected. Then it's the shortlist. Then, in the last week of school, they announce the winner.

The prize is one thousand dollars, and mentoring from somebody applicable to a field you might want to pursue. Steph won it in Year 10 and got mentored by a lawyer for a year, although the relationship tapered off as the year went on. I'm not surprised the school's brought it up with Ash – he's smart, although he doesn't always push himself.

'You should,' I say.

Ash snorts. 'They'll mention it to you, too.'

'They mention it to Riley?'

'He hasn't said anything.'

Riley's smart, but doesn't try, so it's hard to guess what they might've done.

'How was the funeral?' Ash says.

I want to tell him about the thought, but it's stupid and trivial now. Ash never worries about stuff like that.

'It was a funeral,' I tell him, like that sums it all up.

'Can't believe anybody would want to be buried. It's gonna be only a matter of time before we run out of space.'

'What're you gonna do?'

'Stuff me and leave me on the couch. It's not going to make much difference to me.'

'You'll smell, though. Well, *worse*.'

Ash chuckles.

The walk to school isn't long: down onto Highlands Road, then onto Curtis Street, a dead end that feeds into the car park for the Meadow Soccer Club. Meadow shares their soccer ground with one of the semi-professional teams, so the ground's lush. The stands are little, although they're always talking about expanding. The most impressive things are the light towers so they can train at night. The scoreboard's a towering, rickety, decrepit rectangular box standing on a framework of corroding stilts that you can hear screech in the wind. We always joke about it toppling into the creek behind it. The clubroom – with its change rooms, reception, function room, and bar – is this convoluted, snake-shaped building that they've kept adding onto with no real plan. It's also where couples from the school go to make out, using the building as cover.

The creek separates the soccer ground from the Meadow High Football Oval, although the water comes from this concrete aqueduct that cuts right through Meadow. Ash and me followed it once, winding away under the Main Street bridge until it went underground into Greenhills. We didn't go any further, although Ash did walk in about twenty feet, using his disposable lighter as a torch until it got too hot to hold.

Walking down the bank to the plank bridge that crosses the creek is also when Ash takes his cigarettes out of his jacket. He opens the pack. I pop a cigarette into my mouth and we huddle around his disposable lighter, hands up to shield the wind. Then we sit on the opposite bank, smoke with a sophistication that would look cool if we weren't fifteen, and talk about stuff that's important to us.

'Yesterday?' Ash says. 'Kat. Tight faded jeans.'

Kat is Katrina Byers, the *it* girl in Year 10. Conversations are filled with how her arse sits pear-shaped in tight pants, or how rounded her boobs look in tight tops, or the glimpse you might get of her cleavage if her blouse is a little bit low. There are pretty girls, and then there's Kat. And, yes, this is the way guys talk – at least, the way teenagers who don't know any better do.

'She's still going out with that private school prat, isn't she?' I say.

'As far as I know.' Ash lies on the bank and blows out a stream of smoke. 'I wonder what she'd be like.'

Like? I stop myself from asking, belatedly getting what Ash means.

'What about Samantha?' he asks.

Samantha Mrakov. She's had a thing for me since primary school.

'You gonna make a move on her or something?'

'Or something,' I say.

'What's that mean?'

'I don't feel anything for her.'

'I'm not asking you to marry her. Have some fun. See how far she'd go.'

I see Samantha in my head: cute, with a broad face,

high cheekbones, her chin the point of a triangle, looking at me with unquestioning trust, like a puppy waiting to be fed. It doesn't seem right to take advantage of her.

'I bet she'd go all the way with you,' Ash says.

'No way.'

'Easy. What're you looking for?'

I see someone in my head: pretty, but in a cute way; somebody I can talk to like a friend; somebody who'll be supportive and nurturing and pick me up and push me in the right directions. It's stupid. At fifteen. Too much thought. But it's there all the same.

I shrug. 'What about you?'

'I don't care. As long as she's not prudish.'

'Classy.'

'You worry too much about stuff like that.'

'If you had a choice of any of the girls—'

'Not counting Kat?'

'Whoever.'

'Rachel.'

Rachel's one of Kat's friends – small like a pixie, and the quietest of the group, except when she's laughing. Then she's this shrill trumpet that's too undignified for the popular girls, although she's a lot more approachable – I've joked around with her a few times in class. And it can almost go without saying that she's pretty – it's natural selection, as high school goes on.

'She's been looking at me – I *think*.' Ash finishes his cigarette and flicks it into the stream, although he does it violently, dismissively. 'But who wouldn't? Come on.'

I drop what's left of my cigarette and grind it out with my foot.

4

We come to school from the back. It's several long, mucky-brown, L-shaped buildings bookending a courtyard sprinkled with atriums and benches, the canteen in the middle, toilets and lockers to either end. Meadow Primary School next door isn't much different, except it's mucky-orange. Grass stretches across the front of both – grass and gum trees – like the builders made some belated attempt to try and pretty the schools up for passers-by.

Kids cluster in groups: the sporty kids, the popular kids, the nerdy kids, the misfits – I won't name them all, because it's confusing. In the courtyard, Mickey Purser and Lachlan Kinsey are tossing a book back and forth over Deanne Vega's head. Deanne's tiny and wears shapeless clothes that make her almost androgynous. She flaps about, trying to get her book back, forcing a smile like she's being good-humoured about this all, but her face is a blink away from cracking. Mickey and Lachlan – both tall, hard-muscled, popular and on all the sports teams – don't care, because that's the sort of guys they are.

'Hey!' Ash calls. He stops, hands on hips, me behind him. Mickey and Lachlan don't flinch. Now it's a staring contest. But I've seen this with Ash before. Mickey and Lachlan might be big, strong guys, and everybody knows they're cruel and stupid, but there's a pettiness in that. There's no pettiness in Ash.

Lachlan dumps the book into Deanne's hands. 'Getting boring anyway,' he says.

Mickey and Lachlan slink away (although Mickey sneers at Ash), while Deanne smiles shyly at Ash, mouths the words *thank you,* and waves, the oversized cuff of her sleeve flopping back and forth over her wrist. Ash is almost embarrassed by the attention and nods, like he thinks that's the thing he's meant to do. His focus shifts to Kat, almost double-taking as he notices her over by the lockers, talking to her friends Rachel and Gabriella. Gabriella has this wealth of wavy black hair that could be a mane.

Riley comes out of the adjoining girl's toilets, his shock of red hair so bright it's a bloody wound in the world, the hint of a swagger in his walk – he could be a cowboy in the old west. Moments later, his girlfriend, Felicia Del Deo, emerges from the toilets, face held high, almost haughty, like she'd come out of an exclusive club the rest of us can't get in.

'Hey,' Riley says, and holds up his fist to knock Ash's, then mine – not because Ash or me think it's cool, but because that's the sort of thing Riley likes. 'Felicia told me about a party coming up – a sixteenth. One of Kat's friends. Not for a while yet, but you interested?'

'Gonna be drinks?' Ash asks as the bell sounds.

'Sure.'

'I'm sold.'

We stroll to English class and sit at the back as everybody files in and Mr Baker writes *THEMES* in big letters on the board and underlines it. Then he folds his arms in a way that's almost effeminate and taps his foot as he waits for everybody to sit down. You wouldn't think he'd be intimidating – he's middle-aged and thin, even if he's always wearing big, ugly woolly jumpers, and his hair insists it's going to bald into a mullet – but when he scours the room, chatter falls quiet.

'Okay, good. Great!' he says. 'Everybody remember their book reports are due today?'

We rifle through bags and folders. Homework is passed to the person in front, until it gradually makes its way to Mr Baker. He piles it on his desk, then sits alongside the pile, one leg folded over the other.

'What does everybody think is the principal theme behind *I Am the Cheese?*' he asks.

'Crime?' Jake Fichera asks.

'Crime isn't so much a theme but a genre.'

'Loss?' Gabriella asks.

'Loss is one of the themes.' Mr Baker gets up and scribbles *Loss* under his heading of Themes.

'Love?' Ethan May asks.

'Love,' Mr Baker says, and writes it on the board.

Now everybody's throwing suggestions out, one after the other: *family, friendship, mafia, grief, growing up, dealing with problems, violence, conspiracy, anxiety, trust, betrayal* – Mr Baker repeats the themes, and writes them down, and everybody laughs at the couple that are intentionally silly.

Samantha Mrakov, seated in the corner, fixes her gaze on me. When somebody likes you, their eyes change – physically, they're still the same eyes, but they soften. I can't hold her gaze long. It always makes me feel like I'm meant to be somebody I'm not.

'One important one nobody's said, though…' Mr Baker says.

Identity. I want to say it, but I'm worried it'll be wrong. Mr Baker folds his arms across his chest again. The silence has created pressure. Then, sure enough, he writes on the board in the biggest letters of all: *Identity*. I berate myself for not saying it.

'At its heart, this is what *I Am the Cheese* is about – who *we* are.'

A knock interrupts him, the door opens and Counsellor Hoffs pokes in her head, the blonde topknot she wears bouncing girlishly, although she must be forty or so.

'Can I borrow…?'

Her voice trails to a whisper as she points me out. Mr Baker nods. Only moments later, I sit in Counsellor Hoffs' office, which is cluttered with bookshelves and ferns in the corners, the window covered in venetians that belong in a private detective novel.

'I understand you were at a funeral yesterday,' Counsellor Hoffs says.

'My aunt.'

'How do you feel about that?'

'Well, she wasn't really my aunt – she was like my mum's cousin. But we still called her an aunt…'

I'm rambling. Counsellor Hoffs blinks at me. I'm not sure what to say. Does she expect me to be moved? Will it seem cold if I come across ambivalent? I'm sad Aunt Mena died, but it's one of those things that happens, that you absorb and then move on from, isn't it?

'I'm okay,' I say.

'All right.' Counsellor Hoffs folds her hands on top of a

file on her desk. 'How about everything else? How're you doing?'

The thought. That's the first thing my mind goes to. But now, it's like the memory of a nightmare – an event stripped of all the terror that made it unsettling in the first place. I find relief in that. How the hell did that scare me?

'Everything's good,' I say.

'As you may be aware, I've been talking to the students about where they see their lives going.' Counsellor Hoffs opens the file and flicks through it. 'You get great marks, especially in English. Have you given any thought to what you'd like to do when you finish school?'

It's Jim all over again. Should I know at fifteen? Like anything at fifteen is going to be permanent. Steph told me she wanted to be a surgeon at fourteen, a lawyer at fifteen, a police officer at sixteen, a teacher at seventeen, and then she studied business for two and a half years before deciding that wasn't for her. My right hand tightens around the armrest of my chair.

'No.'

'Do you have any particular interests?'

'Movies.'

'You like watching them?'

'I like thinking about how things work in them.'

'What else?'

The conversation drifts meaninglessly: I like sport, I like books, I like hanging around with friends, I like playing games on the computer, I like music – just silly, nothing things. Counsellor Hoffs nods as I babble. She occasionally jots down a word or two. It makes me feel like she's taking me apart.

'It's normal not to think too deeply about what you want to do – especially at your age,' she says. 'But I've been challenging the students to let the question gestate in their heads. Don't spend too much time on it but be aware it's there. We'll talk again later in the year, and see if there's been any development, okay?'

'Sure.'

Counsellor Hoffs folds her hands on her desk again. 'I also want to talk to you about the Boland Fellowship,' she says. 'It's open to everybody, obviously, but there are certain students I feel have a better chance of being considered. I think you would be one of those students.'

She lets that sink in. Steph got a similar talk and worked furiously that year – although she throws herself into everything furiously.

Counsellor Hoffs smiles and sits back. 'I had this same conversation with your sister,' she says. 'I know you're as smart as her and you work as hard – your academic record speaks for itself. Just keep doing what you're doing.'

'I'll try,' I say, because it *does* appeal to me – an accomplishment that'll show Mum and Dad and the Jims of the world I'm going somewhere, even if Mum and Dad only had a lukewarm reaction to Steph winning. Steph could've brought home a gold star for finger-painting and it would've had the same impact.

'As you'd know, there'll be one Boland assignment slipped in with your homework,' Counsellor Hoffs says. 'Even we don't know what it is.'

This is part of the Fellowship: they judge you on all the stuff you'd expect them to judge you on – grades, attendance, behaviour, and all that, but they also slip in an essay assignment that masquerades as a normal homework assignment. It's usually an English piece – usually, but not always. When Steph won it, they judged it on a Legal essay – how civilians could become morally responsible to build a better society.

'If you need to talk to me about any aspect of the Fellowship,' Counsellor Hoffs says, rising from her chair, 'feel free to call on me.'

She dismisses me, so I hurry back to class as Mr Baker's handing a homework assignment around.

'What I want you to do is write a creative essay about *your* identity,' he says. 'It's not just a case of details you might fill out on a form when you go to the doctor. I want you to think about this laterally – don't be afraid to explore themes behind your identity. You can undertake this assignment as an essay or a story – let your imagination run wild.'

He hands me a copy of the assignment and his gaze locks with mine in a way I'm sure is meant to be meaningful but makes me uncomfortable. Riley snorts once Mr Baker has moved on. I study the assignment – a list of the criteria Mr Baker is explaining to the class. I don't tell Ash or Riley that the assignment excites me because I get to do something creative. Already, my mind's ticking over.

'This will be for one of your major marks this year,' Mr Baker says.

Besides the homework that's scattered throughout the year, there are the big assignments in every class that are meant to be handed in at year's end and constitute a big chunk of your mark.

Mr Baker sits on the edge of his desk as the bell rings. Everybody stuffs their books back into their bags.

'Now that we've finished *I Am the Cheese*, *To Kill a Mockingbird* is next,' he says. 'If you didn't order a copy with the rest of your books, buy one now, or borrow it from the library. Class dismissed.'

I follow Ash and Riley out, but not before I notice Mr Baker look at me again.

5.

It cools down as autumn marches towards winter and the days grow shorter.

Mum and Dad score a part-time contract to clean a small office building two evenings a week. They're always on the lookout for extra money and have done a number of these short-term contracts in the past, but when they tell Steph – who would usually help them – her response staggers them.

'I don't want to,' she says.

'What do you mean you don't want to?' Mum says.

'We got this for you!' Dad says.

'I didn't ask you to get it,' Steph says.

'For extra money!' Dad says. 'Money! Do you understand?'

'I've got a job, and I've got better things to do with my time.'

'Better things!' Dad says. '*Better* things.'

'This is for your future!' Mum says.

'I. Don't. Want. To,' Steph says.

'I'll go!' I say.

Mum and Dad are surprised. Ash helps his dad – an electrician who wires a lot of new houses – part-time, so he's always set for money. I don't know where Riley gets his – probably pilfers it from his Mum and Dad. I rely on an allowance, but things like cigarettes aren't cheap.

It's not as glamorous as I think it would be – the location's a three-storey building shared by accountants on the top floor, a design business in the middle and a travel agent on the bottom. Although I've known Mum and Dad do cleaning work, I've never understood what that meant until now. We empty bins, vacuum the carpet, mop floors, wipe windows and desks, wash up the bathrooms, and clean up any messes. It's physically tiring, but leaves my head free to wonder about other things.

I also spend too much time working on Mr Baker's 'Identity' assignment. I wonder if it's the piece they'll judge the Boland on – so far, none of the other classes have issued homework that you could consider meaningful. The Boland essays are always meaningful. So that gives me more incentive but there's lots of false starts.

When I'm not working, I catch up with Ash, or Ash and Riley, and we sit in the creek aqueduct and smoke. When Riley's involved, these conversations are always simpler – usually, they don't gravitate too far from anything related to sex.

'See Madonna in her new clip?' Riley says. 'Her boobs are awesome.'

Ash sits up. 'Which clip?'

'"Like a Prayer",' Riley says.

'You don't see her boobs.'

'She's wearing this low-cut top,' Riley says. 'She'd be awesome to fuck.'

'How would you know what awesome sex is?'

'I'm getting close, you know?'

'To sex with Madonna?' I say.

Ash laughs.

'Felicia,' Riley says, his tone flat. He doesn't like being made fun of. 'She went down on me.'

'No way,' Ash says.

'You see Felicia around, you think she's up herself or whatever. But she lets loose in private. Other night, we were on the couch in her lounge. Her parents had gone to sleep, so we were making out. I had my hand down her pants. She was so wet. She gets *so* wet. And she came – she tensed up and moaned then shook all over. I thought she was having a fit or something. When she recovered, she unzipped my pants and…' He shrugs.

I visualise it all – I don't mean to, and I don't want to, but it unfolds in my head and clashes with the way I see Felicia: that pretty, pristine, proper way she carries herself, and I can't imagine how she could become so wild, although I guess there's every chance she would, if she does stuff like make out with Riley in the toilets. You look at people every day and you never think of who they are behind closed doors.

'She's a fake,' Riley says. 'She's different when we're alone.'

'Never thought she was a fake,' I say.

'I thought she was a bit of a snob,' Ash says, 'but not a fake.'

'Am going for it Saturday at this party,' Riley says. 'Either of you want to bring somebody?'

'Like?' I ask, expecting Samantha's name to be thrown out.

'Mr Baker maybe,' Riley says.

'What?'

Riley smirks around lighting a fresh cigarette. Here's his comeback for my Madonna joke. I don't even think he realises it's payback. It's instinct with him.

'Stupid fag,' he says. 'The way he looks at ya. I think he's got something for you.'

Speculation surrounds Mr Baker's sexuality. He can be camp, like that's a qualification for homosexuality. And we all talk because that's what we do. For most, it's *only* talk, the way guys talk about Kat or who might win the football that week. With Riley, it's nasty.

'That's not funny,' I say.

'Just kidding,' Riley says quick, maybe working out he's overstepped. He opens his cigarette packet and thrusts them towards me and Ash, so some of the cigarettes shoot halfway out. We smoke some more and retreat to safer conversations, like the new Batman movie that's coming out that everybody's talking about, and how the singer Collette looks amazing in tight lycra in her hit 'Ring My Bell'. Once we've finished our smokes, we flick the butts into the creek and watch them sail away.

Riley gets up and pats down his pants. 'I'm taking off,' he said. 'I'll see you at this party. Felicia's friends will be there. It'll be a good night.'

Of course, when I tell Mum and Dad at dinner – Mum loading our plates with chops, mashed potatoes, and steamed vegetables – about the party, they tell me why it mightn't be a good night. Steph shakes her head at Mum's predictions of doom.

'I saw on the *News*, a boy was killed,' Mum says as she

sits down. 'They punched him in the head when he wasn't looking.'

Dad laughs ruefully. 'Kids drink too much, they get too drunk, they do stupid things.'

'It's not safe to go out at night,' Mum says.

They're not telling me I can't go. Despite their ways, Mum and Dad can be liberal. Like, despite me chewing gum, I'm sure they can smell that I've smoked. But they let it go. And they'll let me go out after they've warned me about all the risks – real, exaggerated and imagined.

'There are always stupid people out at night,' Mum says.

'He's going to a party,' Steph says. 'It's normal.'

Mum scowls. Bad mistake from Steph to get involved. Now Mum broadens her sights.

'And you, Aunt Toula rang me today,' she says. 'About Jim's wedding.'

'And?'

'She wants to know if you're bringing anybody.'

'No, Mum, I'm not bringing anybody.'

'You don't have a nice boyfriend?'

A dangerous question. Steph's not expected to bring *just* a boyfriend. She's had boyfriends and could find somebody for the night; what she's expected to bring is *the* boyfriend, the one who'll become her husband. In fact, it'd be best if they were engaged. You don't take a partner unless you're serious about them.

'Well?' Mum asks.

'I've been seeing somebody.'

'You're seeing somebody and you don't bring him here?'

'Mum, I don't know what's going to happen with the relationship.'

'You should bring him here,' Dad says.

'Why?'

'What do you mean "why"? So we can meet him!'

'It's a long way from being that serious you should meet.'

Mum pouts – her heart, her hopes, her very life, shattered. She sighs. Then sniffles. 'People talk. They look at you and wonder why you're not married. They say I've failed you.'

'Mum, nobody cares.'

'Your cousin Malinda is married with a baby and she's only twenty-one – a year younger than you!'

'Mum, she's like one month younger than me!'

'See her nice house. You can't compare to Malinda?'

'It's not that I can't, Mum. I don't want to.'

'I was married to your father and pregnant at about your age.'

'You were ten years older!'

'It's the same thing.'

'Do you want me to get pregnant?' Steph says.

'That's not funny!' Dad says. 'You'll get married first.'

Steph stays amazingly calm. 'It's 1989, you know.'

'This is what's wrong with this country,' Dad says. 'Everybody's too stupid. They want fun and not hard work.' His voice drops now to a whisper, the way it always does when he's serious. 'Do you know, in Greece, when I was saving money to come here, I walked five miles every day in the snow to work. It's lucky I wasn't eaten by a bear.'

'There are no snow bears in Greece!' Steph says.

'Everything's too easy for you!' Dad says, and now it's

back to shouting. 'We gave you that bungalow, we let you drop out of school, we pay for everything–'

'Forget it.' Steph's chair grinds across the floor.

'Finish dinner!' Dad says.

But Steph's already out of the kitchen. I know the beats now: back door slams; Steph's feet thudding down the stairs; light, as the motion-activated light on her bungalow comes on; her bungalow door slams; then music – Bon Jovi's 'Livin' on a Prayer'. The motion-activated light goes off.

'You didn't have to shout at her like that,' Mum says.

'She's a stupid girl.'

'Because you shout at her like that.'

'She should know what it's like to work hard and have to earn things.'

I switch off. Or try to. Mum and Dad argue, a ping pong game where it's impossible to follow who's played what and where. I eat quick, excuse myself and close myself off in my bedroom, then pull out my schoolbooks. Mum and Dad keep shouting. I flick my clock radio on and turn the volume up to drown them out. If you saw and heard their arguing for the first time and didn't know any better, you'd be pencilling in a divorce, but this, this is normal.

I read Mr Baker's criteria for the 'Identity' assignment to distract me, pick up a pen in my left hand and push it to a blank page, but still have no idea what to write.

6.

Getting ready to go out is a ritual. I shower and put gunk in my hair, although my style isn't anything more than straight but messy. I shaved last week and the stubble, dark and thick for my age – I usually pass for being a couple of years older – has come in stylishly. Then I get dressed. My jeans are always scratchy and I dread that first contact between them and my skin. Once they're buttoned up, I jump around to loosen them. Next is my overcoat – well, Dad's overcoat, something old and grey that I found in his wardrobe and had probably been sitting there since before Steph was born. But it looks cool and that's more important than anything else.

I go into the lounge to announce I'm leaving. Mum's lying on the couch, like the weight of all her worries pins her there. Dad's slumped in one of the other chairs, leg cocked over the armrest, looking at the form guide for the horse races. The gravity that sits in the room makes everything else heavier.

This probably happens in just about every household – a teenager tells their parents they're going out. And then they'd get a response like an encouraging 'Have fun' or 'Have a great night' or a joking 'Be good!' Or, if the parents are a bit warier, it might be something like, 'Don't stay out too late' or 'Don't get too silly' or 'Be responsible'. There's a scale of what to expect.

Mum and Dad sit under that.

'I'm go–'I begin to say.

'Be careful!' Mum says. 'There's lots of stupid people out there.'

'It's not safe out at night,' Dad says.

Possible dangers jump in my head: fights, getting hit by a car while crossing the road, having my drink spiked, having a bear eat me – I've heard warnings about all these things. The way Mum curls into herself, twisting with fear, almost makes me want to stay home to assure them.

I duck out, thinking I should hurry, but the light's on at the door of Steph's bungalow and Olivia stands there, hand held up, just about to knock. She wears tight jeans and a denim jacket and her short hair has been spiked up. She smiles at me. I blush but hope the night hides it. The motion-activated light goes off.

'Hey,' she says. 'Going out?'

'Party.'

The light flashes back on as the door to the bungalow opens and Steph comes out. Her hair's pulled back and she wears a big, woolly jacket.

'You going?' she asks.

'Yeah.' The light goes back off.

'We're going to see *Rain Man*. You want a lift?'

'It's okay. I have to meet Ash.'

'Have a good night,' Steph says.

'Have fun,' Olivia says.

I spot Ash at the corner by the glowing ember of his cigarette. He offers me one and we hurry over to Riley's.

He's waiting out front, hands shoved in his pockets, shoulders hunched into himself, like he's brooding – that classic James Dean pose. A two-litre bottle of Coke sits on top of his mailbox.

As we walk, I tense every time a car passes, expecting it might skid to a halt and its occupants will jump out to ambush us – not that that's ever happened, or I've ever known it to happen. But it could, surely, because otherwise Mum and Dad wouldn't warn me the way that they do.

Riley opens his Coke, takes a swig, then offers it to me.

'No thanks,' I say.

'Have a drink.'

It's not just Coke, but something with a bitter tang.

I grimace. 'What's that?'

'Scotch. Swiped some from my dad's liquor cabinet.'

Ash takes a bigger gulp, then another. The bottle's passed around until I'm giddy, and my fears ebb away, so all I have to deal with is the length of the walk: through the back streets of Meadow, cutting across Greenhills, then into the long, narrow streets of Hampton Park. We chain-smoke and finish the Coke.

'Down here,' Riley says.

We hear the music, faint, distorted, but building as we plunge into a long street. Then it's the cars, parked everywhere. One house stands out like a lighthouse. People huddle out front. Others spill from the drive. Now that we're closer I see them – kids like us, although most are a bit older. I don't recognise any of them.

Riley threads his way through them to the garage, which pulses, the heartbeat of the party, kids a blur of shapes as light flashes. The music's deafening now – Michael

Jackson's 'Smooth Criminal' pumping everybody with energy. A lone figure detaches from a group of dancing girls – Felicia, all spruced up in a little skirt, a jacket with puffy shoulders, and bouffant hair. She kisses Riley. His hand roves down to her hip. She knocks it away, but does it casually, like she doesn't want to bring attention to it. Irritation flickers across Riley's face. She says hi to us, although it's lost in the warble of the music.

Riley leans in towards us. 'Help yourselves!'

He lets Felicia lead him to the dancing, while Ash finds the bar like he's sniffed it out – although it's just a long table with an assortment of spirits and under that, cans of beer in tubs of ice. He grabs us each a beer and we find two vacant chairs nearby.

My eyes adjust to the light and I make out the faces I know – Kat, in a body-hugging blue dress, dances with some broad-shouldered blond guy. He's stiff in his movements. Rachel and Gabriella, both in skirts, their hair unmoving, dance together. I seek out Riley and Felicia but they've already gone missing – maybe Riley's made his move on her, although where would they go? Inside the house? Down the street somewhere? I wouldn't have a clue what the strategy should be.

I don't know anybody else, but I make out details – the brand clothes that have marched straight off racks; the hairstyles with the shaven undercut Ash and me have long associated with yuppies; even the way nobody gravitates to Rachel and Gabriella. Kat's boyfriend is the private school prat; these are his prats; it's Prat City.

Ash shoves another beer in my face. I scull the first and start on the second. Ash rests his beer under his chair and struts up to Rachel and Gabriella. They look at him as if a dog is in the process of humping their legs. But then Rachel laughs. They're not getting attention from anywhere else. And Ash doesn't take himself seriously.

I drink and drink until my head spins, and stumble up to the house so I can ask where the bathroom is. People frown at me and I'm self-conscious now of my dad's old coat. I couldn't have picked anything worse to make me stand out. But then I feel guilty about thinking poorly of the coat.

In the bathroom, I splash cold water on my face. I've never felt comfortable in crowds, but tonight it's worse. Tonight, my mind and body have come alive and I'm feeling everything too much. It has to be the alcohol, although I've drunk before and it's never made me feel like this. Usually, it makes me feel *more* relaxed. Maybe I need something else to drink.

I blunder outside. Back in the garage, I grab another beer, although I gag when I swill it down.

But swill it down I do.

7

Gabriella takes the empty seat next to me. Her dark hair stinks of hairspray, but it looks good the way it bounces around her – not just a mane, but a crown that makes her look like a beautiful sorceress who's stepped out of a fantasy novel.

'You going for the Boland?' she asks.

I don't understand the reference – not right away. I'm at a party. I'm not thinking school. I'm thinking the roof might cave in and my parents will be proven right about going out.

'I was thinking of going for it,' Gabriella says, 'although…'

Now my mind ticks over: she means the Fellowship.

'I think it's gonna be you, Ethan, Deanne or Samantha.'

Samantha's smart, although Deanne's the runaway brain. She's terrible socially, like she's spent so much time studying that she hasn't developed her social skills (not that I can judge). Ethan May is one of those kids who's good at everything. That wouldn't be so bad if he wasn't such a nice guy, too.

Gabriella's eyes narrow – she's grown tired of waiting to get something out of me. And then it occurs to me that when she was suggesting who might win the Boland, I should've countered that she might be a chance, too. She *is* smart. I open the mouth to suggest it, but it's too late.

'You drunk?' she asks.

'No.'

Gabriella reaches out and pushes my hair clear from my forehead. 'You ever thought of doing something with this?'

'What?'

'Your hair. It's like a tribute to The Beatles.'

I try to think of a response to that.

'You don't talk much, do you?'

I want to say something witty but nothing comes. I do work out now what I should've said in response to the Beatles comparison – yeah, they were famous and idolised and all the girls loved them. Too late now.

Gabriella laughs. 'See?'

I lift my can to my lips, but Gabriella intercepts it, sticks it on the table and yanks my hands.

'Let's dance,' she says.

So, I dance – not well, but well enough that I don't look the total idiot. Gabriella makes constant eye contact – not like Samantha does, with that soft, sparkly look, but I still wonder am I meant to take the initiative?

I get sweaty dancing in my overcoat and am thinking of ways to excuse myself when Ash and Rachel come into the garage. Ash's hand is low down on Rachel's hip, and Rachel's hair is mussed – that's the only way to describe it, like it'd gotten wet and dried funny. Gabriella frowns and Ash gestures he's going to have a cigarette. He grabs a couple of beers, drags me out front and we sit against the house's front wall to smoke.

'Where'd you go?' I ask.

'Round the side of the house.'

I blow out a stream of smoke.

'We fucked.'

'Get lost.'

'We did.'

'Just…what? Like that?'

'We were going at it and then…we went at it. Against the wall.'

Yeah, guys tell each other these things. Actually, on a scale of disclosures, Ash is being restrained, like him and Rachel might've only shared a kiss. I wonder what Rachel's protocol is with Gabriella, Felicia and Kat. But then I wonder about Rachel having sex just like that.

'So, you're like boyfriend-girlfriend now?' I ask.

'Steady on.'

'Then you–'

'Hey!'

A voice behind us from the drive – one of the prat people, with that undercut blond hair and a button nose, flanked by three guys to either side. I stiffen as I get up, but Ash sits there, takes a last drag of his smoke then flicks it onto the grass. He takes a long drink. Other people in the drive and out front stop what they're doing to watch.

'How many of those beers you had?' the prat asks.

'Don't know,' Ash says. He finishes the beer, crunches the can, and rests it on the wall.

'We brought beers and left them in those tubs under the table,' the prat says.

So many things jump through my head – that this is the night my parents' warnings are going to come true; that these guys don't want to beat us, but humiliate us; that I have only five bucks in my pocket, so it's not enough to pay for the beer; that the beer's probably not even theirs and they're just marking their territory; what it'll be like to show up home with bruises on my face.

'We thought they were for anybody,' I say.

'You're wr–' the prat begins.

The words die because Ash shoves off from the wall and marches up to the prat. The prat falls back a step, but knowing that's made him look weak, straightens back up. He stands a few inches taller than Ash but is whippet-like – maybe he's a swimmer or something because he has that sort of build. But Ash doesn't care. Ash glowers at him with unblinking eyes.

'You got a problem?' the prat asks, but if you listen closely – and I do – you can hear the tremor in his voice.

I rest the beer on the wall and sidle up to Ash, putting a hand on his chest to push him away. His nostrils flare – this is Ash; he doesn't back down and when people get in the face of that, it's scary. But the prat has the numbers.

'Don't worry about it,' I tell Ash. 'Come on.'

I coax him away and he takes a step. But the prat decides to show he's going to win this pissing contest, so he shoves Ash. Ash grabs him by the scruff of his shirt and thrusts him into his friends. Several of them go down. I try to corral Ash. Somebody throws a punch and pain explodes in the bottom of my nose.

'Hey!'

A man in pyjama bottoms and a singlet charges down the drive with a golf club – it's probably the father of whoever's party it is. He's middle-aged and tubby, but he carries the authority of age. The music from the garage has stopped. Everybody's crammed out front – even Rachel and Gabriella, as well as Kat and her pratfriend.

'What's going on, Stuart?' pyjama man asks.

The prat gets up and brushes his pants. 'These wankers came here to fight.'

'No, we didn't!' I say.

'Bullshit!' Ash says.

The man with the golf club takes a couple of steps towards us. 'You two, get the hell out of here.'

'We didn't do anything,' Ash says.

'Go!' pyjama man says.

'Come on,' I tell Ash.

Ash is unflinching.

'You heard,' the man says. 'Or do you want me to call the cops?' Now even his voice has a tremor.

Ash takes a cigarette out and lights it up. 'Fuck you, mate,' he says.

I grab him by the sleeve and pull him away. He comes reluctantly, holding pyjama man's eye until he's visibly uncomfortable, but then we're swallowed into the darkness. Ash doesn't speak until we're out of the street.

'Your nose,' he says.

I dab my nose and pull away my hand to see blood. 'Shit.'

I find a handkerchief in my overcoat and hold it to my nose – my left nostril is trickling blood. It doesn't hurt – at least not much.

'Fucking heroes,' Ash says.

And that's the extent of our conversation. Since Riley's not with us, we can take a direct route, through the school, stop on the bank by the bridge and light up a cigarette. My nose has stopped bleeding, although the left nostril throbs.

We don't talk through the first cigarette, or through the second, although I look to Ash regularly. We've been friends all through high school, we talk lots, but I don't know why he gets like that. After a third smoke, we continue on walking until we reach the corner where our streets meet.

'Your nose okay?' he asks.

I wiggle the tip. 'It'll be fine.'

'See ya.'

'See ya.'

Mum's waiting in the hall when I stagger into the house.

'How dare you stay out this late!' she says.

Well, she doesn't *say* it, because that would suggest she's being calm.

'Do you know what time it is?' she shouts.

No, I don't, and it wouldn't be wise to admit it if I did. That'd be like putting the bomb she plans to kill me with in her hands. I sidestep her to get to my bedroom, anticipating she might swipe me across the back of the head – she doesn't, but I expect it all the same.

'You smell of alcohol! That's why you've stayed out this late? To get drunk?'

'Just…quiet, okay?' I say. 'I'm not–'

'Don't you tell me to be quiet! You do this again, don't come back home!'

A nothing threat. They'd never kick me out – not that I'm complacent or say that like I plan to take advantage of them; they'd be happy if we lived with them forever, although they'd never let us forget it.

I slip into my bedroom, close the door and change into

my pyjamas. Within moments, I can hear Mum ranting at Dad – the plaster walls that separate our bedroom aren't thick, although even if they were, her voice would still pound its way through.

I turn off the light and go to bed, listening to Mum and Dad arguing until I fall asleep.

8

Sunday, the first thing I do when I wake mid-morning –
fuzzy-tongued, bleary-eyed and edgy – is sneak into the
bathroom to check my nose. Last thing I need is blood
or bruises. But there's nothing. I wash my face, then fix
breakfast in the kitchen. Mum's displeasure radiates from
her as she prowls around me, but Dad is good-humoured.
Still, when Ash rings and tells me Riley's suggested going
to Toppy's after lunch, I take it as a reason to get out of the
house.

Toppy's is a two-storey parlour behind the High Street
hub of shops. The bottom floor has a kiosk and is filled
with arcade games – new ones and classics, like Space
Invaders, Pacman and Galaga. The top floor has rows of
pool tables. You don't get many kids from Meadow High
there. It's mostly a rougher crowd: older kids who flirt with
the law, might have a habit or two, or just like trouble –
people Riley knows through his older brother, Ray, who
served a two-year probation for breaking and entering.

Steph has an afternoon shift so offers to drive me.
We pick Ash up from the corner. He's bright and relaxed,
which is great because I was worried he'd still be sullen. It's
about a half-hour walk to Toppy's but a five-minute drive.

Steph drops us off on High Street. We thank her and get on our way.

'How's your nose?' Ash says as we cross the street.

'Don't feel it at all.'

A layer of smoke hangs over the floor of Toppy's and the pudgy old guy behind the kiosk (you'd think he'd have a cool nickname, but he's just Johnny) scowls at us as we come in. Everybody jokes that he's in the mob or something cool like that because, with his slicked-back hair, dark, beady eyes and craggy face, he looks like one of the mobsters in *The Godfather*.

Ash and me search the bottom floor, weaving our way through the regulars who park themselves at the same machines, then hurry upstairs. Riley's playing a game of pool by himself. He doesn't interrupt his shot as he talks to us.

'You two get into a fight or something last night?' he says.

'Wasn't our fault,' I say and recount what happened.

Riley snorts once I'm done. 'Fuckheads. What're you two gonna do?'

'For?' Ash says.

'Your sixteenths.'

'You want me to have a sweet sixteen?'

Riley laughs. 'Have a party. Have everybody over.'

'I don't turn sixteen until December.'

'So? It'll be in summer. You have a pool. Have a pool party.'

'Don't think so.'

'Think of the girls in bikinis.'

'Maybe.' Ash's turnaround is so deadpan it can be hard to follow – but he does that a lot. 'What about you?'

'At my house? No thanks,' Riley says.

'What's wrong with your house?'

'Stuff with Mum and shit.' Riley turns to me. 'What about you?'

'With my mum and dad?' I say.

'You embarrassed of your mum and dad?'

'We don't do things like that at my place.'

Riley leans over the table. 'Gonna be the year of sixteenths anyway. Everybody in our year is turning sixteen. Plenty of parties.' The smoke from his cigarette curls up. He squints as he strikes the cue ball, sinking the black. 'Plenty of parties.'

I empty the pockets of balls and Riley sets them up. Ash takes a cue, so I sit on a stool. There's only a handful of other people playing pool and the clash of balls is relaxing. Pool is all angles – hit something right, you get it in. But there are different ways to pocket balls and you always have to think about where you're leaving the cue ball – in a good position for yourself, or a bad position for your opponent.

'Am done with Felicia,' Riley says as he breaks.

Riley and Felicia have been going together since the summer holidays – three months. That's like dog years to human years for teenagers.

'Had like World War Three trying to go all the way,' Riley says. 'Fuck her.'

We light up and Riley leans against a neighbouring table. He has a very conceited way of smoking, trying too hard to make it all look cool – from the way he holds the smoke like the pin from a grenade, the way he drags the cigarette in and squints, and the orgasmic way he exhales a stream of smoke.

'So that's it?' I ask. 'For good?'

Riley shrugs. 'She's a moron.'

We play pool and finish our cigarettes. Riley beats Ash, but I beat both of them twice, then relinquish my cue and volunteer to get another packet from the supermarket across the street. Toppy's has a cigarette machine but the prices are outrageously marked up.

The cashier at the supermarket is a plump older woman with dyed hair who frowns at me as she hands across the cigarettes. I shouldn't be smoking – none of us should. But it's *cool*. Well, at least that's what movies and TV's been telling us. Like James Bond. He smokes. And right now it's cheap. Smoking's made for teenagers right now. Maybe it'll change one day, but right now this is how it stands.

I've just ducked out of the supermarket when I see Samantha among the stream of Sunday shoppers coming towards me. There's an awkward moment when I debate if I'm going to acknowledge her or pretend not to see her and hope she doesn't push it. Just to clarify, though, there's nothing wrong with Samantha. She's not somebody you'd ignore because she's loopy or trashy or anything like that.

So, I look at her as she approaches and she's the one who's not looking the right way and is going to pass me, but then maybe she feels my gaze because she turns. Eyes widen. Smiles. Tilts and lowers her head. And then we're in that awkward moment where we work out whether it's going to be a wave, a soundless 'Hi' as we pass one another, or if we're going to stop and talk.

She slows – a bit. That's when I'm left with the choice to put on a burst of speed and burn past her, or to slow and meet her. Of course, this is all being worked out in my head almost instantaneously. But I do stop, and she reaches out and pats my wrist while shifting her weight from one leg to another.

'You're all right,' she says.

'Why wouldn't I be?'

'I heard you were in a fight last night and ended up in hospital!'

Here's the typical teenage grapevine, the story getting embellished with each retelling.

'I was breaking up a fight and got hit,' I say. 'It was nothing.'

'It doesn't look like you got hurt.'

Witty banter would be good. But all we share is silence, at first respectful (like we're each waiting for the other to speak) and then awkward (neither of us knows where to go). Worse, her eyes beam at me. She relishes this time we share.

Don't worry about me – I'm indestructible! That's what I could've said. Or, *My face broke the other guy's hand.* Or, *I'm a quick healer.*

'You shopping?' she asks.

'I'm with Ash and Riley. They're across the street.'

'Across the street?' Samantha frowns.

'Playing pool in Toppy's.'

'Oh.' Crestfallen. 'I caught a bus down to do some shopping. I should let you get back to them.'

'Sure. I'll see ya.'

'Bye.'

Her last word scatters in the wind as she hurries off, small, disappointed and vulnerable – well, that's what I think. She might be a tyrant behind closed doors. It doesn't matter anyway, or shouldn't, but that she might be that fragile and I might've hurt her nags at me in a way I struggle to shake.

I run across the road back to Toppy's.

9.

That Monday, when I get up, I have that same edginess tingling all over so that everything is pronounced – noises too loud, lights too bright, and clothes too scratchy. I wash up, then gawk out the kitchen window, feeling something's wrong but unable to place what.

Ash isn't at the corner when I get there. I wait a few minutes and when I'm sure he's not coming (or that he's going to be late), I hurry off to school. It seems like any other day. Kids float around with that unbridled enthusiasm they have when they're not in the classroom.

When I come into the courtyard, I spot Gabriella sitting with Rachel on one of the benches, Rachel pasty-faced and wild-eyed. Gabriella sees me and scowls. I do a sweep of the kids around me, seeing the usual clusters, but no sign of Ash and Riley, which can mean only one thing.

Sure enough, they're in the toilets, smoking.

'Hey,' I say.

'Sorry I missed you,' Ash says. 'I had to get here earlier to talk to Rachel.'

'About…?'

'Just that Saturday night was Saturday night. I think she thought we were, like, married or something.'

In the history of my life and all the stories I've scribbled throughout my A5 exercise books, I don't think I've ever used this word, but Riley *chortles*. Like, *heh heh heh*. He drags from his cigarette, squints the way he does and throws the butt into the sink.

'You're better off,' he says.

I wonder if he would've said that had he not broken up with Felicia. He must've encouraged Ash. Ash always had that thing for Rachel, but for some reason now he's ditched her.

'You sure?' I ask Ash. 'Rachel's nice.'

'What're you?' Riley says. 'A girl?'

'Just…Rachel's nice.'

'They change when you get in a relationship.'

'They can't change that much. You were with Felicia three months.'

Riley's nostrils flare. 'You weigh up what you get out of it and what you want out of it.'

'So, like that, it's over?'

'Live and love,' Riley says.

'Live and lust,' Ash says.

During classes we have with the girls, they glare at us. Riley's unfazed. That little wry grin tugs at the corner of his mouth. Ash doesn't care. He behaves like any other day. I'm not sure what to do. There's solidarity and there's decency.

Gabriella tracks me down at lunchtime, when I'm coming out of the line at the canteen with a hotdog and orange juice. Her eyes note the fringe of my hair in a way that makes me self-conscious.

'Ash can be a real prick,' she says then.

And that's it. That's the extent of the interaction over

the whole thing. The girls stay cool towards us, but after we've eaten, Riley, Ash and me stroll out to the back of the school, where some of the kids play soccer. We sit on the grass, check for teachers and light up cigarettes.

Ethan canters past as he calls for the ball. If God had chiselled a teenager from marble who was the aspiration and envy of every other kid, it'd be Ethan. He pauses, holds a thumbs up to Ash, and then jogs on. Ash is a celebrity now because he's had sex. If I'm to give Ash credit for anything, it's that he doesn't bask in it – he's even surly. It stops the chatter from becoming gossip. I don't even know how it came out. He tells me on the walk home.

'Riley,' he says. 'Felicia told him. Sorta. Rachel would've told her friends and Felicia told Riley I was a bastard. And Riley told everybody.'

'What did you think was going to happen?'

'When?'

'You have sex with her and then you tell her that's it. How did you think she was gonna handle it?'

'Now, when I can stop to think about it, yeah, I know that's how she'd react. But when I have my hand under her skirt and she's pulling down my zip, I'm not stopping to think about those things. Maybe in twenty years, when I have a bit more experience, I might.'

'You really believe that?'

'Fuck no. Don't worry about it. She'll get over it.'

When I get home, I hear the shouting the moment I reach the drive – Mum and Dad screaming, and not the usual shouting that's the way they talk but screaming that lifts the roof. I think they must be shouting at one another but then I hear that they're shouting in concert at somebody else.

'Are you stupid?' Mum asks.

'How can you be so irresponsible?' Dad says.

'You're going to embarrass us to everybody,' Mum says.

With stuff like that being thrown around, I think about the possibilities. *Steph's crashed her car*. But, no, it's parked on the front lawn. *Steph's run up some huge debt*. But she barely spends on anything. *Steph's pregnant*. That makes the most sense. And, inevitably, she wouldn't be able to hide it.

I slide open the kitchen door. There's no dramatic entry. They don't stop. They keep shouting, Mum and Dad launching these condemnations at Steph. She sits in Dad's chair, expressionless, arms folded across her chest. Most of the time she'd retreat to her bungalow. But in this case, that's only a temporary out. So, she's decided to weather it.

'What happened?' I ask.

'Your sister is stupid,' Dad says.

'I'll be ashamed to be seen at Jim's wedding,' Mum says.

'Mum, that's months away,' Steph says.

'What? What? What's going on?' I ask

'Your sister,' Dad says. 'She quit her job.'

'That's it?' I say.

Which isn't a very smart thing to say.

I duck out of there as the shouting bounces off the walls, dump my stuff in my bedroom, then retreat to the garage. I put the radio on – *LOUD*, to drown out the shouting – set up the pool table and play game after game after game, until the door opens. Steph peeks her head in and turns down the radio.

'Can I come in?'

'Sure,' I tell her.

'You want a game?' she says.

'Okay.'

I gather up the balls and set them up as Steph grabs a cue, the mood all sombre – it's not just us, but what we're carrying over from Mum and Dad.

We play for a few minutes, wordlessly. Although we'd do anything for each other, we're not close – not in the way that you'd share things and talk to one another. Maybe it's the different genders. Or maybe the seven-year age difference. But I decide to broach it.

'What're you gonna do now?'

'For a little while?' Steph says. 'Nothing.'

'That's it?'

'I finished high school, I worked for a year, then went into university and then when I dropped out, I went back to work. I've never had a break just for me. I want to be able to take some time to work things out.'

'Jim had things worked out when he was fourteen, you know.'

Steph laughs and hugs me impulsively – a rarity. Like we don't talk, we don't hug either. Then she tousles my hair.

'It's getting long,' she says.

'You think Olivia would cut it?' I ask.

10.

Come Sunday morning, I head next door and knock on the kitchen window. It's only moments before the screen door swings open, and Olivia smiles at me, long, long legs poking out of a pair of khaki shorts, arms bare in a sleeveless blouse, the top two (of five) buttons undone showing a glimpse of cleavage.

'We'll go in the garage,' she tells me.

She guides me into the little set-up in the back of the garage – a mirror on the wall, a storage trolley with all hairdressing equipment, and a kitchen chair. I sit down. She curls a towel around my neck, then drapes a cape around me. I smooth it out over my lap. A radio sits among some books on a shelf in the corner. She turns it on. I expect rock or pop, but it's classical.

'You okay with this sort of music?' she asks.

'Sure.'

'You know what it is?'

It opens with strings going through a slow build-up. It's very moody but moving. I shake my head.

'Beethoven's "Ode to Joy".' She runs her hands through my hair. 'First time you've come to me.'

'I usually go to the hairdresser my mum does…'

In terms of relativity, the words come out of my

mouth before the embarrassment hits, but when the embarrassment hits it stops me from finishing the sentence.

'She's old,' I say. 'I don't think she knows much about styles.'

'What are you thinking about?'

'I'm not sure.'

Olivia grabs a big hardcover book from a shelf in the corner and leans over me as she flips through it. Her perfume's sweet. I don't even know what it smells like. But it's sweet. Maybe raspberry? Or maybe that's her shampoo. Whatever it is, she smells better than hanging around Ash and Riley.

'Take a look at these,' she says, flicking through the book.

The pages contain pictures of models with different styles: spikes, flat tops, undercuts…things I don't even know the names for.

'I don't want anything fancy,' I say. 'I just want to stop looking so Beatley.'

'Beatley?'

'Like one of The Beatles.'

'The Beatles were the biggest band in the world.'

'Like one hundred years ago.'

Olivia smiles. 'You trust me?'

'Sure.'

She puts the book aside, then picks up a spray bottle. I think now that the music might be a little joke from her – as she works, the music ramps up and becomes heady and uplifting. Her hands are light, and fingers cool as they work in rhythm with the music. The scissors snip repeatedly. Hair sheds from me – I've never lost so much.

Locks of it bounce off my shoulders and slide down my arms and chest.

'How's school going?' she says.

'Good.'

'Schoolwork not too tough?'

'No.'

'What about the girls – got a girlfriend?'

'No.'

'How're your parents?'

'Okay.'

She hums in melody with the classical music. I berate myself for my monosyllabic answers. It must be a skill for her to pick up a conversation with anybody and that's the best I have: *Good. No. No. Okay*.

'You've probably heard the shouting lately,' I say.

'Um, yeah.'

'They probably heard it on the moon,' I say, trying for a bit of wit, but now that I hear it aloud, I cringe.

'That's what they're like,' Olivia says, orbiting around me to work on my side. 'Parents are parents,' she says. 'Yours are like mine. They blow up because they're scared.'

'They seem angry.'

'They get angry because they're scared that things aren't going to work out.'

She's in front of me now so she can work on my fringe. I take a deep breath. Her nipples poke through her blouse, and between the tents of the buttoned lapels, the rim of her violet bra and the swell of her left breast flash at me. When she continues her orbit of me, in the mirror I see the shape of her butt in her shorts, how they ride up in a way that's indecent when you stop to examine it, and the faintest outline of her underwear. I'm not breathing. Or I haven't since she got in front of me. And I'm sweltering. When she sprays water onto the other side of my head, it's refreshing.

I don't mean for this to sound so...so...so...I don't even know the word. Lecherous? Sexist? Just seeing her as a body and not a person? But I'm fifteen. The extent of my experience is making out with a few different girls, stories from Riley and general guy chatter. This is the closest I've been to a beautiful woman. I adjust the cape so it's rumpled over my crotch.

She's behind me now. All I can tell is my hair's short and I panic that she's cut too much. I can't show up at school with this much of a makeover, although that had been the plan. I hear kids laugh at me, idiots like Mickey and Lachlan, and Rachel and Felicia scoff at me. It's almost enough for me to forget how close I am to Olivia, and how unsettled.

Almost.

She grabs clippers from the trolley and shaves the back of my head and a fade into the sides. Then comes the straight razor. She dabs hot shaving cream onto my neck, then shaves away what's back there – I wouldn't know, I've never looked. The back of Dad's shoulders and neck are hairy, but he's in his forties. I can't be that bad...can I?

When Olivia's done, she wipes away the foam, rubs wax into my hair, and quickly runs the hair dryer over it. What's left is a mixture of a spikey flat top, but with this natural mess about it. My worries about it disappear. If anybody mocks me, it's not because it doesn't look good.

'All done,' Olivia says.

I get up and rifle through my pockets for money Mum gave me – two tens. Olivia takes only one from me.

'Keep the rest for yourself,' she says.

'You sure?'

'Keep it.'

I thrust it out to her.

'Really.'

'Thanks.'

I stuff the money in my pocket and check out all the hair on the ground, like a sheep has been shorn. A black sheep.

'Can I help you clean up?' I ask.

'It's fine. One of the perils of the trade.'

'Thanks for cutting it on a Sunday.'

'Better here than the salon.'

'Will you…will you cut it next time?'

Olivia smiles as she grabs a broom. 'Sure.'

I should leave, but I don't want to go, knowing this is a MOMENT – an instant I don't want to end because it's just me and her, and I've shared something with her, something sweet and that littlest bit intimate. She mightn't know that, and for her she was just doing me a favour (or doing Steph a favour), but it's something to hold onto.

The screen door rattles. Her boyfriend Mario doesn't so much come as spills in. He's a slab that blocks all the light, with curly hair that should be used to scrub dishes and this caterpillar of a moustache that crawls down to his jaw.

'Hey,' he says to Olivia. His greeting goes through me. I might as well not be there.

'I should get going,' I say. 'Thanks again.'

'Any time,' Olivia says.

Once I get home, I shower because I hate that prickliness you feel in clothes after a haircut.

And I masturbate.

11.

The kitchen is quiet when I go in for lunch. Whenever Mum, Dad and Steph are together now, it's like magnets pushing against each other.

Steph smiles at me. 'Looks good,' she says.

'Thanks.'

It's easy to say a shadow hangs over Mum in moods like this, but that's too simple and it's using a cliché – Mr Baker says never to use clichés when writing. Mum generates the shadow that hangs over all of us. But now, she brightens; it's the first time this week a smile touches her face.

'You are so handsome.' Mum grabs my face and kisses my cheek. 'You should be getting married.'

'Mum, I'm fifteen!'

'It doesn't matter! You are so handsome!'

I see Ash the next day, meeting so we can walk to school. He frowns, then nods.

'Cool,' he says.

The reactions differ at school. If I was Ethan May or Jake Fichera, I could get away with such an audacious change. People would tell me it looked good even if it didn't. Mickey and Lachlan jeer – no words, just, 'Ohhhhhhhh.' Morons. Gabriella gives me a half-smile, which disappoints me because I expected something bigger from her. Samantha's always sneaking looks at me but now she's wide-eyed, like the haircut and a bit of style transfixes her. Riley's the worst – typically, maybe, because it's often your closest friends who say the worst things. He comes out of the toilet and throws his arms out, the way he might to royalty.

'George Michael!' he says, loud enough that he draws the attention of everybody in the courtyard.

'What?'

'You look like George Michael,' he says.

'I look nothing like George Michael.'

'You,' Riley throws a finger forward, 'look like George Michael.'

I become self-conscious through the first two periods. Mr Tan, who takes Computer, is as unobtrusive and deadpan as you can get and even he jokes that I've had an upgrade. Mrs Grady, who takes Legal Studies, is tall and intimidating and she always wears dark colours that make her look grave. She gives me a wolf whistle, which gets a laugh from everybody.

At recess, as we sit on one of the courtyard benches, I wonder if girls are looking at me more. That'd be stupid, of course. I'm just me, like I was last week. Of course, women do their hair and it changes the way they look, so maybe the same happens for men. I hang onto that because it makes me feel good. Things get a bit embarrassing in third-period English, though.

'It seems we have a new student,' Mr Baker says.

The announcement hangs there and we wait for somebody to be trotted in, the way new kids are marched in by the vice-principal but instead, Mr Baker comes up to the back desk and narrows his eyes at me.

'And your name would be?' he asks.

My face goes hot. Some kids titter. Mr Baker flashes a smile at me as he returns to the front of his class to sit on his desk the way he does. Riley rolls his eyes and holds his left hand limp. Ash smirks.

'I've had a few people come talk to me about the identity piece,' Mr Baker says, 'unsure what I want. What I don't want is this: "My name is John Smith. I'm 15. My parents are Mr and Mrs Smith. I live at Blah Blah Street. *The Wonder Years* is my favourite TV show." That's a dossier and it's not interesting. Do people understand?'

Nobody says anything.

'Look at me,' Mr Baker says. 'What do you know about me?'

Again, nothing.

'Oh, come on – say anything!'

'You're tall,' Jake says.

'Okay, I'm tall. That's a detail about me. It's not who I am.'

'You're a teacher,' Samantha says.

'Better, but can we expand on that?'

Riley writes across his notebook, *FAG! FAG! FAG!*

'You're a teacher because you like to teach?' Deanne says.

'And why would I like to teach?'

'Because you want to help kids?' Ethan says.

'Good. Now do you see how we've peeled back the layers? What might the next question be?'

'Why you want to help kids,' I say.

'Right! Again, we peel back the layer. And we can keep

doing that. This is what I'm challenging you to do. Look insides yourselves. You might even learn something.'

Riley's unimpressed at lunch as we walk down to the hamburger joint, Max's, by the supermarket down the road from the high school.

'Felt like saying he wants to teach because he wants to touch kids,' Riley says.

He pauses, leaving a gap for the laughter. But Ash has his eyes fixed right ahead, like he mightn't have even heard Riley.

'What a crock of shit,' Riley says. 'What's he want me to say in this stupid fucking assignment? Probably just wants to get in our heads.'

'I think that identity essay is what they're gonna judge the Boland on,' Ash says.

'More bullshit,' Riley says. 'You see the way they set it up – they don't even tell you which piece is gonna be the one, so you have to work hard at everything to cover it. It's just another way of brainwashing us into doing more work.'

And that's probably true to some extent, although the other side of it is they don't want you focusing especially on just one piece of work. I don't want to say that, though, because Riley's on a rampage. He goes on about it, too, after we eat our burgers and retreat to the aqueduct to lie down and smoke, until it grates on me and I wonder if I should tell him to shut up.

'Why're you two so quiet?' Riley says, when he gets no response.

'Wondering,' Ash says.

'If it's about that fucking assignment–'

'You ever thought about what you want to do once you get out of here?'

'Fuck. Now you're Counsellor Hoffs?'

Ash sits up. 'Not so much about who I am. But who I'm gonna be. Only a couple more years. Who will I be in five years? Ten years? Twenty years!'

My future flashes in my mind like a film on the big screen: wife, kids, steady job. At fifteen. That's already in there, and I recognise that's not me. That's Mum's and Dad's programming. That's not to say I don't want those things eventually, but I've never thought about anything else.

'I want to fuck,' Riley says. 'I want to be happy. I want to have a good time.'

'How long'll that last?' I say.

'Forever.'

'How long's forever?' Ash asks.

'What the fuck's this now? You're turning into Mr Gayer? Forever's forever. Whether it's one day or fifty years. It's your forever.'

'And then you die.'

'And then you die, and who knows what's next?'

'Might be nothing,' Ash says. 'Like sleeping without dreams and never waking up.'

'I'll make a deal – if I die first and there's something afterwards, I'll come back and let you both know. If one of you dies first, you come let me know.'

'What about you?' Ash says to me. 'You thought about it?'

'What? About death?'

'About what you're gonna do next.'

'Who knows?'

'You play pool.'

'Not gonna make a career playing pool.'

'You could if that's what you focused on.'

I shrug.

'You like to write.'

'Yeah.'

'That's something you're good at.'

'Thanks.'

'That's what he does,' Riley says. 'It's not who he is.'

'Maybe,' Ash says. 'Maybe it's like being a superhero.'

'What sort of stupid thing is that to say?'

'Like Superman – Superman's not what he does. Superman's who he is. What he is.'

'That's stupid.'

Riley's not going to be flipped. But I think about what Ash has said. He's right. I do like to write. I think about that day of the funeral, of coming home and losing myself in my writing. I don't do that with anything else. Maybe I should take it more seriously.

For the rest of the day, we're all quiet for different reasons – Riley because of his mood, while I'm thinking about my writing. Ash is pensive; Mr Baker's assignment has gotten to him somehow. I know not to push it; that's when Ash totally shuts down.

When the bell rings to signal the end of the day, Riley skittles off, and I tell Ash I want to go to the supermarket.

'You want me to come?' he asks.

'You go ahead – I want to get something.'

'Sure?'

I nod.

The supermarket is packed with parents who've picked up their kids and have now ducked in to do a bit of shopping. I see Ash's dad, who's only ever been known as Mr Handley to me, chatting with a familiar blonde woman – some kid's mother, although I can't remember whose – outside the chemist. He sees me and grins, this bigger version of Ash with a weathered face and scraggly beard, and I wave, then slip into the supermarket. The blonde woman is in her forties and aging well – she probably doesn't work and instead does aerobics and hits the gym.

Stationery's in aisle five, the stack of orange A5 exercise books high. There's also a stack of aqua A4 books. My cousin Jim would tell me that writing's stupid. Mum and Dad would tell me it's impractical. But as I pick up one of the A4s and flick through the blank pages, I see nothing but potential. This is what life is, isn't it? Making something from nothing?

I take the exercise book to the checkout, pay for it and walk home.

WINTER

June — August 1989

12.

I jolt awake and sit up as terror blisters through my body.

Logic tries to poke its way through. I've been scared before. Everybody gets scared. But this isn't just scared. Something's broken inside my head, some switch that usually controls this, and now it's spilling out and all I know is fear.

The room's darkness closes around me, except for the clock radio's neon numerals on the bedside drawer: 1.11am. That means everybody's asleep. So, it's just me.

And this.

I should call Mum. I'll knock on their door, rouse Mum and Dad and tell them. They're parents; that's what they're there for.

No. The whole idea's stupid. I'm going to tell them I'm frightened? They won't understand. They'll take any explanation literally. I can't explain this to them. I don't understand it myself. And what're they going to do? I'm not a kid who should be screaming for his mum. It's embarrassing.

I sit on my bed and draw my knees up to my chest as I try to work this out. Something's changed. Like getting sick. Like a flu. You go from healthy to infected. Something's happened inside me. That's why I'm feeling this.

I crawl under my covers but can't lie still. The panic throbs. I get out of bed, grab my new A4 exercise book, and flip it open. I don't know what I'm going to write. I just want to find a way to escape. Thoughts flit around in my head. The pen trembles in my left hand. I scrunch up the A4 exercise book, shoving it from the bed, and drag *To Kill a Mockingbird* out of my bag.

The words ripple, like they're printed on water. I force myself to read the first page, then the next, and the next, but nothing sinks in. The sentences don't make sense. I close the book, drop it on the floor and crawl into bed. I need to make sleep happen. There's escape in sleep. When I wake up, this'll be gone.

The lamp goes off and the darkness swamps me.

Relax, relax, relax, I tell myself, but the panic is everywhere. *Relax. Relax.* There must be some explanation for this. *Relax.* The library at school – there'll have to be something there.

Now, some small relief punctures the dread. Although I never fall back into a deep sleep, I do sleep, uneasily, with this suffocating me and I wake to enjoy an instant of hopefulness that this is gone, that this will be like a nightmare that I don't recall happening.

But, no, it's there. Dimmer, but there.

During the morning routine, everything seems too loud. The water from the shower stings. As I wash up, the clatter of plates and cutlery in the sink is too shrill. I should tell Steph but, free from her working life, she no longer shares the morning with me. Would she understand? Maybe Steph will look at me like I'm crazy. Tell Mum and Dad. No. That's not embarrassing. It's humiliating.

Ash. It has to be Ash. And that's the plan as I wait for him on the corner and watch him lumber up. But with each step, my intent dissolves. How can I talk to Ash? Ash, who walks up to a cluster of guys and faces them down? Who tells bullies like Mickey and Lachlan to behave? Ash doesn't know what it is to be afraid. Or weak.

'Hey,' he says.

'Hey.'

The walk to school is quieter but we still stop on the bank by the bridge to have a smoke. The first few times I inhale, my chest tightens up and I hiss out the smoke. Ash is oblivious. He lies back, cigarette poking from the corner of his mouth, and folds his hands back behind his head.

'Parents are arguing again,' he says matter-of-factly.

'Yeah.'

'Why do you think people stay together?'

'Because they love each other?'

'Your parents love each other?'

'I guess.'

'I think sometimes it's habit. Like these.' Ash holds up his cigarette and blows out a stream of smoke. 'You know it's bad for you. But you do it. And you don't stop doing it.'

'Maybe.'

'Marriage should come with a warning, like cigarettes do. It probably wouldn't stop anybody. But they should be warned, all the same.'

We're quiet for a bit, Ash tearing at grass from the bank.

'I was thinking about Rachel, too,' he says.

'Yeah?'

'She seemed okay to you?'

I imagine Rachel but I don't see her smile or that easy-going nature that makes her stand out from her friends. I see her friends crowded around her, the way they were Monday after the party.

'Well?' Ash says.

'Okay?' I hold onto Rachel's face, because at least that forces me to think. 'Like okay as in to hang around with? Or okay because you shattered her?'

'Easy.'

'Which one?'

'Because I shattered her.'

'She hasn't been the same since then.'

'Yeah, I thought so.'

Ash sits up. Maybe he's feeling the guilt. Or it might just be pouring off me.

'You thinking–?'

'Of Deanne.'

'*Deanne?*'

'I wonder what she's like under all that nerdiness.'

'I've never thought about it.'

'I'm curious.'

'You were *just* talking about Rachel.'

'So?' Ash blinks. 'Live and lust – remember?'

Most of my cigarette's burned down to ash. I flick it into the stream and watch it get carried away. If nothing else, Ash has annoyed me enough that the fear's dropped into the background, but as soon as I think that, it bounces back and now it's in my head and all over me again. I jump to my feet as if I could jump out of it.

'Let's go,' I say.

13.

Mrs Grady could be the Grim Reaper the way she looms at the front of the class, tall and dark in her black blazer and slacks, her hair drawn back.

'Justice is meted out differently all over the world,' she says. 'We have prisons, although some may argue the merit of rehabilitation. Some prisons have education programs. Some countries still have the death penalty. And some still carry out an eye-for-an-eye justice – punishing the offender similarly to how they've offended. We also have public demonstrations, such as floggings. Does anybody think there's a better method?'

I try to hold onto her words, like each is a life buoy bobbing in the ocean. Usually, she's telling us to read from the exercise book and then quizzing us. Now, her question fires imaginations in the classroom.

'Hard labour,' Jake jokes.

'Community-minded hard labour,' Deanne says.

'Screw that,' Ethan says. 'Punishment.'

I can't find my way into the conversation that ensues. Each voice speaking is like shearing metal. When somebody says something funny and everybody laughs, it's broken glass tumbling around in my ears. I see myself leaping to my feet and shouting, 'Shut up! Shut up!' Of course, I don't

– and I won't – but the image leaps into my mind all the same.

Faces are alien around me. Samantha looks at me, eyes big and round. I see her earnestness, how she wears her emotions openly. Gabriella catches my glance and smiles, and maybe I imagine it or *want* it to be there, but I see that twinkling and softness in her eyes. Even Riley's face is intent.

'One thousand words,' Mrs Grady wraps up the discussion, 'on how you would shape our legal system, given the opportunity.'

Needless thoughts invade my head – observations of tiny things; extrapolations of what those tiny things mean; a response to how I feel about those things; then the image of me jumping up on my table and screaming until I've got no breath left. The urge goads me.

The next period, I have an Open Room – a class where I'm allowed to do my own homework or work on an Open Room project. Almost everybody does nothing in their Open Rooms (which is why they brought in Open Room projects). I get permission to go to the library.

Ash watches me pack my bags. 'Everything okay?' he asks.

'Sure. Why?'

'You've been quiet today.'

'Didn't sleep so good.'

Ash can tell there's more but doesn't push it. Riley's oblivious to us, already working on his legal essay.

At the library, I go over to the catalogue and look at all the little drawers. What is this? *Fear?* Is that what I look for? I check and find titles. Lots of them are novels. I write down the nonfiction titles and their reference numbers and go check them on the shelves. Unfortunately, fear relates in lots of different ways to everyday life, ranging from politics to phobias to…and that's when I find it: to *psychology*.

The books in the psychology section are fat, dreary, lonely hardcovers that are stuck together. Flicking through them doesn't teach me much and I'm too impatient to read them thoroughly, but at least I identify what's going on: *anxiety*. Giving this thing a name reassures me. If it has a name, then others have dealt with it. If others have dealt with it, then I can, too. It's not some bizarre new condition that they won't know how to treat and which'll be named after me when I die.

I keep flicking through books, reading passages but unable to make much sense of the clinical language. Another book identifies what happened to me as a 'panic attack' – being struck by sudden, debilitating anxiety. Here's something else with a name. *Panic attack*. That fits. As I read about them, I grow worried that another one will hit. What if one hits in the classroom? What would I do? How would the other kids look at me?

The preferred treatment is counselling. I can't go to Counsellor Hoffs with this – there's no way I'd be able to hide that from Ash and Riley, even if I could hide it from the other kids. I have no idea where I'd find a psychiatrist or psychologist, or how I'd afford either. Medication is also mentioned. Various books stress antidepressants must be taken for at least eighteen months before a condition stabilises.

Exercise is advocated as good treatment for anxiety –

even just a walk. Another recommendation is meditation and the book details a progressive muscle relaxation exercise. This seems the only doable thing right now. You tense your feet, count to five, and when you relax, imagine the tension pouring out. You work your way up the body – calves, thighs, buttocks, stomach, and on and on you go.

A hand closes on my shoulder. It's Ethan May, holding a copy of *To Kill a Mockingbird*. He looks at all the books I've drawn from the shelves and sat on the floor around me in various piles like I'm building Lego towers. I'm suddenly self-conscious that my secret is going to be out. Which fifteen-year-old would be reading stuff like this?

'Whatcha reading?' he asks.

'Was doing research for an Open Room project.'

'Ah, okay. I'm turning sixteen – not for a while. Like three months. August.'

'My birthday's in August,' I say.

'Mine's end of August – last day of winter.' Like that's so cool. Like they decided winter should come to an end once Ethan was born. 'I'm telling everybody *way* in advance because I want you to block the date out,' he says. 'It's gonna be big. *Huge*. I'm inviting everybody.'

'Oh. Cool.'

'So, I'll see you there, right?'

'Where?'

'Still tossing up between home and the soccer club. I got a job there part-time cleaning up and stuff, but I have access to their social club.'

'What if somebody trashes the place?'

'Yeah, yeah. Good point. Better dealing with Mum and Dad. Okay. Home, then. Thanks.'

Ethan leaves me to go to the counter to borrow his novel. And although he's never been anything but nice to me (and he was even sympathetic when my girlfriend Mary Hatchet dumped me for him), I resent him. I resent him because he doesn't have to deal with this. That his grand concerns are being fit for sport, planning parties and being popular. I resent everybody in the library – kids borrowing books, flicking through magazines or sitting around chatting.

They're oblivious.

And I resent them and envy them for it.

14.

The weeks trundle by as we plunge deeper into winter. The cold comes. The greyness of the days reflects how the world's come to look to me, the anxiousness like the static on a radio between stations, every now and then blaring to remind me of what it can do. Sleep disintegrates into restless splotches and I amble through school and home and those two days working with my parents, always trying to say and do the right things so nobody knows what's going on but feeling that my mask is shredding.

Homework becomes hard, although I can still lose myself in the creative aspects of it. When I write, there's somewhere my mind retreats that is immune to this. But the more practical homework – like Mathematics and quizzes that need definite answers – becomes scrambled.

One day after school, I come home and find a car I don't recognise – a blue Subaru – parked in our drive. The windows are tinted, although the driver's window is rolled down. The interior of the car is immaculate, and the stereo system is this complicated thing. A packet of cigarettes and a fancy silver lighter sits in the change compartment.

In the lounge room, Mum and Dad sit with Steph and a guy with wavy blond hair who looks like he was dragged through a wringer by the nose and came out all sinewy.

He holds Steph's hand – something Mum periodically frowns at. On the coffee table are cups of tea and plates of chocolate biscuits.

'Hey,' Steph says. She pats the guy's hand. 'This is Todd, my boyfriend.'

'Hey,' Todd says, with a nod of his head. 'How're you doing?'

Steph's introduced two boyfriends previously, and only when the relationships have gotten serious. Those guys had also been Greek and this guy obviously isn't. He's Australian. If you took a snapshot, you might see a set of parents meeting their daughter's boyfriend for the first time. It would happen frequently in families everywhere. But poor Todd doesn't know what he's got himself in for. I excuse myself and retreat to my bedroom.

I close the door and lie on my bed, practicing the progressive muscle relaxation exercises that have become more like exercises in futility. This isn't going to be the quick-fix I'd hoped. As I try, tremors pulse through my body – little hits that threaten to become big hits.

I hear somebody knock at the kitchen window. Then, 'Hello!'

Olivia.

Footsteps through the hallway – not just Olivia's. Somebody cloddy. The kitchen door slides open. A round of greetings. Now I hear Mario's voice rumbling through the kitchen. I listen and piece things together: Olivia and Mario have come for Steph and Todd. They walk through the kitchen. The goodbyes from Mum and Dad are terse. Footsteps back down the hallway. The screen door at the back opens and closes. Olivia, Mario, Steph and Todd are gone. They must be going to dinner or a movie or something together. So, Olivia must've already known about Steph and Todd. Mum and Dad traipse back into the kitchen. I expect arguing about Steph's choice of boyfriends, but nothing.

Already, I feel calmer because I was able to focus on something else. Then I resume the progressive muscle relaxation: my feet, my calves, my thighs, my butt, my stomach and my chest. I tense each too tight, trying to will this anxiety from my body.

The door opens and the light comes on, shattering it all.

'What're you doing sleeping at this time?' Mum says.

'I'm not sleeping. I'm lying down.'

'Why're you lying down? Are you sick?'

'No…'

'Steph isn't going to be here for dinner. She went out with her boyfriend. Did you see him, with that big nose of his?'

'I'm sure he's nice.'

'He's not one of ours.'

And Steph will pay for that. He's not Greek. He's not a member of the tribe. Mum and Dad will ride her over it. The shouting will resume. As if things hadn't been bad enough.

'So, what do you want to eat?' Mum says.

'Anything. I don't care. Can you…?'

She closes the door.

I can't recapture any feeling of peacefulness and after dinner – a plate of spaghetti that could've fed four of us – I excuse myself and slip out into the night. It's cold enough that I draw the zip up on my jacket and flip my collar. I think I'm walking aimlessly, just to have something to do, but I end up at Ash's. I ring the doorbell and his mum answers. She tells me Marcus – in terms of age, he's the next down from Ash – has a basketball game and Ash's dad has taken them all to watch. I thank her and walk on, not wanting to go home, not really wanting to do anything.

I end up at Riley's and walk up to the veranda through his unkempt yard. He answers the door with that sullen look which is his trademark. He beckons me in, and I follow him down the hallway into the lounge. The place is a mess – clothes lie everywhere, the sink's filled with dishes, and there's a faint odour of something damp. His mum sits at the kitchen table, smoking a cigarette. Her blonde hair is like straw and she wears a pink bathrobe drawn tight.

'Hi, Miss Seger,' I say as Riley plonks himself down on the couch.

'Hello.' She blinks at me, the way you do when you're not sure who you're seeing. Either she doesn't know who I am, or she's got a problem with her eyesight and can't tell from that distance.

Riley opens a pack of cigarettes and offers them to me. I look nervously at his mum. He waves her presence away.

'Don't worry about it,' he says.

So, we have a smoke, sit on his couch and watch TV. It's not long before Riley's mum gets up and disappears into one of the other rooms.

'Where's your dad?' I ask.

'Gone.'

'Gone?'

'He's got somebody else.'

'He's got somebody else?'

'What're you – a parrot?'

'Sorry.'

'Want a drink?'

'Sure.'

I expect Riley will come back with Coke, but he brings two beers back from the fridge. He opens them, hands one to me and then toasts.

'Dad's had somebody on the side for five years. Mum's shattered.'

I look around the house. There are pictures of Riley's parents' wedding – both so young and hopeful – hanging from the wall, along with pictures of Riley and his older brother Ray. Other family pictures sit on the mantel. They all beam with a happiness that's empty now.

'Why didn't you tell me?' I ask.

'What would you have done?'

A good question. So many people insert themselves into situations they can have no influence over because they want to feel useful, or they're self-important enough that they believe they can fix somebody else's problem. But the truth is, most of the time, what can you offer but the appearance that you want to help?

'Shit, I'm sorry,' I say.

'Dad's a dick. That's all there is to it.'

My issues seem so trivial given Riley's announcement. What would Riley say if I told him? If I said I had a panic attack and felt anxious? How much is he going through? It plays out in my head, his dad telling them he's going off with somebody else, somebody younger and prettier than Riley's mum. There'd be shock. Shouting. And here's Riley, stoic.

The truth might be that I need to toughen up.

15.

I shuffle through the morning and stumble out of the house. Every step feels like it's coming off the back of some hike that's already exhausted me.

Ash is waiting at the corner, hands shoved in his pocket. 'My mum said you dropped around last night.'

'Yeah. Didn't plan to. Went for a walk.'

'What did you end up doing?'

'Went to Riley's.'

'Is–?'

My mind does the calculations quick. Ash is going to ask, *Is everything okay?* I jump in with question.

'When's the last time you've been to Riley's?' I ask.

'A while.'

I tell him what Riley told me about his dad. It might be confidential, but it keeps Ash from asking about me.

'I wonder why he didn't say anything,' Ash says when I finish.

'Don't know.'

We stop on the bank by the bridge and smoke, although we can't sit because the grass is wet with morning dew. A cold wind funnels down the aqueduct and hurries us on our way.

It's the usual activity in the courtyard, the same everyday

clusters – except for Lachlan sitting with Felicia, chatting and laughing. I don't know what Lachlan's saying. It can't be smart, on account of him being an idiot. But Felicia regularly throws back her head and laughs.

Ash and I slip into the toilets. Riley sits against the sink as always, smoking and blowing rings. He offers us a cigarette. I take one and light it, but the stench of smoke is cloying and my chest seizes up. The fear that I'm going to choke EXPLODES in my head – I can't stop it and my heart *thumpthumpthump*s a warning that has the toilet sway in front of me. I lean against the wall.

'What's up with you?' Ash says. 'Why didn't you tell us about your dad?'

'It just is.' Riley spits in the sink.

'It's a pretty big just is.'

'Not like you could do anything.' Riley spits again in the sink. 'Mum's struggling to keep it together. Dad should be strung up by the balls.'

'For cheating?' Ash says, his voice tense.

'Yeah. Why? What's the problem?'

It hangs there, waiting to be challenged. But Riley doesn't really want to have a conversation about this. He wants to be the final authority, like what he says *can't* be questioned. We've learned just to shut up, for the most part.

Riley throws his cigarette into the urinal like he's ditching everything associated with the topic.

The bell rings.

Ash takes a last puff of his cigarette and then also throws it in the urinal. He and Riley head for the door.

'I'll catch up,' I say, stepping up onto the urinal.

Once they're gone, I go straight to the sink and splash

cold water on my face. Riley's two gobs of spit stare up at me like a pair of unsightly eyes. I pull back and my chest scrunches up. Irrational possibilities blare through my mind: *heart attack, emphysema, cancer*. I tell myself they can't be the case – I'm too young for a heart attack and emphysema and cancer don't work like they've just been switched on. Unfortunately, I'm imaginative enough to poke holes through logic. I don't know how emphysema and cancer work. Maybe they toil quietly away at your body until they hit a breaking point. Aunt Mena only discovered her cancer when she went to get a check-up because she'd been feeling tired. As for a heart attack, I might be young, but young people can have congenital heart defects. Anything could be happening inside me.

I sit on the toilet seat, doubled over, smelling the urinal cakes and feeling the cold seep through my clothes. But it's good, because now I'm not focusing on what's going on inside my head. Slowly, my breath evens out, although my chest is still tight. I get up and feel okay – or at least okay as far as my new baseline goes.

As I emerge from the cubicle, the main door opens and Mr Baker comes in. He puts his hands on his hips.

'You've missed half of the class,' he says. 'Your friends said you were in here. What've you been doing?'

'I…have an upset stomach.'

Mr Baker's face doesn't twitch. He must know it's a lie. If I'd had an upset stomach, the toilet would stink. But he nods.

'You okay to come back to class? Do you want to go to the sickbay? Or perhaps I can call your parents?'

'I'll be all right.'

'Okay. But tell me if you feel unwell again.'

It's awkward coming into class when it's halfway done, but given Mr Baker's absence to come find me, everybody's gotten noisy. Samantha watches me with concern as I take my seat next to Riley. Gabriella glances at me. Kat and Felicia are oblivious. Only Rachel sits quietly.

I struggle through the rest of English and feel little better in Mr McCready's Social Studies class. At recess, drizzle is a drumroll across the courtyard, so kids hang around in classrooms or take refuge in the locker rooms. I'm in the toilets, of course, with Ash and Riley, but being here worries me that there'll be a repeat performance of what happened this morning. I tell myself over and over that I'll be okay, like the sheer weight of repetition can brainwash my thinking back to where it belongs.

But as the day goes on, I know it won't.

Whatever this is, I can't keep facing it alone.

16.

The new morning routine helps my plan – Mum and Dad have already gone to work and Steph sleeps in now that she no longer has a job. That means when I pry myself from a restless sleep at 5.30 am, nobody's around to question me.

I eat a quick breakfast, shoulder my school bag and set off. It's still dark outside and my breath mists. The GP clinic Mum and Dad bring me to is just ten minutes away, but I can't go there. The family doctor is Dr Stathakis – he's from the same Greek village as Mum and Dad and whenever they've taken me to see him, there's always socialising. If I see him, there's the chance the reason *why* I've come to see him will get back to Mum and Dad. I know there's meant to be doctor-patient confidentiality, but you never know.

So, instead, I plan to go to the new 24-Hour Super Clinic over in South Mernda, which is maybe ten or eleven kilometres away. Nobody knows me there. I can go in – at this time of the morning there shouldn't be any problem seeing somebody quick – and then I can be back in time for school. On the off chance I'm late, I'll say I had to see a doctor because I didn't feel well yesterday. That means I'll need a note from Mum. If that's the case, maybe I'll skip school, be sick the rest of the day, and she can write me a note. It's complicated, but that's the only way I can see to do this.

The walk up to High Street is about twenty minutes and I'm tired and puffing when I get there – too much smoking and not enough exercise. I catch the 537 bus all the way down High Street, jump off and catch the 944 that runs down Childers Road, past the Super Clinic and to a hub of shops.

I feel a lightness on my trip, knowing a solution's waiting. The only worry is if the doctor wants to talk to my parents. Maybe parental authority will be needed, although at fifteen, I'm legally allowed to move out of home and get a job. This shouldn't be much different, should it?

When the bus stops at the hub of shops, I get off and walk back to the Super Clinic. Daylight seeps into the neighbourhood and cars fill the streets. I don't have a watch but guess it's about 7.00. Everything has that new feeling, like there's so much of the day ahead that it can't help but be filled with promise.

The Super Clinic is nondescript and lost behind some gum trees. You wouldn't know it was there if not for the big sign that proclaims that bulk billing is accepted. The parking lot is empty except for a handful of cars.

Inside, it's prettier than Dr Stathakis's clinic – rows of plush chairs, a long counter with a marble top, and hallways shooting off in various directions. Big TVs hang in the corners. There's even a pharmacy in the lobby. They haven't spared any expense in putting this place together.

'I'd like to see a doctor,' I tell the receptionist, a pretty redhead who can't be long out of high school. A gold nametag on the lapel of her black shirt identifies her as Bella.

'Have you been here before?' she asks.

I shake my head.

Bella hands me a clipboard and a pen. 'Only Dr Kuruvilla and Dr Prashad are on.' She gestures to a board behind her that lists the names of all the doctors – eight of them, all Indian. Some of the names are followed by titles. The last is a psychologist.

'Anybody's fine,' I say.

'Do you have a Medicare card?'

I hand her the family's Medicare card and she instructs me to sit down and fill out the form. It's all basics – name, address, phone number, height, weight, date of birth and a list of existing conditions. I can't help but think of Mr Baker's identity assignment. Is this who I am, written over this form?

I fill it out, retrieve my Medicare card and sit down. There are only a few other people in the waiting room – a young mother nursing a sniffling baby, a guy clamping a bloodied handkerchief to his hand, and an old guy who nods off in his chair, rouses himself, then nods off again.

It's not long before a plump, middle-aged doctor wearing a striped poncho and a round bowl-hat with a flat top comes out from one of the hallways. He calls a name and the young mother follows him. A few minutes later, the other doctor comes out from an opposing hallway – he's about the same age, but wears slacks and a cardigan. He calls in the guy with the bleeding hand.

It's not long before the young mother comes back down the hallway, rocking her baby. That means the first doctor will come out and call the old guy but instead, he calls my name. I look at the old guy, who's still nodding off. The doctor is already walking down the hallway, so I follow him to a gold door that's closing. He's already seated at his desk when I get inside, his hands resting on a manila folder with just a single sheet in it.

'I'm Dr Kuruvilla,' he says. 'Please, sit down.'

If he has an accent, it's something faint but not Indian – British, or maybe something a little more exotic, like South African.

I sit down in the chair opposite him. His office is smaller than Dr Stathakis's but has just as many degrees hanging from the wall and bookshelves overflowing with books. It doesn't feel like an office. It feels like a room somebody put some equipment in.

'How can I help you?'

I almost cry then. The first word chokes out of me. I pause, swallow and try to compose what I want to say.

'I'm not sure what's happening,' I say, 'but I woke up the other night and I was very scared.'

'Scared? How?'

'I don't mean scared like…you know, how people would get scared. I was terrified. I couldn't shake it.'

Dr Kuruvilla gets up. 'Is it still there?'

'Not at the same level – not most of the time. But I still feel it.'

He takes his blood pressure cuff, gestures for me to remove my jacket and wraps the cuff around my arm. As he takes my blood pressure, he probes me with questions – if I'm at school (yep), if there's problems or pressures at school (none more than usual), if I have problems at home (nope), if I take drugs (nope), if I smoke (yes – a little bit), if I drink (a few if I go out but not regularly), if I have friends (yes), if I have a girlfriend (no), what my interests are (reading, writing, movies), and if there's been any changes in my life. I tell him about Aunt Mena's funeral and how my older sister quit work. As we talk, he flashes a light in my eyes, has me track his finger as he waves it in front of my face, and listens to my breathing through a stethoscope. When he's done with his physical examination, he sits in his chair and leans back.

'Do you think your aunt's death affected you?' he asks.

'We weren't close,' I say. 'I did wonder when I died if people would gather for me like they did at her funeral. It's stupid. It's just a stupid thought that popped in my head. It didn't mean anything. Not that I wasn't sorry my aunt died…but, like I said, we weren't so close that it would affect me like that.'

I clamp my mouth shut to stop my rambling. Dr Kuruvilla's unflinching as he studies me. I wonder what he's thinking. So many different possibilities fire through my head. He thinks I'm on drugs. He thinks I'm crazy. He thinks I'm cold. He thinks I'm an idiot.

'Why didn't you go to your own GP?' he says.

He must see this a lot – people coming here to escape attention: pregnant teens, kids with drug habits, who knows what else? A bluff's not going to work.

'My GP is friends with my parents,' I say. 'I don't want my mum and dad to know about this. They wouldn't understand. They just won't…' Again, my voice chokes up. 'I didn't know what to do.' Then it occurs to me maybe he wants my GP – and my parents – involved for other reasons. 'Is it bad?' I ask.

Dr Kuruvilla smiles. The sternness falls away. 'Physically, everything's good. By the sounds of it, things that are going on in your life are affecting you more deeply than you realise. Sometimes, it might not be one thing specifically, but a collection of things. Your sleep's not good?'

I shake my head.

'I'm going to prescribe you a mild sleeping pill.' Dr Kuruvilla reaches for his prescription. 'Take one about ten or fifteen minutes before bed *when* required. Do you understand? Not on a whim. *Only* when you need it. Once you get rested, I think things will fall into place.'

He tears the prescription free but pulls it away from me as I reach for it.

'This is a tremendous responsibility,' he says. 'Do you understand?'

I nod.

Dr Kuruvilla hands me the prescription. 'You're young, you're healthy, you have your whole life ahead of you – try not to worry. Life's too short to be worrying about things that don't deserve it. Okay?'

I nod again.

'If you need to see me again, you come back.'

I clutch the prescription in my hand. 'Thanks, Doctor.'

17

I almost bounce from Dr Kuruvilla's office, excited to have an answer at hand – *in* my hand. All this time, just soldiering through this and here I've been examined by a doctor who's shown no alarm, and now I've come away with a prescription that'll fix this.

I sign the Medicare receipt at reception, then hand my prescription in at the pharmacy. The bottle I get back is plastic and costs fifteen dollars. I scrounge through my pockets. With all my change, I only just have enough – that's a sign, isn't it?

At the bus stop, I twist open the bottle and tip one of the pills onto my palm. It's the size of a small pea but oval, with a glossy finish, and makes me think of Mum's pills. She's taken them for as long as I remember, usually when she's sick and lying on the couch. Maybe it's this, although she powers through everything when she needs to. I dunk the pill back into the bottle, shut it tight and stuff the bottle into my jacket.

The first bus back is crowded with people going to work and a handful of uniformed kids going to school – who knows where they go to school if they catch buses this early? Their blazers are a royal blue, their ties striped blue and yellow. The second bus has more kids going to school – a different school, these kids don't wear uniforms – chatting, laughing, bustling.

When the bus pulls up at my stop, I ask the driver what time it is. He tells me 8.05. It'd be about a twenty-five-minute walk home – just enough time to unlock the back door, grab an orange juice, then meet Ash at the corner. If I go straight to school, it'll be fifteen minutes, and I can sit around and wait until everybody arrives. Going home's the better option – nobody will have any clues about what I've done this morning. But the tiredness burns behind my eyelids, so I end up at school, sitting on one of the benches in the empty courtyard.

The quiet is a comfort that wraps around me. Peaceful. When the first kids show up – Lachlan and Mickey, kicking a football around – the school seems to lament their arrival. I hear it sighing that it's subjecting itself to another day of being taken for granted, of being dirtied, of being mistreated. It's another stupid thought, but I can't help but feel sorry for the poor school.

Other kids arrive, first in dribs, but growing busier until the courtyard's bustling. Then it's Riley. He's about to head straight for the toilet for his morning smoke, but sees me, starts to come over, then stops again and holds his hands out as if to ask, *Hey, why aren't you joining me?*

So, we go into the toilets and light up a smoke, although I hold mine between my fingers more than I puff on it.

Riley leans on the sink. 'What're you doing here so early?' he says.

'Couldn't sleep. Didn't want to hang around the house so I came here.'

'You nerd.'

When Ash shows up, I repeat the story. I don't feel any guilt about lying to my two best friends. and they don't push it, either because they think if I wanted them to know something, I'd tell them, or they're just not observant enough to know that I'm hiding something.

The rest of the day moves with that slowness that time does whenever you're waiting for something. I yawn through the classes and almost drift off in Mr Malon's Art class, only jerking awake when it feels like I'm falling from my chair. The pills are also a worry. I keep checking my pocket to see that I haven't lost them, and a few times they rattle when I move, and I'm worried somebody's going to ask what they are. I toy with putting them in my bag, but don't want them out of my sight during recess and lunch. Most of all, I just don't want to be discovered with them. They have my name on the label, since they're prescription and if anybody found them, I'd have to explain what they are and why I have them. When the final bell rings, I almost fly home.

'What's your rush?' Ash says.

'No rush.'

'You're walking quick.'

'Am I?'

We separate at the corner and I slow down as I approach home because I see Mario's brutish purple Ford – some classic model from the sixties with stripes down the middle and big silver rims – parked next door. He leans against the hood, his arms around Olivia as they kiss. I taste him on her, something like overcooked lasagne. Don't ask how that comes about, or what's the association. Olivia steps back, and he pulls her into him. It'd be romantic if most boyfriends did it. With Mario, it's violent. Olivia plants a hand in his chest. One of Mario's hands – his left – clutches her arse. She shrugs him off, catches sight of me, then smiles.

'Hi,' she says.

Mario's hands fall from her. He nods at me, as if to say, *How're you doing?* The Marios of the world are too cool to waste that much time on me.

'Hi,' I say, directly to Olivia.

Then I turn into my drive.

18.

That evening, when I try to meditate, I'm so tired I fall asleep. It's Mum knocking on the door and coming in that wakes me.

'What're you doing asleep?' she asks.

'I'm tired.'

'Why're you tired?'

'I just am.'

'You don't work. You're young. You're healthy. You shouldn't be tired.'

'Okay. All right.'

'Dinner.'

Dinner is two big steaks, vegetables and a mountain of mashed potatoes surrounded by a forest of peas, corn and carrot. Dad eats wordlessly. Steph's chair is empty. Mum sits down and pours herself a water.

'Where's Steph?' I ask.

'With that boy. Do you see who she brings home?'

'Mum–'

'Don't *Mum* me. She should bring home a nice Greek boy.'

'She should already be married,' Dad says.

'We should have a grandchild.'

'You better not ever do that,' Dad tells me.

'Have a grandchild?'

'Don't be funny.'

Mum rubs her chest. 'My heart hurts so much.'

'Do you see how she makes your mother feel?' Dad says. 'You bring home a nice Greek girl. You get a nice job. You study, be a doctor like Jim.'

'A doctor?' I say.

'What else are you going to do?' Mum says. 'Sell furniture like Stephanie?'

'I could write?'

'Write?' Mum says. 'What?'

'Stories.'

For a second, silence. Then Mum and Dad chuckle, like I'm five and just told them that I want to hunt dinosaurs when I grow up. It goes on, the same stuff I always hear – that Steph always hears. I race through dinner – eating as much as I can – then jump up from my seat. The pills rattle in my pocket. I've forgotten they're there. Mum and Dad don't notice.

I excuse myself and hurry to my bedroom, searching for a place Mum won't find the pills. She's always going through my drawers, putting clothes away. And I can't stuff it under the mattress because you never know when she's going to change the sheets – it's regular, and sometimes even sooner than that. But the bookshelf – she never goes through that.

I draw all the books on the second shelf out six inches, stick the bottle behind the books, then stack some magazines on top of the books to disguise they're not pushed right against the back wall of the bookshelf.

The rest of the night, I fidget and count down the time

until I can go to sleep. This is what life's come to: this sleeping pill. I watch TV for a bit but when Mum and Dad start yammering, I go back into my bedroom and open my A4 exercise book, thinking I won't be able to write, but I do – the words flow from me, Jean Razor fleeing down a deserted street when he sees the minions of his enemies, the Grave Shadows, rise. I scribble lots of corrections but keep writing until my hand grows stiff.

Just after eight, Mum and Dad go to bed – they always go early because they wake up so early for work – and I go back into the lounge and watch some TV. Before too long, the back door opens and Steph comes in and sits on the couch. She's made up, with her hair all frizzy, her make-up artful.

'You're home early,' I say.

Steph cocks one shoulder. *So?*

I can only take that to mean the date with Todd didn't go well. I should ask her, see if she's okay. That would be the normal thing to do. In other families, do they talk about things like this? Does Riley talk to his brother Ray about this stuff? Or does Ash talk to his brothers? You see it in soaps, like on *Neighbours* and *Home and Away*, but they're fiction, right?

Steph yawns around 9.30, says goodnight and leaves. The back door closes. Then I hear her bungalow open and close. She'll probably read or something for a while, like she usually does. The bungalow has everything she needs – bathroom, a little fridge – so there's no reason she needs to come back up. But then I hear the gate open and the motion-activated light come on. I jump to the window: Olivia. Steph's bungalow door opens and Steph lets Olivia in. Olivia must've fought with Mario. She always comes over after they've had a fight.

I lie back on the couch. The minutes tick away. About 9.50, I creep into my bedroom, remove the pill bottle and tip one onto my palm. My heart thuds. Salvation comes in such a tiny package – and I don't doubt it's come. If there was anything to be worried about, Dr Kuruvilla wouldn't have just let me go.

I grab a glass of water in the kitchen, swallow the pill and wash it down. Now my heart's faster. I lie on the couch and keep watching TV, but then worry I might fall asleep and Mum and Dad will find me here and not be able to wake me, so I turn everything off, go to the toilet, change into my pyjamas and climb into bed.

Already, everything feels heavy. A calm takes hold of me that's so beautiful – something I've never felt before, even before *this* began. This is why people do drugs. I understand it now. Because it *can* feel so good.

I flip onto my side.

Everything's going to be okay.

19.

I wake earlier than usual – 6.30 – and blink at the ceiling. The first thing my head does is turn inward. Since this began, the anxiousness has been parked next to my mind, as if to crow the moment I wake up, *Good morning!*

Now, there's quiet.

I sit up and wait for it to rush in.

Nothing.

I swivel out of bed and land unsteadily. There's a lethargy in my arms and legs, like they're too heavy and uncoordinated. It's not unpleasant and I enjoy the sensation as I make breakfast, shower and get dressed. Because I woke early, it's too early to leave for school – I don't want to miss Ash at the corner again. He'll wonder what's up. But I'm eager to get going because I want to be able to face the day feeling good for the first time in weeks.

To kill time, I go into the garage and play a game of pool. I've just broken for a second game when the garage door swings open. Steph stands there in an old woolly bathrobe, hair all messed up. She yawns.

'What're you doing?' she says.

'Sorry. I had some time to spare – I woke early.'

Steph closes the garage door and grabs a cue.

'You want to play?' I say.

'Sure.'

I rack the balls into the triangle.

'How's school going?' Steph says. 'Any idea if they've assigned the piece for the Boland yet?'

I tell her about Mr Baker's identity essay and Mrs Grady's alternate justice piece – that so far, they feel the most likely candidates.

Steph nods as she breaks. 'It mightn't be either,' she says. 'The essay I had to write was assigned in the last third of the year.'

We play the game, making small talk about school – about the teachers we've shared, the homework and what's changed over the years (not a lot). We don't usually do this, so it's nice to talk without judgement or expectation or condemnation – the sort Mum and Dad usually impose on us.

'Another game?' I say after I pot the black.

'Sure.'

We empty the pockets and I draw the balls to the back cushion between my arms so the balls form a triangle. Then I put the triangle over them and set them up. Steph's not as good as me, but she is *good*, and she pockets a striped ball on the break, then pockets two others.

'Written anything new?' she says.

'Some stories. And I started something I want to be big – like a book.'

'That's great. Let me read the stories?'

'Sure. You know where my exercise books are.'

Steph pockets another of her balls. 'Keep something between us?'

'Sure.'

'I'm thinking of moving.'

'Where?'

Steph shrugs. 'Anywhere. Just out.'

'You're not working.'

'I've saved up. I was thinking maybe doing a holiday, then finding a place.'

'On your own?'

Steph stops in the middle of playing her next shot. Of course not on her own. She'll go with Todd. Although it's quick, that's a next step in a relationship – if not getting engaged and all that, then moving in together. Mum and Dad will freak. It'll be an embarrassment beyond all embarrassments for Mum. I can see her collapsing, clutching her heart.

'I'll see,' Steph says. 'You could have my bungalow.'

'Mum and Dad would love that.'

'Yeah but think of the freedom you'll have.'

Steph must be inspired by what she's talking about or something, because she beats me – and she rarely beats me. I check the little clock radio we have in the garage and see that it's 8.40 – I've gone from having plenty of time to running late.

'I've gotta go.'

'Okay – have a good day.'

I start for the door.

'Hey!'

I spin.

'Don't tell Mum or Dad, huh?'

'Sure.'

I run into the house, grab my bag and a jacket, lock up and jog to the corner. The cold freezes the tips of my ears and burns the breath in my lungs. Ash is already waiting, jacket zipped up to his neck, and hands shoved into his pockets as he pivots back and forth to keep warm.

'Where you been?' he says.

'Got caught up talking to my sister,' I say. 'You talk to your brothers?'

'About?'

'Stuff.'

'What stuff?'

'Personal stuff.'

'Marcus asked me about girls. And Luke asked me about a kid bullying him once. Tom's never asked me anything major.'

Ash is two years older than Marcus, four years older than Luke, and eight years older than Tom – not that their ages are that important, or you need to remember them. It's just to give you some context. It must be cool to have little brothers who look up to you.

'What did you tell them?'

'I punched Luke in the stomach and in the shoulder, told him that's what stood between him being bullied and standing up to this kid. It's just pain.'

'Pain…hurts.'

'You deal with it. If you don't worry about getting hurt, you can do amazing things.'

I see Ash stand up to those kids at the party. So, this is the logic behind it. How'd that stand up to the stuff I'm going through? Fortunately, I don't have to worry about it now that it's gone.

'What about Marcus – what did you tell him?' I ask.

'What's there to say? You find out on the way.'

I frown. 'Find out what?'

'When you're with a girl, what do you think's gonna happen?'

'I don't think anything – other than worry I'm gonna screw up.'

'See, that's stupid. Just go with it.'

'Go with what?'

'Wherever it takes you. If she's not interested, she's not interested. You can try to nudge it the way you want it to go, but if it doesn't, just let it go.'

'That what you did with Rachel?'

We get to the bridge, but the grass is wet, so we sit on the top of the concrete aqueduct, exposed to the relentless wind. Water gushes down the creek, all swampy and dirty and gurgling. The reeds on the bank flutter and you can hear the scoreboard in the soccer ground groaning and creaking.

'That's what I did,' Ash says.

'That's why you're the success you are today, huh?'

Ash laughs. 'Life's about the *me*tails: the details that are about *me* – well, in your case, *you*.'

I balance on the top edge of the aqueduct, holding my hands out. If I jumped now, I'm sure the wind would pick me up and carry me into the sky. All it takes is the belief, as well as the confidence to let go of everything.

Ash gets up, too. He flicks his cigarette into the creek, then grabs my arm and shoves me forward. The panic is fleeting but I'm sure I'm going in. Ash yanks me back, and I take a step back off the aqueduct.

'Saved you,' he tells me.

20.

Over the next few weeks, winter hits us with storms, rain pounding until gutters in the streets overflow and the concrete flanks of the aqueduct are lost under a torrent. Thick jackets come out of closets, along with beanies and scarves and gloves, and noses grow red as everybody's breath mists.

Homework piles up so any major assignments – like Mr Baker's identity essay – are pushed to the side. I take the occasional sleeping pill when I feel any anxiousness, but otherwise bounce from one class to the next and enjoy the little respite we get at recess and lunchtime, or the weekends at Toppy's

'I'm thinking I should give it another shot with Felicia,' Riley tells us one afternoon over a game of pool.

'So, like you said, live and love, huh?' Ash asks.

'Live and fuck,' Riley says.

'So that would be it?' I ask.

'What?'

'If you got her back, once you had sex, then it'd be over again?'

'Who knows?'

'Then what's the plan?'

'I should've taken more time with her.'

'But that's all you're thinking about – the sex?'

Riley's answer is too forced: 'Of course!'

At home, the mood is sullen because Steph spends so much time with Todd. Mum lies on the couch, asks for her pills and bemoans what people will think. Her encounters with Steph are bizarre – Mum all scathing, Steph amazingly relaxed as she lets things wash off her in a way she never has before.

'Are you going to bring him to Jim's wedding?' Mum asks at one of the few dinners Steph makes it to.

'I'm thinking about it.'

'You need to tell me,' Mum says. 'They want to know who's coming.'

'Yes, then. Okay?'

I hold my breath. There's no explosion. Mum slumps in her chair. Dad continues to eat, dipping his bread into the juices of the stew Mum made.

'But first we're going away,' Steph says.

Mum straightens up. 'Away?'

'All of us – Todd, me, Olivia and Mario. Eight weeks. First the US, then Europe.'

'Where do you get the money for a trip like this?'

'I've saved.'

'And now you're going to throw it away.'

'Not throw it away. It's something I want to do. Live a little.'

'Live. *Live!*'

'Mum–'

'Don't *mum* me! Then when you come home, you'll have nothing!'

'I'll work again.'

'How, without a job?' Dad says.

'I'll get a job.'

'You had a good job and you quit it!' Dad says.

'What job?' Mum says. 'Selling furniture! She was studying! She could've had a career.'

It goes on, Steph showing that new patience that I guess means she's happy, and she's not going to let anything bother her. When Mum and Dad settle down, Steph tells us everything's booked and she's leaving in a week. That leads to a whole new set of arguments: how she hasn't given us enough warning and how it's irresponsible to just take off and leave. Steph sighs and rolls her eyes, but she doesn't blow up, like somebody's constantly whispering in her ear, *Keep calm, keep calm.*

Her flight is at 4.00am Wednesday, and she tells us not to bother coming to the airport. Olivia's driving them to Mario's, then they'll leave her car there – Mario has a two-bedroom unit that has a garage and a carport – and grab a taxi to pick up Todd.

So, Steph hugs us all the night before. Mum sobs and Dad kisses her on each cheek. Mum thrusts some money in her hand – a roll of hundred-dollar bills, and Dad tells Steph to be careful and warns her about all the crooks who might try take advantage of her. On and on they yammer, changing between tears and advice and sometimes offering both. By 9.30, they're yawning and Dad keeps nodding off and jerking awake in his chair. Finally, their tiredness wins out. Mum and Dad give Steph one final kiss then go to bed, which leaves Steph and me in the lounge.

'You gonna be okay here on your own?' Steph asks.

'I guess.'

'Of course you will be. If you want to use my bungalow, you know where the spare key is.'

I can't imagine why I'd use it, unless it was to sneak a girl over and I'd never bring a girl anywhere near Mum's vicinity. She'd be proclaiming my wedding.

'Just don't go through any of my things,' Steph says.

'Awww,' I say.

'Funny. Anything you want me to bring you back?'

'Surprise me.'

We watch TV and talk about nothing important, although tiredness settles over me, so I lie on the couch. A few times I drift off.

'You can go to bed,' Steph says.

'I'll wait until you go.'

'You've got school tomorrow.'

'Doesn't matter.'

Steph says she expects me to be well into my big story by the time she gets back, and that she'll have her own stories to tell me. Again, I struggle to stay awake and the next thing I know, Steph's leaning over me and shaking me.

'It's time,' she says.

Olivia's at the back door, in jeans and a shirt. Steph's not dressed much more warmly, although I guess where they're going, they don't need winter-wear.

I help carry Steph's bags from her bungalow to Olivia's car. The night raises the hair on my arms and the straps of the luggage cut into my palms. Olivia has her car parked as deep in the drive as she can. Her own luggage is stuffed in the back, so I hoist Steph's luggage into the boot. Olivia slams the boot closed.

Steph hugs me tight and kisses me on the cheek. Thoughts

jump in my head then. The plane will crash. Steph will get attacked somewhere overseas. This is the last time I'll see her alive. Mum will be shattered. She'll cry uncontrollably. None of these are premonitions – at least as far as I know. They're just stupid thoughts that make me squirm.

'I'll send you postcards,' Steph says.

'Okay,' I say.

Olivia hugs me – tight – and kisses me. I close my arms around her waist – loosely – and can even imagine sliding my hand down onto her butt. Stupid. But like the other thoughts, it shoots in. It doesn't even feel like it's sexually motivated.

'See you in eight weeks,' Olivia says. She tousles my hair – which she cut yesterday, although a bit shorter than before. 'Just in time for your next cut.'

Olivia and Steph get into the car, and Olivia backs out of the drive. Mum and Dad have come out onto the back veranda in their bathrobes, arms hugged tight, Mum sniffling. They wave as Olivia's car arcs back onto the street. The headlights come on. Olivia beeps her horn. Then they drive off into the night.

I duck back into the house, shivering, and lock up. It's just after 1.00am, which should leave me six hours of sleep before school. I climb straight into bed, but the shadows of those thoughts darken into something I can't shake.

My chest tightens until there's a cramp in the middle where my heart would be. I know it's nothing. I tell myself it's nothing. But I can't lose the feeling, so I get up, take a sleeping pill, drink some water directly from the bathroom tap, then go back to bed.

I'm asleep shortly afterward.

21.

I'm tense the whole day at school and when I try to work out why, I can only guess it's because of Steph. Who knows what could happen to her? Planes crash. Tourists are robbed. Raped. Murdered. They can go miss–

I stop myself. This isn't what I want to be thinking. But it's so it's hard to ignore. I find some peace the next morning when Steph rings from New York.

'Hey,' she says, 'tell Mum and Dad we made it! I'll try and call later when they're home.'

'Okay.'

'What's it like there?'

'Cold.'

'Beautiful here. I'll talk to you later.'

I feel more relaxed about going to school, although when Ash and me file into the toilets, there's no sign of Riley puffing away on his morning cigarette. We wait, light up a smoke, expecting he'll show, but when the bell sounds, he still hasn't appeared. He doesn't show up for Maths first period either, so he must be sick, although I keep thinking he'll show up for Legal second period. Nope. Nothing.

At recess, I'm following Ash into the toilets for our recess cigarette when Gabriella pulls me up. 'Hey,' she says.

'Hey.'

'You going to Ethan's party?'

I'd forgotten all about Ethan's party.

Gabriella's smile flickers. 'You were invited? I thought everyone was invited.'

'Oh. Yeah. Sure. Sorry. Been thinking about other things.'

'Like…?

Like… Something witty. I don't want to blow the rapport like I've done the other times. And if it were Ash or Riley, I'd be witty – or at least try to be. But my mind freezes. A pain throbs in my chest and cuts off my breath.

'Stuff,' I say, and I groan inwardly, like my head's caving in.

'Like the Boland?' she says.

I don't think she'd understand how little that's been on my mind.

'You're not taking History this term, are you?' Gabriella asks.

'No.'

'They assigned us a hypothetical creative essay: what if Australia had been settled when explorers landed on the west coast, instead of the east coast? I wondered if it's the Boland essay. Your sister won it, right?'

I nod.

'She give you any tips?'

'All she said was when she won it, the essay was assigned in the last term.'

Gabriella's lips purse as she thinks about it. 'That's interesting. I wonder if they do that regularly.'

'Don't know. Anyway, Ethan's party, when is it? Next Saturday?'

'Not the one coming up, the Saturday after.'

'Next Saturday.'

'Next Saturday is this one coming up.'

'Anyway, it's not this one.'

'No.'

Gabriella hugs her arms to herself. I think about what Ash told me at the creek. I should ask her if she wants to take a walk with me. We could sit in the canteen.

'Anyway, I was curious if you were going. I should…' Gabriella cocks a thumb back over her shoulder, like somebody's waiting. Nobody is.

'Sure,' I say.

In the toilets, Ash claps me on the shoulder as I light up a cigarette. 'She's interested,' he says.

'You think?' And this isn't even sarcasm. I'm genuinely unsure.

'Make your move at Ethan's party. You want a condom?' Ash thrusts a hand into his jacket pocket.

'You have a condom here, on you, now?'

'Always be prepared.'

'You're buying condoms?'

'My dad gives them to me. He wants me to be careful.'

I can't envision the way that plays out. Dad pesters me – the way all the aunts and uncles hound their kids – to get married, buy a house, have kids and all that, but it's conversation on such a surface level. I could never talk to Dad about something as personal as having sex with a girl, let alone expect him to give me a condom.

At lunch, I hope that Gabriella might seek me out again. She sits in the corner of the canteen for the first half hour and I detain Ash by eating slowly and making several trips to the counter, right past Gabriella, to pick up things I don't need – a straw, some salt, a napkin – just hoping I'll get noticed. Nothing, though. Maybe my lack of interplay killed any interest she had in me.

But I think about her the rest of the day – and it's nice to think about her. When I get home, I lie on my bed and instead of meditating, I think of talking to Gabriella, of putting my arms around her and feeling her soft and warm against my body. It's all silly and romantic. Riley or Ash wouldn't think this way. They'd be thinking about sex.

Come night-time, I take out my sleeping pills and don't know whether I should take one. Dr Kuruvilla stressed I should only take them when required. I put the bottle back but when I'm in bed, I toss and turn for an hour. Thoughts whiz around in my head. They're not bad thoughts, just stuff like which homework's due, the Boland being something I should be mindful of, how I should continue my Jean Razor book, Steph telling me she's planning on moving out, and maybe having Todd as a brother in-law – on they go, first with some order, but then flitting around so I can't track them.

I give up and take a pill. The heaviness falls on me over the next fifteen minutes. Those racing thoughts slow, then still. And then it's sleep, although this time I wake around 2.30 am. I flip onto my side, wide awake. There's nothing else, though – no anxiousness or anything. I close my eyes and must be asleep not long after, because I wake before the clock radio buzzes.

Again, I perform a check of myself. Now, I sense an unease that something is going to return. I can't shake the certainty of it. I know it's not how I should be thinking, but there it is. At least it's faint enough that I can distract myself.

The real distraction comes when Ash and me arrive at school and Riley's nowhere to be found again. In English, Mr Baker even asks about him, but nobody has an answer. At recess, Ash and me skip out of school and jog to the hub of shops. There's a string of telephones out front. Ash tries to call Riley, but no answer. We have a smoke, then try again, but still nothing.

'I hope he's okay,' I say.

'He'll be fine,' Ash says.

Through third period Mathematics, Counsellor Hoffs calls students in for evaluations again – partly a nuisance, but partly a relief because it gets us out of class. On this occasion, I'm one of the first ones up.

'Last time we spoke, you were unsure where you wanted to go with your life,' Counsellor Hoffs says. She has my folder out again, her hands crossed on top of it, but I can't get over her glasses – she has this new horn-rimmed pair that are purple. Somebody must've told her they were trendy. 'Have you given that any more thought?' she goes on.

'I was thinking about writing,' I say.

'Journalism?'

'No.'

'Technical writing?'

'No.'

'What then?'

'Stories.'

'Fiction?'

'I guess.'

'That's a difficult field to make a career in – at least one from which you can support yourself. I know that.' Counsellor Hoffs says it with a tinge of frustration. She must be a writer herself, or *was* in the past. But now she's a counsellor. That doesn't sit well.

'The percentage of authors who live off writing is tiny, and the ones who make a great living tinier still. Most of them hold primary jobs, sometimes in a field involved in writing – like publishing, editing or even teaching. Do any of those interest you?'

'No.'

Counsellor Hoffs smiles. 'That's something you need to think about. How about the writing itself? Have you thought about how you plan to make that a reality?'

'Don't I just do it?'

'Just do it?'

'Like, I've written lots of short stories – I've handwritten them in an exercise book. And I'm writing something new.'

'I'd be happy to look at them for you if you're interested.'

'Yeah. I guess. Maybe.'

'If you want to go into writing, it's best to consider some tertiary schooling. Perhaps I can gather some literature for you?'

'Sure.'

'At least that creative side should hold you in good stead for the Boland. Your sister was creative.'

'Was she?' That's not something I've ever connected with Steph. She's always seemed pragmatic. Like the career pathways she chose – They were all very practical.

'The Boland Fellowship lends itself towards people who are imaginative,' Counsellor Hoffs said. 'That doesn't necessarily mean creative writing, but creative thinkers – people who might tackle entrenched problems from a lateral perspective. I remember one student won it with an essay about restructuring the working week so that people could focus on family and community. It was very inventive.'

I wonder how that would work with Mum and Dad being home more.

'Think about it,' Counsellor Hoffs says. She rises with practised fluency. 'And good luck with your writing! Just keep in mind what I've said.'

I leave her office flat, although I know she's being practical. That's her job. And I have that tightness in my chest again – the one I felt when I spoke to Gabriella yesterday. It spider-webs into my ribs, tight and cramping and I take a deep breath to prove to myself everything's okay.

22.

As me and Ash walk home from school, that pain in my chest throbs. *Heart attack*, the fear pops up. Like my grandfather and Uncle George. Maybe it runs in the family. Of course, neither of them were my age. I struggle to squelch the fear that takes hold.

'What would you do with the money if you won the Boland?' Ash asks.

When Steph won the Boland, the money went into the bank – that's Mum and Dad's influence: *Save! Save! Save!* Mum and Dad barely made a fuss about the award itself – they looked at it like some minor school prize. They weren't meaning to be condescending. They just don't understand those sorts of things.

'I don't know,' I say. 'What about you?'

'I'd put the money down for a car,' Ash says. 'I don't know about the mentoring – I don't know what I want to do. Not that I'm much chance.'

'You're a chance, though.'

'Yeah. We'll see. I think it'll be Deanne, Ethan or you.'

'Me?' People keep pointing at me. I don't get it.

'Deanne probably gets the best grades and Ethan is the best all-round, but I bet they'll like that you're creative.'

That's what Counsellor Hoffs said. The winners of the

Boland Fellowship are listed in the offices. Each winning essay is printed out and framed. I wonder if it would be worth going to read them, just to see if there is a familiar pattern.

We reach the corner where we separate. Ash pauses.

'Hey, I'm gonna call Riley when I get home,' he says. 'See what's up.'

'Sure.'

'I'll let you know what happened.'

'Okay.'

It's only about an hour later that Ash calls me. 'No answer,' he says. 'I'm going over after dinner. You wanna come?'

'Yeah.'

'Drop around about seven.'

'Okay.'

When Mum and Dad get home, I tell them that Steph called in the morning, which annoys them that she didn't call when they were around. I tell them Steph said she'd call back, but they're not happy until Steph does call at 6.00, telling them New York is amazing, her hotel room is gorgeous and she can't wait until they see the rest of the city.

We eat shortly afterward and once I'm done, I tell Mum and Dad I'm going to Ash's. They grunt and tell me not to be late, so I grab my jacket and jog there. Ash opens the front door before the doorbell's chime has stopped echoing in the hallway.

'Sorry – still eating,' Ash says. 'Mum was late home from the nuthouse.'

I feel uncomfortable sitting in the lounge, Ash, his

brothers, and their dad crowded around the kitchen table, Mrs Handley – still dressed in her nurse's uniform – fluttering about, trying to answer their demands for food, for drinks, for serviettes.

'Can I offer you anything?' she asks me.

I wave her off. 'No, I'm fine, Mrs Handley. I ate.'

'How's school going? Ash says so little.'

'What's there to say?' Ash asks. 'It's school. You work with loonies–'

'Ash!'

'It can't be much different.'

Chuckling, Mr Handley gets up and grabs a beer from the fridge. On the way back to his chair, he passes Mrs Handley, who's reaching up to a high shelf in the pantry to grab some more serviettes. Mr Handley smacks her right buttock, although he claws her for a second too. Mrs Handley yelps and Mr Handley laughs and leers at her as he sits back down. I can't imagine Mum and Dad ever acting like that.

'Behave yourself,' Mrs Handley says.

Mr Handley grins.

'It's gross,' Tom – Ash's youngest brother – says. The others laugh.

They've all got Mrs Handley's sandy hair, although Marcus and Tom have Mr Handley's curls. They all look so alike and you can feel the friendliness between them.

Ash shoves his plate away. 'Gotta go now.' His chair screeches. 'Be back in a bit.'

'Not too late,' Mrs Handley says. 'You've got school.'

'I know, Mum.' Ash grabs his jacket. 'Come on!'

We're walking to Riley's before too long, the zippers of our jackets up and hands numb in the cold.

'Do you think something's happened?' I say.

Now I get thoughts about Riley: cold, measles, broken leg, sick, so sick he's in hospital, cancer – maybe they just discovered it and he's been busy with tests the last two days. They all seem impossible. Riley's indestructible. But that's a lie. He's not strong like Ash. Riley's just… *sullen*. I can't imagine that ever changing, and since I can't imagine that ever changing, I can't imagine anything ever getting in.

'He'll be fine,' Ash says.

'Then why doesn't he answer the phone?'

'We'll find out.'

Once we get close to Riley's, we slow down. The grass at the front is overgrown, and the bins in the drive are overflowing. A light shines in the window and no car sits in the drive.

'Come on,' Ash says.

Riley answers on the second ring of the doorbell. He's had a haircut and it's spiky – military almost. His socks aren't pulled up so they flop from his feet like wagging tongues.

'Hey,' he says. 'Come in.'

Some things become clear as he leads us down the hallway. Any pictures that featured Riley's dad are gone now. You can see dark square patches on the wall around where the pictures used to hang. Other pictures are gone from the mantel. Some have had Riley's dad torn out of them.

We sit in the lounge and Riley gets us a beer, although

I see when he opens the fridge that the shelves are bare. He offers smokes and we light up like this is our place and we're adults sitting back to chat. His school folder is on the coffee table, opened to the Legal Studies section. He's written pages and pages in green pen, with the heading at the top: *Essay*.

'Where's your mum?' Ash asks.

'Overtime,' Riley says. 'Dad came by yesterday, took his stuff. Mum lost it. I think it finally hit her this is for real. She cleaned out every trace of him.'

'You okay?' I say.

Riley shrugs, then takes a drink. 'Was more worried about Mum, so I stayed home with her. She's coping now – took yesterday off, but she went back to work today. She needs to get overtime. She can't afford the house by herself.'

'So, you might have to move?' I say.

'We'll see.'

'You coming back to school tomorrow?' Ash says.

'I'll see how Mum's doing tomorrow. Not really a priority – if it ever was.'

'What do you mean?' I say.

'What are we learning? Like, name me one thing you learned today that you need.'

'We had meetings with Counsellor Hoffs.'

Riley rolls his eyes. 'Careers again?'

'Yep.'

Riley lifts his feet onto the coffee table, planting them right over his essay – like he wants to hide the work he's put in. 'What a waste.'

'You're gonna have to think about it sometime.'

'I *do* think about it – *sometimes*. But it's not that important right now. Not like… Guess what?'

Ash and me stare at him.

'I'm back with Felicia.'

'Really?' I say.

'Spoke to her – I apologised.'

'*You* apologised?' Ash asks.

'I apologised.'

'You apologised?'

'I apologised – what's wrong with that? It's not like I did anything wrong, but it's what she wanted to hear. You should apologise to Rachel.'

'Why?'

'Because she's mad at you – they all are. Felicia told me.'

'And then what?'

'Just to get them back on side.'

'I'll see,' Ash says. 'So, where'd you leave it with Felicia?'

'Going to Ethan's birthday together. We should get him something. We'll chip in, right?'

'Sure.'

'Felicia and me will organise it and you can fix me up.'

'Cool,' Ash says.

'Speaking of birthdays,' Riley lifts his can of beer towards me, 'yours this week.'

'Already?'

Riley chuckles. 'It's *your* birthday – how don'tcha know when it is?'

It's not that I don't know but time's just become a mess. But he's right – it's my birthday this Sunday. An occasion that should bring some joy and anticipation means so little right now.

Riley toasts his can of beer against mine. 'We should do something.'

'Like?'

'We'll see.'

We talk for the next twenty minutes about little things – about who else is going out with who in the school, who's reported to like who, who has it in for who, and equally meaningless stuff that's mostly gossip. But it fills the time as we finish our beers, at which point Ash shoots to his feet.

'We should go,' he says.

Riley walks us to the door and we say our goodbyes just as his mum pulls up in the drive in her little brown Civic. We smile and say hello but once we've left Riley's house behind, Ash grows surly and he doesn't talk much, which is okay because my chest has grown tight again. It's not until we get back to Ash's house that I find the courage to prod him.

'You okay?' I ask.

'Sure. I'll see you tomorrow, huh?'

I nod and head off into the night.

23

Over the rest of the school week, the chest pains grow, sometimes so painful that they bring me to my knees until they pass. The first time it happens at school – on the way out of Social Studies – I kneel and tie my shoelace to cover what's going on.

When I get the chance, I duck into the library to research what I'm feeling, but it's the worst thing I could do. There's way too much information. Angina – when the arteries that supply the heart grow thick – is possible. Or it could be congenital. I find out there are a lot of heart conditions.

I could see Dr Kuruvilla, although I don't feel up to an early morning jaunt. So, I book in Saturday morning to see Dr Stathakis, our family doctor, because I'm sure something physical is going on.

Dr Stathakis has sharp features set in a constant state of disapproval. I tell him my chest has been tight lately and sometimes it makes it hard to breathe. He nods throughout and when I'm done, he takes my blood pressure, then has me sit on the cot at the back of his office and listens to my breathing the way Dr Kuruvilla did. He takes his stethoscope off and pulls a white plastic case out from under his cot about the size of a shoebox.

'Take off your jacket and t-shirt,' he says.

I do that as he unclasps the case and pulls the lid off. Inside is a monitor of some sort. There are electrodes connected to it with long, long wires. Dr Stathakis attaches the electrodes to my chest and runs the machine for a minute. It beeps steadily and shoots out a ticker of paper. Dr Stathakis yanks it out and studies it briefly.

'All fine,' he says. He scrunches up the page and tosses it in a bin under the cot, then pulls the electrodes from my chest. 'So's the breathing.'

He packs up the machine as I sit up and put my t-shirt and jacket back on.

'Then what is it?' I ask.

'How's school? You worried about that?'

'Not really.'

Dr Stathakis sits back in his fancy leather chair; I sit in the simple chair opposite him. 'Nothing's physically wrong,' he says. He taps his temple. 'It's all in here.'

I have the chance now to tell him everything about this but don't have the courage. He'll tell my parents. It'll get out. I'll look weak.

'What should I do?' I ask.

'Take it easy,' Dr Stathakis says.

'That's it?'

'That's it.'

As I leave the clinic, I try to absorb what he's told me but nothing wants to sink in. It's so easy for somebody to tell you that you have nothing to worry about. It's something else when you don't know *why* you're worrying and you can't convince yourself that you shouldn't be.

Then I notice the most amazing thing: the tightness in my chest is gone. I take a deep breath and feel it flow deep,

deep down. It can't be that simple. It *shouldn't* be that simple. But it is. Knowing this isn't – or wasn't – something physical has dissolved it. It's a relief that I'm fine but a worry that this will come back in some other form.

I head home, each step quicker than the last, until I'm sprinting, the wind cutting through my hair. I get home, puffed, hardly able to catch my breath, and I worry that I won't. This'll be it. An asthma attack, although I don't have asthma. I go inside, lie on bed until I catch my breath and tell myself I'm okay. This is all I need to keep doing: *reminding myself.*

Sunday's my birthday. When I stumble out of bed, Mum – and then Dad – greets me with a kiss and a hug and each thrust money into my hand. Money's their gift for everything. I've just finished breakfast when Steph calls from Los Angeles and after she's done with Mum and Dad, she gets me on the phone to wish me a happy birthday.

'Sixteen!' she says. 'These are your glory years! Live it up.'

Riley calls later, suggesting we go to Toppy's after lunch for a celebration. I agree for the sake of agreeing but would rather crawl back into bed. Something is *off*. I'm unsure what but can't shake the sensation.

Around 1.00, Ash comes and picks me up, but instead of heading for Toppy's he drags me towards the school. I ask him where we're going, but he plays coy, so I follow him down to the bridge, then onto the aqueduct. We walk along the edge until we get to where the aqueduct slides under the Main Street bridge. Riley is waiting with two bulky plastic bags, and a can of beer in hand. He grabs another two beers out of the plastic bag and throws one to each of us.

'Happy birthday!'

Riley pulls something wrapped in blue tissue paper about the size of a book from the bag. He Frisbees it to me; I catch it one-handed against my chest, while holding the beer in the other.

'There's that, too,' Riley says.

'A gift? We never give gifts.'

'Times change,' Ash says.

'You're sixteen,' Riley says.

I tear the wrapping open.

'We didn't know what to get you,' Ash says.

'Ash suggested this,' Riley says. 'Unless you like it, then I'll take the credit.'

I think it's going to be a book, which would be the easy thing to buy me. But it's a leather-bound journal with this old, yellowed paper. In a separate plastic case, there's also a fountain pen.

'I thought it was a little bit gay,' Riley says. 'But Ash said you'd like it.'

'It's cool. Thanks.'

We sit there, huddled under the bridge like trolls out of a fairy tale. The wind snakes down the aqueduct, and every now and then we feel drops of wet, which might be rain or the wind spraying up water from the creek.

'Mum's not happy about the beer I've been grabbing,' Riley says. 'I got Ray to get these – twelve of them.'

'You should've invited some girls,' Ash says.

'Surprisingly, this isn't a hotspot for them. But I did bring this…'

Riley slips his hand in his jacket, then pulls out what I'm sure is a cigarette without a filter, the end twisted tight. But it's not. It's a joint. It takes me a second longer – and Ash's excited reaction – to realise that.

'Where'd you get that?' Ash says.

'Ray.'

Riley pops it in his mouth and lights it up. The smell of it is thick and rich and weird – a cross between tobacco and pine air freshener. Riley takes a deep drag, then lets out the smoke leisurely, savouring it.

'Who's next?'

Ash is – he splutters on his first drag but inhales deep and lovingly on his next. He holds the joint out to me, but I shake my head.

'What's the matter?' he asks.

I light up a cigarette so my mouth will be occupied. 'I'll stick with the beer.'

'I got it for your birthday,' Riley says.

'I appreciate it but…'

I have no idea what excuse to give him – that I don't want to, that my parents will notice me stoned, or (and this rages in my head) I'll have some adverse reaction to it. People can have paranoid meltdowns from something as simple as a joint and the way my head's working, I'm sure that's likely for me.

In understanding that, I also now know what's been misplaced: *this*, whatever it is, is gone, but only as a retreat to work out how it's going to come at me next. It's fine for Dr Stathakis to tell me to take it easy, but I can't.

I need to be on guard.

I stare at the water of the creek rushing by and wonder where it'll carry me if I throw myself in.

Sitting there, under a bridge in the biting cold on my birthday while my two best friends get stoned, life's never seemed emptier.

24.

I wake with a tight band of pain that circles my head. It must be from drinking yesterday, although I only had four. Maybe it was the dope? I might've passively inhaled it and this is the response, but I know that I'm deflecting.

I feel a little better once I've had breakfast and showered and through the day, when I get can get immersed in something – like in first lesson in English when we talk about *To Kill a Mockingbird* – it slips by unnoticed. So, it can't be bad. You wouldn't be able to ignore something truly bad, would you?

In second period, I have Social Studies with Mr McCready. Mr McCready is a bear, his face more hair than skin. He looks like he was left in the wild as a kid and grew up into some fierce, untamed savage who's been packed into jeans, a shirt and a khaki coat. But he's softly spoken and always challenges us to think about the world's problems. Now – as much as I struggle to focus – he talks about means of improving the world and assigns us the essay of finding a unique way to do just that. It's ironic – he wants us to fix the world when I can't even fix myself.

When the bell rings for recess, it sounds so shrill that it slices through my head. We stumble out of the classroom and head towards the toilet, but Riley pulls us up halfway across the courtyard.

'I'll catch up to you,' he says.

Ash and me go into the toilet and light up. The toilet stinks of urinal cakes, their sweetness cloying. I lean against the wall and drag on my smoke.

'You all right?' Ash says.

'Got a headache.'

When we've finished our smokes, we go out into the courtyard. Riley's sitting with Felicia on one of the benches by the atrium, chatting. Me and Ash sit on the bench opposite them.

Ash shakes his head but before he can say anything, Samantha comes skittering up to me like a plane slowing down a runway.

'Hi,' she says.

'Hey,' I say.

'I wanted to wish you a happy birthday for yesterday,' Samantha says.

'Thanks.'

Samantha hovers over me, maybe waiting for an invitation to sit down and join me or something. I don't know what else to say. It's a simple transaction: *Happy birthday. Thank you.* There are not a lot of places to go from there.

'You going to Ethan's birthday?' she asks.

'Yeah.'

'Okay.' Samantha arches her brows. 'I'll see you there.'

She hurries off.

Ash claps me on the shoulder. 'We've had this talk before–'

'I'm not interested in her.'

'Go for it. She'd be willing. Maybe she's even experienced. Then dump her.'

All this time, I've been thinking it was Riley's influence that's shaped Ash's attitude towards girls, but now Riley's chasing Felicia and Ash is the same as ever. This is who Ash is – I'm seeing that now.

'Isn't that cruel?' I ask.

'It's life. And she'll be so angry at you that she'll stop bothering you. Win-win.'

'Do you think there's a possibility some time in the future that some woman might, like, kill you?'

'Hey!' Ash says, as if offended. Then he grins. 'Of course there is.'

When my headache persists, I slip away to the library at lunch so I can read about symptoms. The problem is that a headache could be so many things: neck tension, a migraine, a brain tumour – it's such a big list there's no way to know without going back to the doctor. Anyway, if it was anything serious, it would've shown up when Dr Stathakis examined me. I tell myself this over and over but I can't stop obsessing about it. Other times, my head feels oddly weighted, like moving one way or the other will throw me off balance.

I stumble out of the library, not wanting to be around anybody – at least so I don't have to talk with them. But I don't want to do *nothing* either. I need to occupy my time. Then it pops up in my head: the Boland essays.

The offices are a hub in the central building. It has a totally different feel to the rest of the school – serious and grave. Reception is a square counter that sits in the middle like a fortified trench. Offices surround it – the Principal, the Vice-principal, Counsellor Hoffs, a staff room, and various others. Pictures, certificates and achievements decorate the walls between each office door.

One wall is dedicated to the Boland stuff – framed essays, along with photos of the grinning fellows receiving their prizes. The Fellowship has run seventeen years, so these photos are a chronology of fashion – ranging from the big lapels, psychedelic shirts and overlong hair in the 1970s, to the blow-waves and acid-wash of the 1980s. I see Steph as a sixteen-year-old, smiling, eyes sparkling, a toothy grin. I wonder what she was thinking at that time.

I read Steph's essay first – which is about wealth redistribution – and then skim the others. They all contain some idealistic version of improving our way of life in some way, or how somebody can be an agency for change. They make me think about the homework assignments that have been given out – at least the ones that might fit the Boland. Definitely Mr McCready's today about improving the world, as well as the Legal Studies essay. I now can't see how Mr Baker's identity essay could reach anybody on that sort of level.

I wonder what's become of the winners. Steph has struggled to find direction in her life. Have the others? Has life swallowed them up into some mundane job? Or have they gone onto better things? Are some of them doing – or trying to do – the stuff they wrote about? Or was the Boland the peak of their accomplishments?

I look at last year's winner – Frank Valeri – and then to the space under his picture and his framed essay. I could occupy that spot. People expect it of me. I *should* take the

Boland seriously, work towards it and hold onto that. It can make life mean something more than this.

After school, I go home, eat a sandwich and then Mum, Dad, and me go to clean the little office building they've contracted part-time, emptying bins and vacuuming the floor. But once we're done and driving home, Mum and Dad start on me – the cost of Steph's absence.

'Sixteen now,' Mum says. 'Any nice girls at school?'

'Mum, please,' I say.

'When I was not much older than you,' Dad says, 'I was thinking about settling down. I had a job. I was saving money.'

'I know.'

'You need to know what you're doing.'

'Now? Right now?'

'Don't speak to me like that,' Dad says. 'You've got it way too easy here.'

'I'm helping you with this,' I say.

'You're not helping! You're getting paid! It's work. Easy work!'

'Don't shout at him,' Mum says. 'You don't need to go on.'

'I'm not going on – he needs to know!'

'He knows. Don't you? You know you have to work hard, you get married, you buy a house and you start a family.'

'They have it too easy!' Dad says.

Their voices grate until my headache re-emerges and that good feeling that I carried home evaporates. The moment we pull into the drive, I flee the car and hide in my bedroom. I lie on my bed, fighting the ongoing fears that I have a brain tumour, that it'll pop, that it'll kill me and that'll be it.

When Mum and Dad go to bed, I crawl out into the lounge, lie on the couch and watch TV. At 9.30, I take a sleeping pill. I don't have many left, but it doesn't matter, because they do nothing now and I contemplate taking a second. But I might overdose. Who'd find me? Mum and Dad? And it wouldn't even be until they got home from work. No, I can't take the second.

I go to bed and close my eyes and it takes me so long to get to sleep, but when I do sleep, it's okay. Unfortunately, when I wake, the first thing my mind does is turn inward and find the headache waiting there. I sit up and scrunch the covers in my hand.

It's this or me.

This is not going to beat me.

I clamber out of bed and start the new day.

25

Come Saturday, I shower, put gunk in my hair and get dressed for Ethan's party. Jeans are scratchy. Coat's too hot. It's so stuffy in the bathroom. But my headache's not so bad.

'You be careful,' Mum tells me when I slide my head through the kitchen door to tell them I'm leaving.

'There's a lot of stupid people out there,' Dad says.

'Okay, okay,' I say.

I get out of there as quick as I can. The collar of my overcoat scrapes against my neck, and my t-shirt sticks to the sweat on my chest.

Ash waits at the corner, collar of his leather jacket turned up. He has two 600ml bottles of Coke in hand. 'You all right?' he says.

'Of course. Why?'

'You look a little out there.'

'Got a killer headache.'

'You've gotten a few of those,' he says.

I shrug, unsure how to respond.

'You sure you want to come?' he asks.

'Yeah.

Ash thrusts one of the bottles of Coke at me. 'This'll make you feel better.'

I taste the mix of scotch burn down my throat and almost splutter it back up. Ash laughs. He drinks from the other Coke.

'Riley called me,' he says. 'Told me there's no alcohol. So…' He pulls back his jacket. He has a full bottle of scotch stuffed inside his pocket. 'Took this from home. It's Dad's.'

'What happens when he finds out?'

'He won't say anything,' Ash says.

Ethan lives on what you'd called the richer side of Meadow – houses are double-storey with twin garages, big gardens and cobbled paths. Ethan's dad's a builder and has built a lot of the houses in Meadow, these clones whose only real difference is the shade of bricks or the placement of a window or two. He's done well for himself – well enough for a double-storey, at least.

We go the way we'd usually go to school, cross Main Street and then enter Mountain Park Avenue – a long street that ends in a string of houses under construction. Stretching out beyond that is a seemingly endless paddock where they plan to build even more houses one day. I'm sure Ethan's dad has them pencilled in. His blueprints are probably a Monopoly board.

We hear the thump of the music first – Milli Vanilli's 'Baby, Don't Forget My Number'. Even the trees on the nature strips rustle to its beat. Then it's more and more cars parked on the street, until there's a steady line of them on both sides. Then the chatter, growing louder and louder. Finally, the lights pouring from Ethan's house.

Kids are everywhere. Packed on the veranda, in the drive and in the open garage. We see lots of kids we don't know, mostly guys – probably friends of Ethan from all the sports teams he plays on. Then we see kids from our school –including Deanne Vega, who, you might remember, was being bullied by Mickey Purser and Lachlan Kinsey until Ash stepped in. Deanne's shed the plainness of school; she's blow-waved her hair so it hangs wild instead of flat, and she wears this dress cut low, along with this little pink tux jacket that accentuates something that her usually shapeless clothes hide: disproportionately big boobs. Guys are looking at her like they've discovered that a Playboy model has been coming to school.

Out back, a tarpaulin has been pulled from the house over the yard. People are sprawled over tables. Other tables are used for chips and food, and barrels contain drinks. The light to the back door is on, with a steady stream of people going in and out signalling the house is also open to the party.

We find Riley inside on the couch with Felicia. He gets up when he sees us and does his fist-knocking greeting. He's also holding a 600ml bottle of Coke and toasts us. Over in the kitchen, grabbing a bottle of water from the fridge, is Gabriella. She smiles at me, almost shyly. Behind her is Samantha.

'I got Ethan a boxset,' Riley says. 'From all of us.'

I don't know if all of us means from Felicia, too. She doesn't respond in any way.

Kat walks out of the dining room with her prat of a boyfriend. Everybody's dressed up but she looks like she should be at a formal dinner in a fancy restaurant. Her boyfriend has a hand on her hip like he wants to make sure everybody knows he has a claim on her.

Ash stares at her like he's trying to hypnotise her but she

looks right past him. Somebody claps me on the shoulder – Ethan. He has his other hand on Ash's shoulder.

'Thanks for coming!' he says.

'Happy birthday,' I say.

'Happy birthday,' Ash says.

'Thanks!' Ethan says. 'Have a great night, but nothing silly, huh?'

I'm sure that's directed at Ash. Ash's response is to lift his Coke to Ethan. I down the rest of my scotch. It burns in my stomach and my face becomes all warm.

A familiar woman bearing a platter of sandwiches cut into quarters approaches us. She's impish and not at all sedate like the other parents. Dressed all in white – a woolly white V-neck that hangs low, and white jeans – she seems like she should be much younger, or she's trying to hold onto what she used to be. Make-up hides the few lines around the corners of her eyes. It takes me a moment to place that she's Ethan's mum.

'Something to eat?' she asks.

'I'm good, thanks, Mrs May,' I say.

'Sure, thanks.' Ash grabs a couple of sandwiches.

'Drink, fellas?'

Now it's Ethan's dad standing before us, a little guy, balding, with glasses – you'd never pick Ethan's his son.

'We're good,' Ash says, holding up his Coke.

Ethan's parents head off to do the rounds of the other kids. It's not until Mrs May is in the lounge and I'm seeing her from a distance that I recognise she's the woman I saw talking to Ash's dad that day.

'Hey,' I say to Ethan, 'where's your bathroom?'

Ethan drags me down through the hallway and points

to a bathroom under a stairwell leading to the second storey.

'You can use that one,' he says.

His bathroom should be in a magazine. Everything's white, with a marble finish, and the sink has these little toy soaps that smell like incense. And there's so many towels – little folded ones by the sink, and then small ones and big ones hanging from three gold rings on the wall. We have two towels in our bathroom: one slung over the shower cubicle wall, and a nice cotton one that's decorative and hangs from a rack.

The toilet has a fluffy mat on the floor and the rim is burnished wood. The water's blue. To one side is a bidet. I've never seen one – don't even know how to use it. I wonder how many people don't. It's not exactly toilet training growing up, or even when you're in kindergarten or primary school.

I use the toilet, flush, wash my hands and then sit on the toilet seat for a bit. Again, my breath feels short. But no chest pain. It's the stuffiness in here. Somebody thumps on the door.

'You ever coming out?' Ash says.

I open the door. He holds his empty Coke bottle up to me.

'Didn't want to leave you behind,' he tells me.

There's nothing useable in the fridge but outside in the buckets we find bottles of Coke – these even smaller, like you'd give to primary school kids to bring to lunch. We sneak out to the furthest corner of the yard, out beyond the tarpaulin where you can feel the wind on your face and see the stars, spill out some Coke, and fill in some scotch.

Over the next couple of hours, Ash and me duck back out into the corner of the yard to fill Coke bottles two at a time, until we've made about four trips and the scotch bottle is done. By now, I'm so relaxed it's like I've never known anything different.

No headache.

No anxiousness.

Nothing but feeling warm and secure and happy.

26.

For a while we dance in the garage to music from Roxette, Bros, Johnny Diesel, and others who are hot in the charts, until Kat arrives and everybody crowds around her to watch her dance. Her boyfriend stays close and sometimes rubs against her or runs his hands down her hips – like he's still making those claims – until Kat playfully slaps his hands away. You can see he's irritated but he's trying to contain it because he doesn't want to show he's not a cool guy. Finally, after a couple of dances, he leads her away and that's the last we see of them for the night.

In the backyard, we bump into Rachel and Gabriella. Some of the scotch and Coke from Ash's bottle sploshes onto Gabriella's arm and the sleeve of her blouse. I grab some napkins from one of the food tables and wipe her down.

'Sorry, sorry,' Ash says. 'I didn't see you.'

'Obviously,' Rachel says.

She moves to brush past Ash, but he sidesteps to block her.

'Hey!'

'I wanted to apologise,' Ash says. 'Not for the drink – not just for the drink. But for the way I treated you at the last party. That was wrong. You probably can't forgive me, but I'm sorry.'

Rachel's face softens. 'Okay. Thanks.'

Gabriella shakes her arm. 'This is sticky. I'm gonna find the bathroom.'

'I'll show you where it is,' I say.

I lead her into the house, down the hallway and under the stairwell. If I was Riley or Ash or anybody else, this whole offer to show her to the bathroom would've been to get her alone. Not me. My whole offer to show her to the bathroom is…to show her to the bathroom. It's not until I usher her in – she goes immediately to the sink to wash her arm – and step inside, hovering there like her private security, that I think this could've been a move on my part.

She bends to use the sink, the swell of her butt so tight in her little skirt I can see the outline of her underwear and the crack in her arse. Ash and Riley would be thinking one thing. And she *does* look good. I try to think of something to say. It doesn't have to be witty. It just has to be conversational.

'Close the door,' she says, still washing her arm. She sniffs at her skin. 'What's in that?'

'Coke.'

'And …?'

'Some scotch. Maybe.'

She holds out her hand. I deposit the scotch in it. She lifts the bottle to her lips and grimaces as she sips, then takes a deep drink.

'Better,' she says. 'It's so boring out there.'

She steps up to me as she offers my bottle back. This is so easy in movies. Throw one arm behind her back, pull her in close, and tilt my head – just not the same direction she's tilting. That would be awkward. But it must happen. Maybe I should ask her. That would be polite.

I imagine shoving her to the floor – just thrust my palms into her chest. I know I won't do it. But it's like that stupid thought at Aunt Mena's funeral, jumping in, foreign and sharp. I fall back a step. Uncertainty flickers across Gabriella's face.

This is so stupid. Gabriella's nice. And smart. And gorgeous. Her blouse is the littlest bit see-through – just enough to make out her bra's pink and pushes up her boobs in a way you can see the swell of their shape. Now I'm objectifying her. But my thoughts are all over the place, tadpoles in a pond, dancing to the tempo of my heartbeat.

Somebody knocks on the door. Then it swings open – I didn't lock it, of course. Ethan leads in some kid, then points at us and grins.

'Hey, no making out in the bathrooms,' he says.

Gabriella retreats into the kitchen and through to the adjoining lounge. I follow her – I'd be an idiot not to, but I stutter when I see Samantha's sitting on the couch with Lachlan, one of Lachlan's orangutan arms over the headrest and around her, his other paw on her knee. It shouldn't make me jealous. I've never been interested in Samantha. Never. But I feel a…what's the right word? Ownership? No, that's dumb. She's not a slave. An entitlement? Maybe closer. Given her interest in me, I didn't think she'd become interested in somebody else, although that's dumb again. But it's a night for dumb.

Samantha sees me, and I see that same soft intent in her eyes. But then she turns back to Lachlan and laughs at something stupid he says. His face nuzzles hers. They could kiss now. They should kiss. Like I should've kissed Gabriella.

Something in me splits. It's not Samantha being with Lachlan. Or missing out on Gabriella – a situation I might be able to recover. But it's a guillotine coming down on my ability to connect – not just with Gabriella, but everyone here, and even the occasion. The language becomes something other than English, the setting something other than a party. I'm a blur in a bad photo.

I stumble out of the house, not even sure where Gabriella's gone. Kids dance in the garage – Riley's there and grinds against Felicia. I get angry. No. Not angry. Resentful. Fuck. Other kids are laughing. Having fun. It comes so easy to them. So naturally. So unthinkingly. So *everything*.

I don't even know where I'm going when I leave the house and I drink greedily from my bottle but it does nothing for me. Down the street, it grows darker as I get to the houses under construction. When I first hear the moans, I don't even register them. But then they become unmistakable: sharp, desperate, with some attempt to be restrained – afraid to draw attention.

They're hazy silhouettes on the veranda, a singular blob with a pulsating rhythm – I think she's leaning against the balustrade and he's behind her. They don't see me. At least I think they don't. And I drift across the road and walk and walk until the houses behind me are tiny, lost in the ghostly aura of the few streetlights, while the paddock stretches ahead to a string of tiny lights – the freeway, I think. But it's dark here, except for the stars peeking through wispy clouds, and a shy half-moon that hangs large enough that you can see craters.

I flop down, onto my back, and finish the last of my scotch, my head overflowing with thoughts, self-loathing burning inside me and, seething through that, combatting the tide of scotch that tries to numb it, the anxiousness pokes out its head and grins, as if to say, *Remember me?*

SPRING

September – November 1989

27

The sky's this purplish blue that bemoans the coming morning. Clouds are scattered strands trying to hold onto whatever's left of the night. All in an instant, as I blink my eyes – before I even realise I'm awake and that I should be staring at my ceiling instead of the sky – that I feel nothing but an absence of everything.

Then it floods in.

The headache is a shard of glass that splits my head open; the anxiousness trembles in my shoulders; as I rise, nausea hits, so I double over, but nothing comes out. My mouth is cloyingly sweet. I take a deep breath but it barely sinks into my chest.

I light a cigarette, but two puffs make the shortness of breath worse, so I butt it out, walk on then worry that I haven't butted out the cigarette properly and it'll set the paddock on fire, so backtrack and spend five minutes finding the butt to assure myself it is out.

The party's a dream I recall through splotches that breed other splotches, until a streaky picture is painted. Gabriella. Samantha with Lachlan. Riley all over Felicia. Ash apologising to Rachel. Dancing. Celebrations. Fun. All that stuff. This singular organism with a heartbeat. That'd make me...what?

Nothing more than an infection.

I emerge from the paddock and back onto Mountain Park Road, passing the house where the sex was taking place on the veranda. I imagine them there now. But it's empty. And the rest of the houses are quiet. Ethan's house is dark. Everybody would be asleep. How long would the party have gone on? When did I get out of there? What did people think? Hopefully, I didn't worry Ash. I doubt Riley would've noticed.

The streets of Meadow are empty. Nobody's up this early. It must be 4.00 or 5.00am. Mum will kill me. I'll have to lie, say I slept at Ash's, although that's improbable. I never sleep anywhere. And it's not sleeping elsewhere that's the issue. It's not telling Mum that I was going to do it.

I cut across Meadow High, empty, deserted, even melancholy. I feel it in the bricks. The walls have sad faces. The courtyard is a splattered teardrop. It's all stupid, of course. But I feel like the school has eyes on me as I make my way through, this interloper to its quiet Sunday. Or maybe I give it purpose. It needs kids to be a school. Otherwise, it's just empty buildings.

The bridge is quiet and the creek a trickle. The water smells, too. Or maybe it's the dew on the grass. I try to pinpoint it and then work out that it smells *clean*. Every time I'm here, I'm smoking with Ash. This is nice the way it is – the way it should be.

When I get back to my house, I ease my way through the gate. The motion-activated light comes on. I stop. Steph keeps a spare key in one of the loose bricks that surround the garden. I pick up the brick and fish around in the hole, afraid a spider might bite me and then afraid that Steph might've put the key away while she's on holiday. But then I feel something cold. Carefully, I slide the key out, put the brick back, and let myself into the bungalow.

The bungalow smells like Steph – something flowery and sweet – that perfume she's been wearing since her twenty-first. Olivia gave it to her. Before that, it was all cheap perfumes that were meant to smell like something expensive but smelled like air fresheners.

The bungalow's neat. The bedcover is this generic gold pattern that Mum bought. A small desk holds a sketchpad and resting before it is the ergonomic blue felt chair she got on staff-discount from Furniture Warehouse. There are a few pictures of Paris and the Eiffel Tower. The stereo – another gift for her twenty-first (ironically, from Aunt Mena) – fills the corner. Two towers overflowing with tapes flank it. In the opposite corner is our old television – Steph inherited it when Dad bought a new one for the house. Between the two, books are crammed into a bookshelf and other books are stacked into their own columns. The whole place has the sense of somebody just getting by – except for the books, and they're mostly second hand.

I fall onto her bed and strip off, then fold myself under her covers but I can't get to sleep. The morning filters through the curtains of the bungalow. Then it's the back door and the screen door clattering open. I can't hear her footsteps but visualise Mum shuffling down the stairs. More light coming through the curtains now as the bungalow's motion-activated light comes on. I clench my eyes shut. The door opens – quietly. That's good. Quiet means Mum doesn't suspect I've just gotten in. I sense her standing in the doorway and can feel her indecision. To wake me or not to wake me? I hear the back door and screen door open and the clomp of Dad coming out.

'He in there?' Dad asks.

'*Ssshhhh*!' Mum says with such force she might've put a rip in space. 'He's sleeping.'

Dad chuckles. He chuckles like Barney Rubble: *Hee-hee-hee.* 'Probably drinking, silly boy.'

Mum closes the door quietly and I hear them open and close the gate. Then the car pulls out of the drive. They're going to church – their typical Sunday routine.

I flip onto my back. My head throbs and my skin tingles. Every now and then, the restlessness explodes and my mind distends, then snaps back into place to contain it. I shift, unable to keep still.

What I need is sleep, although I don't feel drowsy. I could take one of the few remaining sleeping pills I have left but I know I shouldn't mix that with alcohol. Is there still alcohol in my system? Obviously there is, but enough to interact with a sleeping pill? What would happen? Would it make me sick? Overdose? No, no to the sleeping pill.

I need to get to sleep. There's refuge in sleep. But the anxiousness keeps at me. I try to think of something else to occupy my mind. Gabriella? No, given how that unfolded – too depressing. My story? No. Olivia? Not even she helps.

Sleep.

I just need sleep, and everything will be okay.

28.

A good night's sleep solves everything. Well, that's what everybody says. It's the ultimate reset, like playing a game and starting over because you're not doing well. Go to sleep. Fall into unconsciousness. And everything starts over.

Except when it doesn't.

I do sleep, at some point. I have no idea when my body gives it up and I must never get too deep into it, because I feel awake the whole time – and there's lots of noise outside: Olivia's dad cutting the grass, Mum and Dad coming home, kids in the neighbourhood kicking a ball around.

Somehow, time judders to 1.00pm.

And there's no reset.

Everything's still the same.

I go into the house, throw some bread in the toaster and pour myself a glass of orange juice. Mum's on the couch, Dad in his chair, watching something on TV that's in Greek – one of their shows.

'What time did you get home last night?' Mum asks.

'One, maybe.'

'Why did you sleep in Steph's bungalow?'

'I didn't want to wake you up.'

'Your friend Ash called,' Mum says.

I wait. Hopefully, Ash didn't say anything about me disappearing last night. Mum says nothing more.

'Okay,' I say. 'Thanks.'

I finish breakfast and call Ash back from the phone in the hallway.

'Where'd you disappear to?' he says.

Anxiousness crawls all over my skin. I'm scared it's going to erupt into something that's going to blow me apart. I even imagine it – my limbs and head exploding from my body. Now I want to be off the phone. I don't want Ash to be witness to that.

'My head–' I say.

'That headache?'

'Yeah.'

'You okay?'

'I'll be all right. Look, I'm gonna go.'

'Okay. You think you'll go to school?'

'Sure.'

We hang up and I shower, which makes me feel better. But I can't calm down. This burns inside of me. I try things to settle down: take a little walk, but get breathless; try to play some pool, but I have a tremor in my arms; crawl into bed and try to masturbate to distract myself, but I can't get excited; try to read, but can't focus on the words; try to write, but can't get my imagination started.

I yank my school folder from my bag and open it up. Homework. That'll work. I do my Maths. It's a struggle to focus, but I manage it because Maths has fixed answers. I only need to think enough to confirm my solutions on a calculator, although my fingers tremble when they hit the buttons.

Then it's a toss-up between Legal, Social Studies and English. That wall of Boland Fellows flashes in my mind – that blank spot that will be filled at the end of the year. I see a picture of myself there. That's the picture of somebody who's achieved something and not somebody debilitated by what *this* is.

I write several paragraphs of the Legal essay, but they become scattered and I misspell words – I rarely misspell. I scrunch up the page. That hope that was a bright spark dims and then – as I misspell 'justice' as 'jutsice' – goes out.

This isn't going to work.

I can't push through this.

Then it hits: like I've plummeted through the floor. My hands shoot out – I want to catch myself. Now it's like somebody comes up behind me and shoves me as hard as they can. I stay standing where I am, but what resilience is left in me flies out. Now, there's nothing but terror. The house rocks and spins. I want to run – run as fast as I can.

I need help.

That's clear now.

It's Sunday. My doctor's clinic is closed. That's the closest option. That leaves the 24-Hour Super Clinic. There's no guarantee Dr Kuruvilla works on a Sunday. I don't even know if I should be thinking about him as a fall-back. Maybe somebody else there. But how's that going to work? I went to that clinic for a quick fix. Am I going again for *another* quick fix? This is no longer quick-fixable.

My thinking forms half-ideas that dissolve. The terror screeches through my body. I clench my fists and wait for it to pass, but it wells up inside my head until I'm sure it'll burst.

I rush into the kitchen, clutching at my temples.

'Mum,' I say, 'we need to go to the doctor.'

Mum shoots up from the couch with an agility that I've never seen. 'What's wrong? What's the matter?'

'I don't know.'

But it's more than *I don't know*. It's also *I don't know how to explain this* – not to her or Dad at least.

'Can we go?'

'Get your keys,' Mum tells Dad.

We're in the car within minutes, Dad behind the wheel, Mum in the passenger seat, me sitting in the back, head in my hands.

'Where are we going?' Dad says, pulling the car from the drive.

'The hospital.'

'Which one?' Dad says. 'St Margaret's or the Western?'

'St Margaret's,' Mum says. 'No. Wait. Jim works there. The Western.' She looks over at me in the back seat. 'Lie down.'

I do that, curling up on the backseat as resignation overcomes me. The terror pokes away, but it's dulled – maybe because something's being done about it, or because of the relief that builds up. They know now. Mum and Dad know. And we're on the way to hospital. They'll fix this. That's what I keep telling myself.

I've been to the Western – when Aunt Mena was battling cancer. It's a fifteen-minute drive, basically down two long straights (the bypass and the freeway, once you get off Main Street) and I try to visualise it as Dad drives.

Every now and again, he curses at the traffic or at lights. But otherwise, it's quiet. Mum looks back at me frequently.

'What is it?' she says. 'Did you take something last night?'

'No,' I say.

'Are you sure you didn't take something?' Dad says.

'I didn't take anything.'

'This isn't the time to lie to us if you did–'

'I didn't!'

'Ssssh!' Mum tells him. 'What is it?' she asks.

'I can't stop my head from worrying.'

'What do you mean you can't stop worrying?'

'It's in my head – it keeps going.'

Judging by the way we slow down and all the turns, I think we must have arrived at the hospital. I sit up. Sure enough, we're parked outside the doors.

'I'll let you off here at the door,' Dad says. 'I'll park the car and come find you.'

Because of those visits to Aunt Mena, we know the way through the lobby and head down the hallway to EMERGENCY. Rows of seats are filled with people. Mum sits me down and gets in a long line to reception.

I double over and bury my face in my hands. My breath comes in rasps. A little blond kid stares at me from the next row of chairs – can't be older than six or so. He pivots back and forth and holds onto his mum, or maybe it's his mum who holds onto him, afraid if she lets him go, he might fly away like an untethered kite. The look on the kid's face is quizzical, trying to work out what's wrong with me. I can't look back at him. He's so earnest it feels like I've disappointed him.

So, I listen to what's going on around me: the murmured conversation of the others in EMERGENCY, footsteps walking away from Reception to sit down (that means Mum's one person closer to checking me in), the doctors who call the patients in, the announcements that blare through hospital speakers. There's an order to it that's calming in an environment so chaotic.

Mum finally comes and sits down, putting an arm around me.

I lie on my side and rest my head on her lap.

29.

Mum strokes my hair the way she did when I was a kid and I was sick. Dad finds us, talks briefly with Mum then walks off. He does this repeatedly. His chatter goes from asking her if she wants a drink or a coffee, to cursing the doctors for the delay. My thoughts slow down, then drift randomly, losing their attachment to the terror and fear. I could go home but I know the way I'm feeling isn't fixed. This will change. Something else will come up.

A doctor calls my name – a young guy, at least for a doctor in a hospital, with sandy hair already thinning, and only half his shirt tucked into his trousers. His appearance doesn't inspire confidence. It looks like he just woke up.

I ease myself up from Mum. She stands and waves to Dad to wait. The doctor shows us into a small examination room – a cot and two chairs, partitioned with a curtain. He instructs me to sit up on the cot.

'I'm Doctor Searcy,' he says. 'What can we do for you today?'

He's pleasant and friendly. That's good. So I tell him about the anxiousness, about the way that I've been feeling, but do so in a way that omits details – like seeing Dr Kuruvilla. I don't want Mum to know how long this has been going on. Mum watches me, frightened. I don't know how much she understands.

'I'd like to examine your son,' Dr Searcy tells Mum. 'If you could wait outside…'

Mum leaves us and Dr Searcy does all the things Dr Kuruvilla did – listen to my heartbeat and take my blood pressure – and more. He has me stand up with my arms out and has me balance on one leg with my eyes closed; he has me hold an arm out and tells me to resist him pulling my arms down; he asks me to close my hand as tight as I can around his finger. There's lots of these little tests. I think I do okay with them.

'Have you taken any drugs?' he asks.

'I saw a doctor who gave me sleeping pills,' I say.

'Not that sort.'

'I don't take anything I shouldn't.'

'You're telling me the truth now?'

'I am. I swear.'

'Do you drink?'

'Sometimes.'

'How much?'

'When I go out, I drink – maybe like once a month.'

'Are there issues at home?'

'No.'

'Nothing?'

'Nothing that's not normal.'

'What does that mean?'

I think about life at home – Mum behaving like she's sick, the shouting and all that, but that *is* normal. And it's not malicious. It's not like they beat me or lock me in closets or anything like that.

'It's fine,' I say.

'How about school? Are you under pressure there?'

'I'm doing well at school.'

'Has anything untoward happened recently? Have you been bullied, for example?'

'I did get in a fight,' I say, thinking about that first party. 'Well, my friend got in a fight and I tried to break it up and got punched in my nose.'

Dr Searcy purses his lips. 'When was that?'

'I'm not sure.'

'Before or after this started?'

'Before – I think.'

Dr Searcy's eyes bore into me.

'Nothing really came of it. My nose bled a bit. But that was it.'

'We never know how the human mind is going to respond to external stimuli – particularly violent stimuli. This could be a result of shock, escalating into a generalised panic disorder.'

'Generalised panic disorder?'

'An anxiety condition, usually marked by anxiety without any real cause and panic attacks. I think it would be good if you saw somebody here – one of our psychiatrists.'

I see myself lying down on a psychiatrist's couch, recounting my problems, going through childhood until I make some stunning revelation – I'm not kidding, either. I almost smile at the prospect that I'll emerge from this fixed, better than I've ever been. This is what I need, what I've always needed.

'Give me a few minutes,' Dr Searcy says.

He slips out through the curtain and I swing my feet

from the cot, almost embarrassed by all this fuss. But being here is reassuring. If anything happens to me here, somebody can treat me. I almost wish something *would* happen, so they could see it in action and do whatever's needed.

The curtain's pulled open and Dr Searcy leads in Mum and Dad. Dad can't stand still. Mum's eyes are misty. Shit, I've made her cry. The shame makes me feel horrible. Dad rests a supportive hand on the middle of her back. I've never seen that from Dad.

Dr Searcy hands me a piece of paper with a date and time written on it. The date's a month from now – a month! I'm coming apart and they're scheduling appointments that far into the future. How am I meant to survive?

'That's an appointment to see one of our psychiatrists,' he says. 'I've spoken to your parents and think that's the best course to take. There's also these.' He hands me a box of meds. 'I've told them I'm prescribing you a mild sedative. Take one three times a day, or, preferably, as needed – but no more than three in total. No more sleeping pills. This should help settle everything down.'

'It'll fix it?' I look dubiously at the box.

'You take the pills,' Mum says. 'They'll make you better.'

'It'll give you some peace so you can do the things you've probably had trouble concentrating on before,' Dr Searcy says. 'It's a good way to help reassimilate back into your normal routine and unlearn the trepidation you've developed.'

'Okay. Thanks.'

Dr Searcy claps me on the shoulder. 'You'll be all right.'

It's dark when we wander outside. Dad picks us up from

outside the entrance. The drive home's quiet. The family's punctured. We're that balloon you see in decorations that's become deflated and sad compared to all the other ripe balloons.

At home, we settle in the way we always would on a Sunday. I retreat to my bedroom and sit on my bed, looking at the box. 'Ducene' is printed on the label. I pop one – it's a round tablet, like an Aspirin – out of its foil and put the rest away in my bedside drawer. I throw the tablet into my mouth and hold it there. Then I head back to the kitchen and pour a juice from the fridge, making it look as if I'm doing nothing more than getting a drink. Dad's on his chair. Mum's on the other chair. The couch is vacant. I lie on it. Dad switches the TV on.

'Don't go to school tomorrow,' Mum says. 'See how you feel.'

'We should call Stephanie,' Dad says.

'No,' I say. 'No! Leave her.'

'But you're sick.'

'Let her have a holiday – don't call her!'

I'm unsure if I'm passionate because I don't want to disturb her holiday, or if it's because I don't want to extend my embarrassment.

'She can't do anything,' I say. 'Let her have her holiday.'

'All right, all right,' Mum says. 'But you keep this between us. You don't tell anybody, all right?'

The sedative is already working – the quiet in my mind is foreign.

'All right?' Mum says.

'All right,' I say.

'Not even Ash or Riley – all right?'

I couldn't – even if I wanted to. Mum's right. Nobody needs to know. I'm faulty. That's all there is to it. *Weak*. Why would I want to share that?

30.

For the first time in weeks, I sleep okay, although I think that maybe it's because I'm exhausted. I wake just after 8.00 and, for a few moments, everything is perfect. Calm. And then it starts: the monitoring of every thought, every emotion, every reaction, like my mind has embarked on some meticulous cataloguing of everything going on inside my head.

I get out of bed, grab a sedative and swallow it in the kitchen with some juice. Breakfast next, as that stillness closes over me. Unlike the sleeping pill, it doesn't make me feel drowsy or heavy about my body. These can keep me going. It'll be no problem to last until the psychiatrist.

Something clanks outside – the clothesline spinning. Through the kitchen window, I see Mum hanging up laundry. She should be at work. But, of course, she stayed home to watch me. Does she think I'm that fragile? I feel resentful but it flattens out into a peculiar resignation. I came in here yesterday telling her and Dad I was sick and needed a doctor. What else is she going to think?

Mum babies me outrageously throughout the day. She makes me sandwiches, cutting them into quarters, and regularly comes into my bedroom – where I work on the book report for *To Kill a Mockingbird* and then on my Jean Razor story – to ask if I want something to drink.

I start my Legal essay and while I'm sure everybody's writing practical alternatives, mine becomes a story where criminals who are found guilty go through a second trial that questions their worth to society, and sentences them to execution if it's decided they contribute nothing valuable. If this is the piece that's used for the Boland, I'm not sure what they'll think of it – or me. My left hand's cramping from writing so much and I haven't thought about the anxiousness once. I still have my Social Studies essay about improving the world to go, but that can wait.

I go down into the garage and play some pool. Mum comes into the garage and asks me if I want an orange juice. I tell her I'm okay.

'Do you want to go to school tomorrow?' she asks.

I don't even need to think about it. 'Sure.'

Mum hugs me. 'Please don't worry,' she says, tearfully. 'You have a house to live in, you have parents who love you, you never have to want for anything – you've got nothing to worry about.'

'Okay, okay.'

She's no sooner left when there's a knock at the garage door: Ash, his school bag slung over his shoulder.

'Hey,' he says. 'Thought I'd check how you are. You don't look so bad.'

Two streams of reality take off. One stream is me with Ash, chatting the way we'd always chat. The second stream is a tension that crawls over me, tightening in my shoulders and chest. It's not severe but it's there, and I worry that something will happen in front of Ash, that *this* will return.

Then where do I run? I took the first sedative around 8.00am, and it's now 4.00pm. I'd be due another one. Dr Searcy said three a day, or *as needed*, and it's needed now.

Ash eyes me from the end of the table as he racks up the balls.

'I took something for it,' I say. 'I might grab a drink. You want something?'

'Sure. Whatever.'

I grab another sedative from my bedroom and dry swallow it, then pour two orange juices and carry them into the garage. Ash has set up the balls and breaks as I enter. The balls scatter across the table and a striped one goes in. I set the orange juices down on a wardrobe in the corner of the garage where Dad keeps his tools.

'So, everything's okay?' Ash says. 'We were a bit worried when you disappeared.' He plays a rebound off the bank and pockets it.

'You and Riley?'

'Riley's fused to Felicia now. I meant Gabriella. When I came back, she was worried.'

'My head was hurting. I didn't know where you were, so I came home.' The lie slides right out of my mouth. But then something else clicks. 'When you came back? From…?'

Ash holds out his arms in celebration, the way a soccer player might appeal to the crowd after kicking a goal. He thrusts his hips forward once.

'You and Rachel… *again*? Is that why you apologised to her?'

'Hey, I resent that.'

'So, you're boyfriend-girlfriend now?'

'Firstly, it wasn't Rachel. I apologised to her because…'
Ash shrugs and plays his shot.

'Because you were sorry.'

Ash rolls his eyes.'Because I didn't want to walk around with her constantly angry at me.'

He plays his next shot, commanding the table. Usually, Ash is too unfocused to be consistently good. But now he's pocketing them from everywhere.

'So, you weren't even sincere about the apology?' I ask.

'Of course I was sincere. How dare you accuse me of *not* being sincere. That apology was sincere. Right from the bottom of my heart.'

'Okay, well, that's something.'

'Sincerity – what a weapon.'

I'm feeling better again – maybe the sedative, maybe this conversation distracting me, or maybe a combination of both.

Ash finally misses a shot and I lean over the table, lining up the three ball in the corner pocket – a long shot across the length of the table, but the way I've been playing today, it should be no problem.

'If not Rachel–' I say.

'Deanne.'

I shank the shot. The white ball comes off the edge of my cue and spirals into the corner, that sound of a mishit – like a plank of wood that snaps – sharp in the garage.

'Deanne?' I say. 'Little Deanne? Nerdy Deanne?'

'Nerdy Deanne is hot – did you see her that night?'

'So, are you a couple?'

Ash splutters. 'Yeah. Right. But she's wild under that nerdiness. She kept seeing us filling those Coke bottles, so she pulled me up in the garage and asked what I was drinking. Then she wants to go out front for a smoke. Then she grabs my hand and pulls me down to those houses at the end of the street.'

Ash and Deanne. That's who was on the veranda.

'It seriously happened like that?' I say.

'We went out front to have a smoke, I told her she looked good, I was sincere and the best thing is, she's happy to leave it at that. Everybody wants to ride the legend.'

'You're a legend now?'

'Not me but my cock,' Ash says deadpan. 'Don't tell Riley, though. He talks. I don't want to embarrass Deanne – it's nobody's business. You know what'll happen if it gets out?'

'Sure,' I say.

He's right. That high school grapevine will blow it up.

We chat and play for the next couple of hours, me able to enjoy something I used to do all the time with him. Mum invites Ash to stay for dinner and heaps steaks on his plates, with mashed potatoes and vegetables. Ash eats it all uncomplainingly.

'See?' Mum says in her stilted English. 'You should eat like Ash.' She tousles his hair. 'None of this *too much-too much.*' She says to Ash with a sense of martyrdom. 'They tell me I give them too much, him and Stephanie.'

'You should give them more,' Ash says.

Mum gives me a smug, victorious look.

Once dinner is done, Ash says he should be going, so I walk him to the corner and we have a smoke there. It makes me dizzy; it's the first one I've had since the party.

'So, you're coming to school tomorrow?' he says.

'Yeah, I guess.'

'You've been out there recently.'

'Out there?'

'Like you're always distracted.'

How much do I tell him? It's awkward; he knows it, too. We don't share like this; guys just *don't*. It's so unfamiliar that it's scary.

'You finally going through puberty?' he jokes.

'Ha. Ha.'

Ash finishes his cigarette, taking one long drag that burns what's remaining to the filter. He flicks it away and blows out a stream of smoke as he looks sidelong at me. *If you want to talk*, I think he's going to say to me. Or, *I know there's something you're not telling me*. But teenagers don't talk like that. It only happens on the TV soaps.

'I'll see you tomorrow,' Ash says.

'See ya.'

Ash heads off down into his street and I make my way back home.

31.

I wake up at 6.50 the next morning. The house is quiet. I get up to check and find it's empty. Mum's gone to work.

Now it's just me.

I grab the sedatives out of my drawer but don't take one. *As needed.* That was the instruction.

I have breakfast, shower, and the closer it gets to the time I leave, the quicker my heart thumps and the clammier my palms get. I go back to the sedatives and break off the cellophane so I can grab two tablets. One I take immediately in the kitchen, and the other I thrust in my pocket. Then I lock up.

Ash waits on the corner. 'How're you doing?'

'I'm okay, I guess.'

But the sedative hasn't taken effect. I feel a mild agitation as we walk and it triples once we get to school. Kids are everywhere. They're always everywhere. But now they're suffocating.

In the courtyard, Riley sits with Felicia. He waves to us but doesn't get up, so there's no morning cigarette. Samantha strolls past with Lachlan, close enough to suggest they're together, which brings up that jealousy again. Samantha glances at me, haughtily maybe – if I'm not going to do anything, then it's my loss. Deanne – now wearing tight jeans and a body-hugging sweater – bounces on the way to class. While her friends are still the same timid, nameless group, she beams.

My chest tightens in that way that it feels like I can't take a deep breath. I go into the toilets with Ash to have a smoke but don't end up smoking much because it makes me dizzy. So I let it burn out, then flick it into the urinal.

Once the bell rings, we go back into the courtyard. Kids scatter, heading to their classes. I want to hide back in the toilet or tell Ash I need to go. It's too risky being out here. I'll blow out here. Somebody will see it. *Everybody* will see it. They'll think that I'm a freak. That I'm weak. That I'm crazy. Then, a tiny, desperate thought questions why the sedative isn't working.

I follow Ash into English class, sit in our usual place at the back – although I almost expect Riley to go sit with Felicia – and fidget with my books.

Mr Baker holds up a stack of homework. 'I'm handing back your book reports for *I Am the Cheese* today,' he says. 'As I do so, please hand in your book reports for *To Kill a Mockingbird*.'

He must've put the homework in order because he moves systematically, working his way from the front to the back. Ash, Riley and me are the last to get our book reports back. It's easy enough to see what marks we got, since Mr Baker always uses a thick red pen and marks homework in the top right corner, along with ticks or some comments. Ash gets a B- and three ticks, Riley a D with the comment *You can do better than this!* and I get an A+, with a *Well done*.

Mr Baker smiles at me. 'Excellent work,' he says.

As he heads to the front of the class, Riley scrunches up his homework and shoves it in his folder. Mr Baker would hear it because half the class turns to us, but he sits on his desk as he always does, grabs a novel and holds it in his lap.

'Final book for the year,' he says, holding up the novel. '*The Catcher in the Rye*. A classic in literature and, arguably, a book some of you will feel you'll be able to relate to.' He puts the novel back on his desk. 'But let's talk about *To Kill a Mockingbird*. What themes does *Mockingbird* explore?'

Suggestions are thrown out – racism, justice, family. Mr Baker nods as the class descends into discussion. I don't say anything, instead only listening. But in listening, something happens. I forget that I'm meant to be panicked. Or maybe the sedative kicks in. Whatever happens, it gives me confidence that this is going to be all right.

When the bell rings, everybody stuffs their bags and Mr Baker dismisses us. But then his voice cuts through the noise of everybody leaving.

'Riley,' he says, 'may I speak to you please?'

Ash and me look at each other, then hurry over to Computers. Mr Tan waits until we've settled. He's only a small man, and often you forget he's there because most of the students are taller than him. But there is always this tremendous sense of patience with him. He's one of the few teachers who never raises his voice – his face will twist into disapproval, but he'll just wait out anything that happens.

'Before we move onto the computers,' he says, 'a homework assignment.'

Everybody groans. Computers is meant to be one of the

easy subjects where we don't have homework. Everything's done in class because it's the only place that everybody has access to these computers.

'Computers are becoming an accessible, everyday item – just like a toaster,' Mr Tan says. 'I want one-thousand words on how you think computers will look in ten and twenty years. What technological advancements do you foresee? How will that impact other everyday technology, like televisions, refrigerators, cars and all those things we use in day-to-day life?'

Riley comes in. 'Mr Baker needed to talk to me,' he says as he slumps into his chair.

Mr Tan nods, repeats the homework assignment, then proceeds with the class as normal, teaching us the programming language Turbo Pascal. He gets us to write a few small programs that use variables and ask the user for their name. There's a logic to it that there isn't in real life. It keeps my mind occupied, although a few times I gasp for breath just to prove to myself that I can breathe.

At recess, we spill from the class and mushroom out into the courtyard. Felicia, Kat, Rachel and Gabriella mill about, chatting as we approach.

'What happened with Mr Baker?' Ash asks.

'Said he didn't like my attitude and if it happened again, he'd send me to see the vice-principal.' Riley snorts. 'I think he's got it in for me.'

'Sure you haven't got it in for him?' I ask.

'What's that supposed to mean?'

'You always seem so angry at him.'

'Just because you love him doesn't mean I have to.'

'I don't–'

'He's a fag, okay? Probably pissed I don't worship him like you do.'

I bite back on my anger. 'Don't get–'

'Forget it. I'll see you later.'

Felicia detaches from her friends, grabs Riley's hand and they head off to the canteen. Kat and Rachel sit on one of the benches in the atrium. But Gabriella keeps standing there, waiting for me. Ash reads the situation straight away.

'I'll see you…' He gestures in the direction of the toilets.

'Sure.'

'What happened to you the other night?' Gabriella says, once Ash is out of earshot.

'I had a bad headache,' I say.

'Not surprised with how much you drank.'

'I had it for a few days.'

'A migraine?'

'Yeah. I guess.'

'You think the assignment Mr Tan gave us is for the Boland?' Gabriella asks.

I think about the other essays, then shake my head.

'Why not?' Gabriella asks.

'I went and looked at the other essays – they have them framed in the office.'

'Oh! That's such a good idea! I should do that, too.'

'They're all about how we can make an impact on the future. The Computers thing is more about something else making an impact on our future.'

'But we don't know what the future is, right? It could be anything. So it might be about how we see the future.'

'Maybe.'

I'm worried something will happen – that I'll freak

and she'll see it. I could tell her the truth. She might understand, but who wants to be laden with somebody who has so many problems? I could apologise for leaving Ethan's party so abruptly. I could ask her to the canteen, to sit and have a drink. I could compliment her on the way she looks. The options pour into my head.

And what comes out is frightened silence.

'Okay,' Gabriella says. 'I'll leave you to it.'

Or I think that's what she says and I think her voice even breaks, but I can't tell for sure because she's already spun and moving away halfway through her sentence. She rushes off to join Kat and Rachel on the bench.

Lachlan and Samantha walk past. Lachlan leers at me, then throws an arm out around Samantha and pulls her close. He grins this stupid grin. Samantha doesn't see it and she's stiff at his side. But then she notices me and melts into him. He says something – I don't hear it. Samantha laughs. It's not fair how easy things come for some.

I hurry off to the toilets to have a cigarette.

32

As I walk home with Ash, I feel a sense of relief and triumph. Today proves I can make it through school. I can beat this.

'You seem happy,' Ash says, as we approach the corner where we part.

'Just feel a bit better,' I say.

'Okay. That's something. I'll see you tomorrow.'

A shoddy bunch of flowers sit on the doorstep of Steph's bungalow – the roses are bruised and the stems wilted. You'd think they'd been sitting here days. I pick them up and find a small card attached. I shouldn't be looking but I do anyway:

How bout we give it another chanse?
Luv,
Todd.

Todd should be on holiday with Steph, Olivia and Mario for another month. If Todd's leaving flowers, then he mustn't be on the holiday. If Todd didn't go, did Mario? Did Olivia? Olivia must've, since she picked Steph up, unless it was all part of an elaborate ruse. Steph might've thought Mum and Dad wouldn't let her go off on her own, so concocted this story of going away with the others. Maybe she went alone and Olivia and Mario went and did their own thing.

I shove the card in my pocket and bury the flowers deep, deep in the garbage – under a whole load of other rubbish, so Mum and Dad won't see them. They won't like that Steph lied. Hopefully, Todd doesn't drop by again. I go up into my bedroom and hide the card in a book on my bookshelf.

The next couple of days are good. There are breathless periods and flighty moments, but I'm able to occupy myself until I stop noticing them. That's the key now, I figure: keep my head busy so I don't let anything else in.

Writing's the best way to do that. First, there's my homework, although I struggle with some of that because it's so dull. I eke out my Social Studies report, writing what I'm feeling: that we could improve the world if we could teach people not to worry, as worry's often what causes stupid decisions. I don't really know what I'm writing – I think it's me trying to make sense of this, and the result is okay without being great, but given how I'm feeling, it'll do.

Then there's my book. Things I was unclear about reveal themselves to me – how the Grave Shadows work for something called the Crimson Tower, and how Jean Razor's one of a handful of people who can shift through dimensions. It excites me that I'm seeing a broader picture and my hand cramps from my efforts. My writing becomes loose scrawls as I fill the exercise book.

Steph calls on Friday from France. Mum gets it while I'm in the garage playing pool. She calls me to come to the phone and after her and Dad are done with Steph, I get to chat.

'Hel–' I begin.

'What's Mum saying you went to hospital?' Steph asks. 'What's wrong?'

'It's nothing,' I say. 'Mum shouldn't have told you.'

'What is it? Tell me. Should I come back–?'

'No. It's…the doctor said it's this thing called Generalised Anxiety Disorder.'

'What's that?'

'Just worrying too much,' I say, wanting to make it seem as meaningless as possible.

'What've you got to worry about?'

'I'm not meaning to do it. It's all right. You stay there.'

'You sure?'

'Totally.'

I hear Olivia's voice in the background. 'Hey, Steph, bus is going.'

'I've gotta go,' Steph says.

I want to tell her about the flowers and Todd's note, and even ask her what's going on, but it's impossible with Mum and Dad in the lounge, so I make a mental note to do it first chance I get. At least hearing Olivia proves she's there.

'Okay,' I say. 'Have fun.' After I've hung up, I glower at Mum and Dad. 'Why did you tell her? I told you not to tell her!'

'She's your sister!' Mum says. 'She needs to know, instead of running around with that silly boy.'

My head throbs, so I take the other sedative – my second for the day, and this time, within fifteen minutes, that peacefulness comes over me.

As spring takes hold, the days grow sunny and the trees

bloom. Winter jackets are filed away and it's no longer a misery to get out of bed to face the cold. I'm sure now that everything's going to be okay. I take the sedatives as needed. That morning sedative is my anchor. That fixes where I should be. Sometimes, it's also one after school. Never has it been three in a day, something I'm proud of.

The schoolwork grows and there's excitement around speculating which piece is going to be considered for the Boland and who the likeliest winners are – Deanne leads, then Ethan, then me, Samantha, and then a group of people that includes Gabriella, Ash and several others.

I work for about another month with Mum and Dad. It's another small victory that I can push myself through it. The contract doesn't get renewed, and I wonder how hard Mum and Dad tried and if they were worried about my ability to keep handling it.

School becomes almost new to me, although little things still nag at me. One lunchtime, Ash and me are out back watching girls play basketball when I spot a couple walking hand in hand across the footy oval. They must've gone behind the Meadow Soccer Club changerooms to make out. It doesn't take me long to identify the girl as Gabriella and the guy as Jake Fichera.

At least she traded up, if anything, but something darkens inside me – not for Gabriella or Jake but for myself – because that could've been me. It *should've* been me. That could be *us*.

They walk around the basketball courts and past us. Gabriella glances at me, but there's nothing there – not the soft gaze that marks affection which I always see with Samantha.

I could be anybody.

Or nobody.

As she disappears from sight, that's exactly who I feel I am.

33.

When the bell goes, we wander over to our Social Studies class with Mr McCready. He loves to pose hypothetical situations to explore, like what would've happened if the South had won the Civil War in the US, or the Germans had won World War I, or Gough Whitlam had never been sacked.

'Essay time!' he says. 'If Germany had won World War II, and what they did in their concentration camps led to cures to conditions such as cancer, AIDS, multiple sclerosis, etc., would that justify what they did? One thousand words!'

As he drones on, I stare out the window at the courtyard when a simple thought pops into my head: *What if the courtyard isn't real?* That courtyard might be a product of my imagination. I know it's real but can't get out of my head the possibility that it's not. And if it's not, what else isn't? Maybe the classroom isn't real. Or Mr McCready. Or the other kids. I might be in some hospital now, strapped to a bed, imagining all this. Maybe I never got up from the paddock the morning after that party. Somebody found me and called an ambulance.

Panic wells up inside me and my hands tighten around my folder. Light shines through the windows and skews off one of the tables, blinding me. I throw my hand up.

'Yes?' Mr McCready says.

'Can I …?' I make a vague gesture.

He nods and I scoot off out of the class and force myself to take my time across the courtyard, since people can see me through the window.

In the toilets, I splash water on my face, then plant my hands against the wall. The bricks are cold on my palms. Obviously real. But if I were imagining this, I'd imagine every sensation. I slap the wall, like a high-five, and feel it sting against my palm, hear the *clap* echo in the toilets. *Real.* Of course it's real.

I pluck the sedative out of my pocket, swallow it, then drink from the tap. I give it a few minutes, although I know it won't work that quick, and check myself in the mirror – I'm wild about the eyes and the fringe of my hair's wet. I run my hands through my hair until it looks normal, take a deep breath and return to class. About ten minutes later, that Ducene calm sweeps over me.

On the walk home, I work out how this has gone in phases. Get over one thing, there's a bit of peace, then something else pops up. What's next, though? Where does this lead? Is it a gradual chipping away until nothing's left?

Getting ready for school the next morning, I feel a lot of the old staples: the shortness of breath, the chest tightening, and a wooziness in my head like I might faint. The Ducene have an effect, and I consider taking a second sedative – I try to convince myself that Dr Searcy said I could take three, although I know he didn't mean at once.

It would be better if I didn't go to school, although the thought of staying home, and telling Mum and Dad I stayed home, fills me with guilt. I don't want Mum thinking that this is so bad I can't cope. So down the stairs I go, down the street, to meet Ash, a cigarette dangling from his mouth.

'What's up?' he asks.

'Nothing. Smoking already?'

'Parents had this big fight this morning. Got ugly.'

'Ugly how?'

'*Ugly.*'

'Over what?'

Ash shrugs one shoulder. 'Their usual shit. Makes me worry they'll turn out like Riley's parents.'

I think of seeing Ash's dad at the shops with Ethan's mum. He wouldn't be that blatant, though, would he? And he waved to me, anyway – not exactly the behaviour of somebody trying to hide something.

'You gonna be okay?' I say.

'Can I tell you something?'

'Sure.'

'I saw Dad slap Mum once.'

'Really?'

'When I was seven or eight. It was late. I got out of bed to get a drink. They were fighting – she was telling him he didn't help out enough, he was saying he was busy working overtime because she wasn't working. They called each other stuff. He was lazy. She was a bitch. It went on and on. And then he slapped her. Everything went quiet. Then he hugged her and kept apologising. I went back to bed, scared, not knowing what to think. Next morning, it was like everything was back to normal.'

'You think he's done it other times?' I ask.

'I don't know. When they argue, my head always goes back to that night. And I wonder. I *do* wonder.'

'My parents argue all the time,' I say.

'Why?'

'It's the way they talk.'

'You think he's ever hit her?'

I shake my head. 'The shouting's their normal.'

'I think Mum and Dad might divorce,' Ash says. 'Eventually. Every argument is worse than the one before it.'

A tremor enters his voice and he draws on his cigarette. He blows out smoke too hard. He was going to tell me something else, but it's gone now – he's decided he's going to deal with this himself, just like he always does.

'It is what it is.' His voice is firm. 'We all have our own shit to deal with. You know?'

I know I'm not going to get anything more out of him, so I nod.

'Yeah,' I say. 'I know.'

34.

When I run out of the sedatives, I take the empty box and make an appointment with Dr Stathakis. I give him a brief overview of what's happening. He sits back in his recliner and holds the empty box in his hand. My account splutters. He radiates disapproval. He drops the box on his desk and takes out his prescription pad but then stops. He taps the empty sedatives box with the top of his pen.

'I want you to be careful with these,' he says.

'Why?'

'You can grow reliant on them.' Dr Stathakis writes out the prescription, tears it from his pad and slides it across his desk.

Steph comes home the day before my appointment with the psychiatrist, tanned and happy and laden with gifts – Mum and Dad telling her she shouldn't have wasted her money, but me appreciative she's gotten me stuff, like an American Football jersey (the Los Angeles Raiders) and soccer jerseys from England (Manchester United) and Italy (Barcelona).

I want to talk to her but she's tired – she says she didn't sleep at all on the second leg of the flight – and goes to bed. But after school the following day, she offers to drive me to my appointment, which is fine by everyone. Mum and Dad won't understand a thing the psychiatrist has to say – not if it's to be meaningful, so the responsibility falls on Steph. Before long, we're contending with peak hour traffic as we head over to the Western.

'So, what's happening with this?' she asks.

'It just came on.'

'Just like that?'

'Pretty much.'

I tell her bits and pieces about being worried, the chest pains and the shortness of breath but I leave lots out – sleeping in the paddock, feeling like things aren't real and hiding in the school toilets. I know my research says this doesn't lead to insanity but all those things sound insane. I could handle it if Steph kept nodding, but if she got a look on her face like she's shocked at what she's hearing, that would just about prove to me that I *am* crazy.

'Let's see what this doctor has to say,' she says once I'm done.

At Western, the receptionist refers me to Outpatients' Clinic C. Several twists and turns later, I come to another reception and three open doorways leading to Clinics' A, B, and C. The receptionist gives me a small yellow booklet to keep track of my appointments and tells me to go through. Then I find myself in a small room with rows of chairs and a couple of doors. That's it. There are three other people waiting. Steph and I sit down.

'There's something else I've gotta tell you,' I say.

Steph arches her brows. They're not as thick as they used to be.

'You got some flowers while you were away.'

Steph's face is unreadable.

'Mum and Dad didn't see them. I found them when I came home from school. There was a card, too. I have it somewhere. But Todd asked if you could give it another chance.'

'I didn't think Mum and Dad would fuss as much if they thought I was going with a group.'

'That's what I thought.'

'I didn't tell Mum and Dad we weren't going out anymore because then they'd start up all the boyfriend shit again.'

'Did Mario go?'

'No. Olivia wanted to take a break. They've been fighting a lot.'

One of the doors opens. A patient shuffles out. Then a doctor emerges, a small, bespectacled man in a navy suit. He calls out a name; one of the other patients follows him through the door. Not long afterward, the other door opens. Again, the same pattern: a patient emerges, leaves the clinic, and then the doctor comes out, this guy tall, wearing a cardigan, with curly hair bunched at his ears. He reels off a name. Another patient follows him in.

'Want me to come with you when they call you?' Steph asks.

I think about the things I haven't told Steph and how I can't have any freedom with the doctor if she's there with us. She must see my uncertainty.

'You probably want privacy,' she says. 'I'll wait here.'

We're quiet, this problem of mine creating a divide between us – she wants to help but she can only do so much. I stare at the way the floor's scuffed. Who knows how many patients have trodden over it? How many of them got better?

'How's this affected you at school?'

I tell her how sometimes I duck out to the toilets or take an extra sedative.

'You don't want to tell Ash or Riley?' she asks.

'They'd think I was weak.'

'I remember what school was like – the groups, the way kids made fun of others.' Steph smirks. 'Olivia permed her hair and the boys teased her for weeks and called her "Mop-head".'

'What did she do?'

'She cried that first week. When it grew long enough, she cut it short. Then they teased her about that. A couple of weeks later, they moved onto somebody else. I understand what kids can be like but friends can surprise you – well, I think Ash could.'

It's not surprising her thoughts align with mine. I don't want to tell her that I think Ash might be having trouble at home and doesn't need my problems.

'What about your schoolwork?' Steph says. 'And the Boland?'

'I'm pushing myself through it. It's hard to pick what essay's being used for the Boland. But I think I'm still doing okay.'

'I guess you haven't had time to write much,' Steph says.

'I've written lots of my big one.'

'That's great. I have your last exercise book. I read it on the plane.'

'Really?'

'I didn't realise I'd packed it with some other books.'

'That's okay. I didn't even notice it was gone.'

'It's great. I can't wait to see what you're doing with this big one.'

'The school counsellor thinks I should do some more studying if I want to write.'

'That's up to you.'

'She says not many people make it as writers.'

'So? You want to spend your life worrying about what's not going to happen? That's Mum and Dad.' Steph sits back and extends her legs. 'Being away from them for eight weeks, I really saw the effect they have on us.'

'What effect?'

'How they expect us to live our lives to their expectations. Mum and Dad are great people – they help us out and they'd do anything they could to make sure we have great lives, but they expect us to be like Jim. That's fulfilment for them. Not for us.'

'You've thought about this a lot?'

'And talked to Olivia. She gets it, too, from her family – not as bad. Anyway, it's something to think about.'

We don't say much more. The bespectacled doctor comes out and calls another patient. Others come into the waiting room. When the other door opens and the curly-haired doctor emerges, I'm already getting up as he calls my name.

35.

The doctor's office is windowless and tiny. He has a cluttered desk pushed up against the wall, his own chair – a plush, leather monstrosity that cradles him like a giant hand – and a plastic chair that he gestures me to.

This can't be the right room. The doctor should have a big, fancy office. There should be bookshelves filled with psychology textbooks. I should be lying on a couch.

But this is it.

The doctor introduces himself as Dr Dimmock. He opens a manila folder that contains my information and gets me to confirm all my basic details. Then he pulls a lined yellow notepad out from under the manila folder and pushes his pen – this fancy ballpoint that looks expensive – to it.

'In your file, it says you've been experiencing some generalised anxiety disorder,' he says. 'Tell me how that felt.'

So I go through it. Again. Answering the same questions that Dr Searcy and Dr Kuruvilla asked. Doctors must have these questions in a checklist or something. Dr Dimmock nods throughout and takes notes and when he's adventurous, he lets out a 'Hmmm', as I tell him about waking up panicked, the chest pains, the headaches, the ongoing agitation, school, life at home, that I write – it spills out. I wait for some question that nobody's asked me – he's the expert, after all. I wait for *the* question that's going to unravel the mess this has become. I wait even for the old movie cliché of getting me to tell him about my childhood. But the closest he gets to anything like that is when he asks if mental illness runs in the family.

'Mum's always stressed,' I say. 'And she takes pills. I've never known what for exactly.'

Dr Dimmock nods.

'I'm worried sometimes I'm going crazy,' I say.

What I want him to do here is laugh and say, *No, don't worry, you're not going crazy!* But he nods again and takes another note. I try to read it but his writing is all scribbles. It might be shorthand.

'I think we have you on the right medication,' he says. 'Do you need a prescription?'

'I got one from my GP.'

'How about we make an appointment in two weeks and we'll see how you're doing?'

'That's it?'

'For now.'

As I leave his office and lead Steph back to reception, I hold onto that *for now*. Of course, what can he do in a single appointment? He needs all the background information. He needs to learn about *me*. Then he'll go from there. And that he *wasn't* concerned should be the biggest reassurance. If he saw anything worth worrying about, he would've done more.

Wouldn't he?

'How'd that go?' Steph says on the drive home.

I shrug.

'You don't have to tell me specifics. I just want to know we're going the right way with this.'

'I guess.'

The lights ahead change to red. Steph stops the car and puts an awkward hand on my shoulder. 'It's going to be okay,' she says. She's trying. There's that much. But she doesn't know how to handle this any better than I do.

We're caught in peak traffic, so we don't get home until after six. Mum's made spaghetti bolognaise, mine and Steph's bowls heaped like bolognaise-topped mountains.

'How did things go?' Mum asks.

Only, she doesn't ask me. She asks Steph.

'I don't know,' Steph says.

'Didn't you talk to the doctor?' Mum says.

'He went in to see the doctor himself.'

'How can you let him go in by himself?' Dad says. 'He's just a child.'

'I'm not–' I say.

'He needs to speak privately with the doctor,' Steph says.

'You should've gone in with him,' Mum says.

'You don't get how this works, do you?' Steph says.

From here, it erupts into typical shouting. Poor Steph. Back one day and already into it. Usually, she'd storm out, but now she weathers it until a tense silence falls over the kitchen, the only sound the *clink* of cutlery against bowls and spaghetti being slurped.

Once we're finished, Steph helps Mum clear up and I escape to my bedroom to work on Mr Tan's essay. I think of the computers as the big things they used to be – like how in films about NASA, computers are shown as boxes the size of wardrobes that line the walls. But now they're getting smaller and people have them in their homes. I write that they'll keep getting smaller and smaller, and they'll become part of every bit of technology we use, until kids in the future won't know what it was like to have been without them.

I think my ideas are good but my writing is scattered. I don't like that I'm the cause of such disruption at home. It would be easier if I were gone. I see the house empty, quiet, Mum, Dad and Steph all in black, moping about. They'd understand then how difficult this is. But then I realise what I'm thinking, and the panic accelerates, with my heart thumping and breath shortening. I fish a sedative out of my drawer and take a drink from the bathroom tap so nobody can see that I've taken a pill.

I lie on my bed until there's not even a whisper of a thought in my head. A knock at my door rouses me. I tell whoever it is to come in, expecting it to be Mum, but it's Steph.

'Game of pool?' she says.

If I'm playing pool by myself, Steph might ask me to have a game to kill some time but she's never, ever grabbed me from somewhere else and asked me to play a game. I can only think that she's that worried about me or wants to talk away from Mum and Dad.

It's only a couple of minutes later that I break and watch the balls splatter across the table. Steph stands in the corner, cue planted between her feet. I blow the fringe of my hair from my eyes as I take my next shot.

'Getting long again,' Steph says.

'My hairdresser's been overseas.'

'We'll get something organised. This weekend?'

'Sure.'

I pocket three balls in a row but miss the fourth, a long shot that I try to rebound into the top corner. Steph examines the table, then lines up a first shot.

'I told you I was thinking of moving,' she says.

I now know why we're down here in the garage.

'I'm looking for a place. And a job. I can't cope here anymore.'

'I understand.'

'I hate that I'm looking now when you're…struggling with this. I was going to try put it off, but dinner convinced me…'

I nod, confused but understanding.

'I'll take you to your appointments – whatever you need,' Steph says. 'Anyway, it's not like it's gonna be straight away. But I wanted to tell you because I don't want to disappear on you without a warning.' She puts her cue on the table and comes over to hug me. 'I'm sorry–'

'It's okay,' I say. 'I'll be okay. I'm sure of it.'

'Yeah?' Steph pulls back and looks me in the eye.

'Yeah.'

And in this moment, I believe that.

36.

As Olivia cuts my hair, classical music plays in the background – she identifies it as Beethoven's 'Moonlight Sonata.'

'How w–was o-overseas?' I ask.

'It's gorgeous.' Olivia's scissors snip away. 'There's a whole world out there of places you couldn't imagine. You ever thought about travelling?'

'No.'

'You should. Steph regrets it took her so long.'

Panic tethers me to home. I can barely survive school. The possibility of going somewhere I can't get back home from in fifteen minutes terrifies me.

'If I could, I'd live somewhere like France,' Olivia says. 'You okay?'

She's looking at my reflection in the mirror, eyes dark, searching. I think I look okay, although my forehead glistens with sweat – of course, that might be spray from her water bottle. I wonder if Steph's told her anything. I feel like Olivia's seeing inside me.

'Sure,' I say. 'Why?'

Olivia resumes cutting. 'You feel very tense.'

'School,' I say, like Year 10 could weigh me down like that.

'How's that going?'

I shrug.

'Don't move.'

'Sorry.'

'Steph said you're going for the Boland Fellowship.'

'Yeah, I guess.'

'You should've seen Steph.' Olivia laughs. 'She was always smart, so she was always a chance. But she went next level.' She steps around to my side. 'How's your writing going? Steph told me about it. She was reading one of your books on the plane. She says you have a lot of potential. She's very proud.'

I weigh up what should mean more to me – that Steph told her, or that Steph's proud.

'I wanted to be creative,' Olivia says. 'I used to write song lyrics. I wanted to sing. Unfortunately, I didn't do either very well.'

A rap at the door: Mario. It gets so much darker when he comes in. Either his head blocks all the light from coming in from the doorway, or he sucks the light out of the room.

'Hey,' he says to Olivia, ignoring my existence.

'What're you doing here?' Olivia says as she swings around front to work on my fringe.

'Thought I'd visit.' Then, challengingly: 'That okay?'

'Sure.'

Mario leans against the door jamb and folds his arms across his chest. I see him in the mirror, the big poser, trying to look cool, like it's the most natural thing in the world to lean against a door jamb with his arms folded. His eyes fix on Olivia's butt in the mirror. He doesn't flinch. Doesn't move. A tiny sneer curls his mouth. The anger that rises in me is brittle. He's not doing anything that I haven't, but it's so cheap and dirty with him.

'What's this crap you listen to?' he says.

'I like it.'

'I don't get it.'

'You don't get a lot of things.'

Mario snorts, perhaps feeling hard done by. Then he lets out a big breath, the martyr.

Olivia finishes the haircut, then shaves the back of my neck before running product through my hair and teasing it delicately, her fingers playful. She makes a big show of it, slower than she's ever done before. I shift restlessly.

'All done,' she says.

'Thanks.'

She undoes the cape and pulls it from me. I get up, facing away from the mirror, her, and Mario, as I fish around in my pocket. I hand my money to Olivia – half what she'd charge in the salon, as always.

'Is that all?' Mario says.

'That's all,' Olivia says, putting the money on the counter like she wants it to be an affront to Mario. She grabs her broom.

'Thanks,' I say.

'You're welcome,' Olivia says with a smile as she sweeps up. 'Can you ask your sister if she wants to catch a movie later?'

'So, you're going out with *her* again?' Mario says.

'Hey!'

Olivia tries to be discreet when her eyes flit to me, as if to say this isn't a conversation to be had in front of me, but I see it, and it makes me not want to leave, although my heart's thumping this crazy *boom-boom-boom* like it wants to beat its way out of my chest.

Mario scowls at me. 'Something else you want, kid?' He draws himself up. He really is a flabby block of lard. It repulses me imagining him all over Olivia, kissing her, being between her legs – but I see it, unbidden in my head, see Mario oozing sweat and melting over Olivia like he was made from wax.

'I should get going,' I say. 'See you, Olivia.'

'Bye. Remember to tell your sister.'

'Sure.'

I leave the room. The moment the door's clattered shut, Olivia's voice rises, angry but controlled. 'How dare you talk to him that way!'

'He's just a kid,' Mario says. 'He'll get over it.'

I move extremely slowly.

'He's a client–'

'A client? With what he paid you?'

'–and a guest–'

'*Some* guest.'

'–and a friend, you prick.'

'A kid's a friend?' Mario scoffs.

'You are *so* narrow-minded.'

'I don't have to listen to this!'

'Then go!'

I hurry off and have just scampered my way around the garage when I hear the door whine open and clang shut. Mario's car is parked in the drive, that big violet Ford. I wish I had a key that I could run down the length of the car. I hear Mario's feet lumbering behind me, so I keep walking.

When I get home, I tell Steph about Olivia's invitation for a movie, then shower, although my hands shake, and my heart keeps thumping. I try to distract myself in usual ways – fantasize about Olivia, try to masturbate and then think about something to write – but nothing works.

It's a long time before it settles down.

37

As it warms up and t-shirts and blouses reappear, the days grow longer. Trees sprout leaves, flowers bloom and things *change*. That's how simple it is, really. Not a lot's unchanging – well, death, maybe. That's a thought that creeps in.

Steph's always up early, looking for jobs. Evenings, she's often out – Mum and Dad think with Todd but I don't know where. She might have another boyfriend she's not telling anybody about. That would be the smart thing with Mum and Dad – don't let them know until the engagement.

School becomes this mishmash of shifting dynamics. There's the world inside my head and the world outside it. Samantha ditches Lachlan, those soft eyes are always studying me in a way that makes me think I could be a god if I didn't have so much trouble being a human. It's not two days after she ditches Lachlan that she tracks me down in the courtyard at recess.

'I'm having a birthday,' she says. 'A sixteenth.' She thrusts an invitation at me. 'Will you come?'

In the instant before I open my mouth, my head's overwhelmed with possible catastrophes: the crowd will make me uncomfortable; the last party I was at, I panicked. Can I drink on sedatives? What if I can't breathe? What if another headache hits? What if I freak out in front of everybody? I'll be trapped, unable to escape. And on it goes.

'I'm inviting everybody,' she says, maybe to assure me it's not just going to be me and her, or just me and her and her friends.

'Sure,' I say.

Samantha smiles and takes off, a firework I've lit up.

Riley and Felicia often take long walks to the back of the school. I can't figure Riley out, if this is some ploy to woo Felicia, or if he's fallen for her that much and, having lost her once, is afraid he'll lose her again. It'd be good to talk to him, too, because his birthday's coming up.

Gabriella splits up with Jake and I see her chatting at times with Scott Marshall, a barrel-chested guy with blond hair tied into a ponytail. I would love to tell you that when each of these things happen, they're momentous, but they're not. This is high school.

And still emerging is Deanne. Gone are the shapeless clothes and unassuming haircut. Now she wears clingy blouses, tight jeans or dresses, and so much crap in her hair a hole in the ozone forms above wherever she walks. She gets a lot of attention.

'See what I did?' Ash says one lunchtime, while we're smoking in the toilets. 'It's like I have a magic touch. But in my cock.'

I shake my head. 'I can't believe you said that.'

'This is a power I need to share. It's a calling. You understand that, don't you?'

The constant in my life becomes the appointments with Dr Dimmock every two weeks. He sits there and listens to me report what the fortnight's been like – usually, it's me listing the symptoms. He'll nod and scribble on his notepad. Sometimes, he'll ask a question and I think we're going to get to the bottom of what's going on.

'What appeals to you about writing?' he says, towards the end of that second appointment.

'I like that I get to make things up,' I say, 'that there's this story I want to tell and I can go anywhere with it.'

Nods. Scribbles. Then he'll ask me if I need a prescription. Even Counsellor Hoffs asked me more about my aspirations than that and Dr Dimmock's meant to be helping me deal with what's going on inside my head, isn't he?

'It gets to me the way my parents shout so much,' I say in another appointment. Then I add, like it's meant to give more weight to my claim, 'It gets to my sister, too.'

'Why does it get to you?' he asks.

'Because they're always looking at the negative of a situation.'

'Why do you think that is?'

'It's the way they are.'

Nods. Scribbles. Prescription?

'Do people get better from this?' I ask, another time.

Dr Dimmock purses his lips, like that's meant to make him look thoughtful, and not like a fish sizing up some bait. 'It is about management.'

'What does that mean?'

'In learning to manage this, you improve your situation.'

Nods. Scribbles. Prescription?

Each time I leave his little office, I can only think that if this is how it's going, it can't be too bad. Steph sits patiently in the waiting room and doesn't press me with questions until we've gotten in the car and are driving home.

'Is he helping?'

'I don't know.'

'You should know. You've been seeing him a while.'

'I guess.'

'You guess?'

'I don't know.'

'This the way you talk to him?'

'Not really.'

'I want to know that he's taking care of you. I want to know that he's helping.'

I sit back and stare at the undeveloped paddocks out here before we get back on the bypass. The truth is, Dr Dimmock is helping by existing because I know there's always an appointment close by where I can check in, talk about which symptoms have been worse in that fortnight, but show I'm otherwise stable.

'Well?' Steph says.

'Sure,' I say.

38.

Shouting wakes me on Sunday morning. I'm sure if the house could, it'd uproot itself, tilt on its side and shake Mum, Dad and Steph out, before marching off.

Stumbling out of the bed, I slip into the kitchen, and start to make breakfast – well, I *pretend* to. Really, I just want to work out what all the fuss is about.

'You're being crazy!' Dad says. 'You don't even have a job!'

'I'm looking!' Steph says.

'How long does it take to find a job?' Mum says.

'You've been looking how long?' Dad says. 'Ever since you wasted all your money overseas!'

'I'll find one,' Steph says. 'I just want to find the right job.'

'The right job!' Dad says. 'The *right* job. You, who dropped out of university!'

'You're being stupid,' Mum says. 'Look at your cousin Malinda–'

'I don't care about Malinda!' Steph says.

'You're such an embarrassment,' Mum says.

'You don't have to worry about that anymore.'

'Of course we have to worry about that!' Mum says. 'You think because you're moving out, people aren't going to talk? You think it'll stop? You, without a job. Who dropped out of university. With that stupid boyfriend of yours you're too embarrassed to bring around.'

Things click then.

'You're moving out?' I say.

'Me and Olivia got a place,' Steph says. 'We're going next week.'

'Next week...? You and Olivia?'

'Olivia! Olivia!' Dad says. 'That stupid girl! She has ants in her bum. She can't settle down.'

'At least she has a job,' Mum says.

'How are you going to pay rent without a job?' Dad says. 'How're you going to pay your bills without a job? How're you going to live without a job?'

'And it's Jim's wedding in a month! What about that?'

'How does me moving out affect Jim's wedding?' Steph asks.

'What are people going to think?' Mum says.

The phone rings – I answer it and, as the shouting continues, hear it's Riley. I excuse myself, hang up and take the call on the hallway phone.

Riley chuckles. 'What's going on? Sounds like the end of the world.'

'My sister told us she's moving out,' I say. 'Mum and Dad aren't happy because she's not working.'

'It's her problem.'

'Doesn't work like that around here. What's up?'

'My birthday tomorrow but I'm celebrating today. Toppy's? Will meet you and Ash there at three. Got something to tell you.'

'What?'

'I'll tell you then.'

'You told Ash?'

'About meeting? Yep. See you at three.'

Once he's hung up, I ring Ash. His brothers scream in the background, playing something or other, but it's a fun screaming – not like what's going on around here. Ash tells them to shut up, then goes into another room.

'What's up?' he says.

'You get Riley anything for his birthday?' I say.

'No.'

'We should get him something.'

'Like?'

'We'll meet up earlier. There are a few shops around Toppy's. We should get Samantha something, too. Her sixteenth is soon.'

'These birthdays, they're like extortion. You get a gift for being born.'

'You'll be turning sixteen.'

'And this is the reason to have a birthday. The gifts.'

'I'll meet you at the corner at one, okay?'

'Sure. What's with all the shouting at your house?'

'I'll tell you later. See you at one.'

At some point, Steph gives up and flees. The back door slams open (Dad shouts that she should be careful she doesn't break it). She runs down the steps and her car revs as it burns out of the street.

I go back into the kitchen but when they start up again – arguing now with one another, Mum telling Dad he mishandled it, Dad insisting Steph's irresponsible so there was no other way to handle it – I make breakfast for real now and have it in the garage over a game of pool. Then it's a case of showering and doing a bit of homework to kill time. It's when Mum calls me in to eat that it occurs to me I haven't taken my morning sedative. I almost pop out of my seat to fetch it out of my drawer, but then plant myself back down. I've gone the whole morning and felt okay. Let's see how long I can go.

I wolf through the roast, then tell Mum and Dad I'm going out. They say nothing as they clean up around the kitchen, chairs screeching across the floor, plates clunking into the sink, water splashing from the tap – everything turned up to signal their displeasure.

While I get changed in my bedroom, my gaze fixes on the drawer where I keep the sedatives. I should do this alone given I've done so well already. But my heart flutters – it's not about going out, but about being underprepared. I tear a tab free and thrust it in my pocket.

Ash is waiting on the corner, smoking already. We shouldn't smoke as much as we do, but at this age we're invulnerable – well, we're meant to be. Cigarettes are cheap, too. *And* cool. These are all the things we tell ourselves because when you're a teenager, life is meant to be forever.

He offers me one from his packet; I take it and light up. As we walk, he asks about the shouting in my house. I tell him what happened. He chuckles ruefully.

'Fucking marriage,' he says. 'I'm never getting married. It's evil.'

'I'm sure it's not all bad.'

'I bet more are than aren't.'

'You don't know.'

'I know it shouldn't be like that.'

'I've told you that's the way they talk.'

219

'When they want to shout, what do they do?'

'They talk quiet, like in a whisper.'

'What the fuck?'

I shrug.

'Riley's dad runs off, your parents are like that, now Mum's gone for a bit.'

'What's that mean?'

'Said she needs a break. That she's rundown. Went to some naturopathic sanatorium in the country for two weeks.'

'She'll be back, though – right?'

'Don't know.' Ash runs his wrist across his nose and avoids looking at me.

'You all right?' I say.

Ash grins at me but I can see now that his eyes are rimmed red.

'Fine,' he says.

We walk on in silence.

39.

The first thing we do once we get onto High Street is use the ATMs to withdraw money. Then we walk down the strip of shops opposite Toppy's. There are cafes, the post office, a big supermarket and a music store. Down the end, there's a jeweller right next to one of those variety shops that has a bit of everything. We go into the variety shop and after a lot of to-ing and fro-ing, pick out a gold Zippo lighter for Riley – the only thing we know he'll use for sure – and, almost as a bit of a gag gift, a matching cigarette case. We try to find something for Samantha, too, but there's nothing suitable, so we go into the jeweller's and settle on a pretty bracelet that costs us twenty-five dollars.

Our next stop is the supermarket, where we buy some tissue paper and tape. Outside, we perform a crude job of wrapping Riley's gift in the one package. Ash folds the remaining tissue paper and thrusts it towards me.

'You'll need this next,' he says.

'Oh. For Samantha.'

'No. Me. We should get something to drink.'

An alarm sounds in my head. If I drink, can I take the sedative? Probably not. As a rule, you shouldn't mix medication with alcohol. Both the Ducene and the alcohol work on my head so there must be a good chance of them clashing.

Still, I relent, even though I feel dread, because I want to be normal and I've been feeling good today, so I should be able to behave my age. The last few months have been nothing but *this*. Time to be like I was before all this began.

There's a liquor shop down the opposite end of the hub that we've had success at in the past. I go in, walk straight up to the counter (if you look like you're loitering, trying to summon up the courage, they know you're underage) and ask for three flasks of scotch. The clerk is a plump old guy, maybe in his late fifties, with bushy sideburns. He looks me over for a second longer than makes me comfortable – all he needs to do is ask for identification. That's it. And it's over. I'll have to say that I left it at home or something. Then Ash will have to try later at some point, once enough time's passed that the clerk won't connect it to this attempt. But he grabs the flasks. I pay him with a fifty. You always look like a kid when you pay with small bills and change. Fortunately, I have savings from my allowance and the part-time job.

Triumphant, I walk from the liquor shop and we go back to the supermarket to buy three 600ml bottles of Coke and use the bottom-floor toilets in Toppy's to mix them.

Riley's already on the top floor, helping Felicia to play pool by standing behind her, one hand on her bridge (the hand that goes under where you slide the cue), the other hand steadying her grip on the bottom of the cue, his crotch grinding into her butt. I don't blame him. She looks good in her little skirt and a loose blouse that she might fall out of at any moment.

Ash and me pull up before we're seen and Ash even takes a step backwards. He probably doesn't mean it to be heard, but he whispers under his breath, 'Holy fuck.' But then he ploughs on.

'Happy birthday!' he says and shakes Riley's hand once Riley detaches himself from Felicia. 'Felicia.'

'Happy birthday,' I say and shake Riley's hand also. 'Hey.' I nod at Felicia.

Felicia forces a smile. It's a surprise her face doesn't crack in two.

Ash gives Riley our gift. Riley lays it on the pool table, rips away our clumsy wrapping and grins. He picks up the cigarette case first. That's the main gift for him. He fills it with his cigarettes and offers them around. Then he takes the Zippo, flips it open extravagantly and lights everybody's cigarettes.

'There's this, too,' I say, giving him one of the bottles of Coke.

Riley takes an experimental taste, then gulps it down. 'Nice,' he says, passing the Coke to Felicia.

Ash holds up his Coke bottle. 'We got a flask each.'

'Should've got a bottle.' Riley scrunches up the wrapping paper and dunks it in a nearby bin. 'Let's have a game – you two against Felicia and me.'

It's awkward with Felicia there. She's hopeless, so it's not a contest. Riley spends a lot of time coaching her and in-between that, there's lots of kissing – nothing too passionate, just pecks on the lips and stuff, but it makes me feel like I've walked into something private and I can hear Ash grinding his teeth. Felicia being here curtails how open we can be.

Ash and me drink quicker than we might usually because it *is* so uncomfortable. Felicia makes no effort to talk to us and at one point, Ash and Riley go to the toilet, leaving me to set up the table as she sits on a nearby stool, staring out the window at the hub of shops, probably longing to be there instead, or maybe she wants to make sure we don't make eye contact because that would mean she has to acknowledge me or talk to me or something.

When Riley and Ash come back from the toilet, Riley lights up a cigarette with his Zippo, leans over to break, then straightens up again and points at Felicia with his cue.

'You come and break,' he says.

The cue's unsteady in her hand and you can hear the mishit. The white ball skews off her cue and hits the ball on the furthest corner of the triangle. A handful of balls trickle loose.

'That's not a break,' Ash says. 'That's a fracture.'

'I tried my best,' Felicia says.

'Of course you did,' Riley says. He glares at Ash, then throws an arm around Felicia's waist and kisses her on the cheek.

I splatter the balls to get them all in the open, knowing no matter how set up they become, there's no way Riley and Felicia are going to beat us. But the five goes in. From there, I go on a run, knocking ball after ball in.

'Oh yeah,' Riley says, sitting on a stool. 'I wanted to talk to you two.'

'Shoot,' Ash says.

'I'm joining the Navy.'

Ash and me exchange a look. I knock the three in.

'Right,' Ash says.

'It's done,' Riley says. 'I'm out of here next year. Already filled out the forms and everything.'

I hit the seven in.

'Bullshit,' Ash says.

Riley keeps straight-faced. Felicia bounces up and down, then hugs him.

'You even old enough?' I say.

'I need to be sixteen and a half – I'm not yet, but I will be just after school starts next year, so no point going back.'

'What the fuck?' Ash says.

'What am I gonna do?' Riley says. 'Stay at school doing that bullshit we're doing? I can get a career out of this. I can mean something.'

'In the Navy?' Ash says.

'Yep.'

I finish up the game, hitting the black in. Riley puts away his cue and sits by Felicia; they hug and kiss and coo at one another. It's like the whole get-together was nothing more than a means to tell us this and now we're forgotten. Ash and me put away our cues and sit down as well. But we're there only a minute or two before Ash gets up.

'We should get going, huh?' Ash says.

Riley doesn't look up – not straight away. Felicia nudges him.

'Riley?' Ash says.

'Sure,' Riley says. 'Thanks for coming. Thanks for the gifts. I'll see you at school, huh?'

'Yeah,' Ash says. 'Sure.'

40.

We stop by the supermarket to buy another bottle of Coke to make our last mix of scotch from what's left in our flasks. Neither of us say anything on the walk home – at least not until we cross the school and get to the bank by the bridge. Then we sit down to finish our drinks and light up a smoke.

'I don't give a fuck about the Navy,' Ash says. 'If that's what he wants to do, that's what he wants to do. But it's the way he's with Felicia that shits me.'

'The lovey-dovey stuff?' I say.

'Not just that. Remember when they broke up, he called her a fake? That's him now.'

Once we're done with our drinks, we throw the empty bottles into the creek and watch them sail away. Then we amble home, separating at the corner. Things are different now. Something's ended.

I puzzle over that as I escape to my bedroom. Then it hits me. It would be easy to blame Riley's relationship with Felicia as the reason he's pulled away, but it's not that. Riley's always coasted in school. Now, he's barely trying. The Navy's an out for him. Ash and me are pushing ourselves. The way things have worked out, we were always going to drift apart from Riley this year.

At dinner, Dad carves his way through the leftover roast. The kitchen light flashes off the knife that he uses in a way that shakes me. I feel the sharpness of the blade, can imagine seizing it and plunging it into flesh, carving through it like a watermelon. I know I won't. But that echoes through my head.

We hear Steph come home – the gate open, the motion-activated light outside her bungalow switch on briefly, and then the door to the bungalow open and slam. Mum, Dad and me freeze in the middle of what we're doing – me with a juice half-lifted to my mouth, Dad's knife paused in the middle of cutting roast beef, Mum holding a plate under the tap. I almost expect the water to stop flowing. But the bungalow door doesn't reopen. Steph's not going to join us. The point of Dad's knife screeches against the plate. Life resumes with the squeaking of Mum's sponge.

I hurry through eating as much as I can. The food's tasteless and every mouthful is a chore. The quiet's too much because it leaves my mind open to indulge itself. This is what it'll be like post-Steph. It'll be just the four of us: Mum, Dad, me and the silence.

Shoving my plate aside, I go to my bedroom to continue my homework but coming off the scotch, I fall into an uneasy nap. I don't wake until I hear Mum and Dad going to bed and then I go back into the lounge room to watch TV.

Now I'm alone.

A detachment falls over me. I know it's because I've been drinking all afternoon, but I can't convince myself of that and the anxiousness rises – not horrible but persistent.

I get up to grab a sedative but stop, worrying again about its interaction with the scotch that's still in my system.

So I flick through the channels as the stupid thoughts run rampant: the fears about the knife, that I'm going to get violent; that things aren't real; that I'm going crazy in such a subtle way that it's escaping Dr Dimmock's attention, and when it happens, it'll be too late, except some tiny part of me will stay trapped but powerless in the dimmest corner of my mind.

A voice penetrates the movie – a shout. Was that real? Maybe I imagined it. That's another sign of craziness – hearing voices. I mute the TV to try to hear it again, to identify it as real. If it's real, I'm okay…although I might just imagine it and not know the difference between whether it's real or not. That's the definition of crazy, isn't it? Not knowing what's real and what's not?

But now I do hear raised voices outside. A screen door clanks – the door on Olivia's garage. Then nothing. I get up, creep to the back door and unlock it, pull it ajar enough to look out.

I can make out the silhouette of Olivia through the screen door of her garage, animated as she talks. Somebody big lumbers past her – Mario, no doubt. He waves his arms as he responds to her. Sometimes, he talks loud enough that I can hear his voice, although I can't make out what he says. The conversation goes back and forth. Lots of waving and pacing. The screen door bursts open so hard it creaks against its piston, and Mario storms out. Only moments later, his Ford bellows as it backs out of the drive then screams down the street.

The light in the back of Olivia's garage goes off and

she comes out. I back away from the door and return to the lounge to sit on the couch, my arms trembling. Then the light from the bungalow activates, shining through the window. I wonder why I didn't hear the gate open, but realise it must've been open already, because I never heard Steph close it when she got home earlier.

I'm back up, pulling the curtain aside. Olivia's at the bungalow door. It opens. Steph steps aside to let Olivia in. The door closes and the bungalow light goes off. The light inside Steph's bungalow goes on, dim through the curtains. They'll no doubt be talking all night, discussing why Mario's a moron – just like they've done countless times before, but the whole episode feels unreal.

I turn the TV off and escape to bed, burying myself under the covers. The night floods in and what I hear isn't silence, but the threat that it might erupt into something to claim me. Something snorts. I hold my breath. Just Dad's snoring coming through the walls. A dull thud. Then a rush of movement. Water through the neighbour's pipes – the sound echoes between the two houses. I hear little things that I never would've noticed once upon a time, but now I catalogue them, prove to myself they're normal, because if they're normal, then I've still got some grip on normal. And if I've still got some grip on normal, then I must be normal.

It's a long time before I sleep.

41.

In the coming weeks it becomes harder to focus. Mr Baker reminds us we have to finish *The Catcher in the Rye*, although I still haven't started it. Mr Tan keeps teaching us Turbo Pascal. Mrs Grady asks us to do an essay on civil law. Things that used to come easy now make no sense. I duck out to the toilets lots to recompose myself and start taking three sedatives a day.

'You expecting or something?' Ash asks me during one recess.

'I think I have a stomach bug,' I say.

The lie slides right out, beautifully wrapped – better wrapped than Riley's present.

'Maybe you should see a doctor,' Ash says.

'Yeah, maybe,' I say.

Ash is the only one who notices anything because most of the school's attention is on Riley. Joining the Navy has made him a celebrity – or a novelty. He lazes in class with a casual disdain for what's going on, sometimes sitting back with his hands folded behind his head like he's preparing for a nap. During the breaks, he holds court; even idiots like Mickey and Lachlan hang out with him as he talks about the places he'll see and the things he'll do.

At home, things stay quiet as Steph packs her things.

We store everything in the garage for the time-being, under and around the pool table. Dad helps wordlessly, while Mum hovers nearby, sniffling, sometimes even sobbing. Then Steph will stop what she's doing and go over and hug her. Next door, Olivia's also packing, although her parents chatter through it and give her advice.

The day before Steph leaves, I walk late into the evening. Thoughts brim in my head – stupid thoughts, panicked thoughts, thoughts that things aren't real, thoughts that I'm going to lose control, thoughts that I might hear voices – and my walking grows quicker, and then I'm jogging, then running, then sprinting until my breath burns, my throat grows dry and the cool night air whips through my hair, and I hope that I can outrun what's going on. And then I get that same thought I had once on the aqueduct, that I could fly, that if I jumped now, the wind would pick me up and I'd soar and leave all this behind.

I run and run, willing it to happen but instead, I run until I have nothing left. My legs give out and my feet pound and I double over, panting, sure I'll pass out – but that's okay, because that'll give me peace. Only, I don't pass out. My breathing levels and then it's back to the thoughts ricocheting through my head, faster than I could ever run.

Disappointed, I go home.

The next morning, we get up early, have breakfast and meet the movers when they pull their big truck into our drive. Dad and I help Steph as much as we can loading the truck, while Olivia's dad helps her. Mum and Olivia's mum cry. Mario's conspicuous by his absence, but between the rest of us and the movers, we make short work of loading the truck.

I jump in the car with Steph and she leads Olivia in her car, the movers in their truck, and both sets of parents packed into Dad's car, as we drive to the new place. We go slow. The movers know their way, but it wouldn't be hard to lose Dad – he's terrible in new places.

'It's not that much different to me in the bungalow,' Steph says.

'What?' I have the window rolled down and my head half tilted out, wanting to feel the wind splash on my face.

'I'm just saying it'll be like before.'

'You won't be at dinner. Or lunch on the weekend.'

'I'm not that much anyway. And I'll visit.'

'How come Mario's not around?'

Steph rolls her eyes. 'They broke up.'

'For good?'

'For good. How about you? You all right?'

As with Ash, it's gone past telling her the full extent of what I'm going through, and I don't want to make her feel guilty now that she's leaving. She's living the life she wants. She should be able to do that without having to worry about me.

'Sure. Of course.'

'I'll take you to your appointments when I can – but I have to tell you something I haven't told Mum and Dad yet because…well, you know why.'

'What?'

'I've got a job as a cashier.'

'A cashier?'

'Just for now. To pay the rent. And stuff.'

'What stuff?'

Steph takes a deep breath. 'I've enrolled in a course –

two nights a week. It's a design thing. That's what I want to do.'

It's a lot to digest. While everybody's been thinking Steph's biding her time, she's gotten on with her life. Part of that makes me sad – she's moving forward, moving away from me. But I'm also proud of her. It hasn't been easy for her with Mum and Dad. And part of me is curious. In all the aspirations she's had over the years, she's never mentioned design.

'Where did this come from?' I ask.

'Growing up, I was thinking of all this practical stuff because of Mum and Dad. I think, actually…'

'What?'

'Watching you write has helped me realise I have a creative side. And Olivia. She's helped me find that in me.'

'So, you've only just started?'

'I've been sketching a while now – nothing I've wanted to share.' Steph laughs. 'Olivia says they're good, but…' She shrugs. 'I don't have the confidence yet to share.'

'Then the Boland was for nothing?'

Steph frowns. 'Why would you say that?'

'You're meant to get mentoring to help you with what you want to do. And you've just realised this.'

'Doesn't mean the Boland wasn't important.'

'How?'

'I didn't know what I wanted back then – most fifteen- and sixteen-year-olds don't. When I was at uni and Furniture Warehouse, I knew they weren't for me. For a little while, I was worried maybe I'd just bounce around, never being able to commit to anything. But then I'd think back to the Boland; that year's proof when I want something, I'll chase it. Now I've finally realised what I do want to do – design.'

We drive on for a while as I think about what she's said. I need to recommit to my schoolwork. And the Boland. It's a life buoy. If I was caught out in a raging sea, that's what I'd be swimming towards.

'Anyway,' Steph says, 'I'll take you to appointments when I can–'

'It's all right,' I say, feeling a surge of independence. I can't keep dragging her down – not when she's finding herself. 'I'll grab a train. It's a couple of stations and a bit of a walk.'

'But I want to take you–'

'Steph, it's okay. If you can, cool, but if you can't, I'll get the train.'

'Thanks for being understanding. If you want to talk to me, you can call any time – well, you'll be able to once we get a phone. And if you get sick of Mum and Dad, feel free to come crash the night.'

She's trying to be cheery, but her eyes get misty and her voice chokes up, so she stops talking and focuses on the road. I try to remember where we're going – down the freeway and over the bypass, over into Brookvale, which is all hills and trees. The roads wind like tangled threads as we cross over into Roseview, until we're taking side streets to a block of units shrouded in gums. We park out front and wait until the others arrive.

The unit – the third in a block of six – is nice, with hardwood floors, a lounge with an adjoining kitchenette, and two bedrooms. The backyard is small, the grass overgrown and weedy, but it has a nice flowerbed full of unruly roses. Olivia's mum and dad examine it and nod, like they're thinking Olivia has done okay, but disapproval is etched on Mum's and Dad's faces.

We help the movers unload, then Dad, Olivia's Dad and me shift things to the rooms Steph and Olivia direct us to. It's a mess, lots of boxes remain unpacked and things are missing – like a good television, a couch, a washing machine, a fridge (although Steph says they've bought a fridge and it'll be delivered Monday) – but you can see the potential of the home it'll become.

Mum cries again and hugs Steph, trying to be discreet as she shoves some money in Steph's hand. Steph puts it in her pocket, then hugs Dad, me and Mum again, while Olivia hugs both her parents together.

Finally, they see us out and we pack into the car – Dad driving, Olivia's dad in the passenger seat, and Olivia's mum, Mum and me in the back.

We drive home in silence, nothing left to be said.

42.

It's around one when Mum nags me about having something for lunch. Because we were helping Steph and Olivia, Mum hasn't had time to cook, so she offers to make me a sandwich. I tell her I don't want anything.

'You should eat something,' Mum says.

'It's all right.'

'You going to lie around all day unfed?'

'I'll make something, okay?'

My whole body pulses with restlessness. Another sedative is an option, but if I have another sedative, I can't drink at Samantha's party tonight. As it is, I'm not sure about the morning sedative and drinking, although surely it would have to be out of my system, otherwise I wouldn't be able to take three a day. I need something now, so I call Ash from the phone in the hallway.

'What're we drinking tonight?' I ask.

'Got nothing here,' Ash says. 'Mum made Dad lock up the cabinet after that other bottle went missing.'

'We should get something.'

'Can meet earlier before Samantha's and get something, I guess.'

'When?'

'Five or so?'

'You can't go earlier?'

'What's the rush?'

'Okay. Sure. Five. See ya then.'

I tell myself I should do some homework, or work on my story, or play some pool – all good options but instead, I find myself hurrying out of the house and down the drive. I stop at the mailbox when I see a thick, rust-coloured elastic band on the ground – it's one of those rubber bands the mailman uses to bundle up the mail when there's a lot of it. Mum must've gotten the mail whenever and let the elastic band drop. It had one purpose. Now it's abandoned. I pick it up and pull it up over my wrist like a bracelet.

The plan is to walk to the liquor shop, but I run until I have no breath left, walk until I recover, then run again. By the time I get there, I'm all sweaty. I give myself a couple of minutes to catch my breath, then go into the liquor shop holding a wad of cash in one hand and twirling my keys around one finger like I've just come from my car.

It's not the same guy behind the counter – this one's younger, a tall guy with big, round shoulders who's probably only in his twenties. I worry because he's closer to my age, he'll know all the tricks and be on the lookout to shoot down anybody trying them. My heart pounds as I ask for a couple of bottles of scotch. But the guy gets them, puts them in a brown paper bag and takes my money.

The supermarket's my next stop. I buy a stack of Coke bottles and a packet of cigarettes and begin my walk back home. In one of the side streets, I make my first mix and take big gulps of it. By the time I've gotten to the bridge, the alcohol has dulled the anxiousness. I sit on the bank and drink and smoke and watch the water trickle down the creek.

The scotch goes down easy and the more I drink, the more courage I get, thinking I'll swagger into Samantha's and make my move with Gabriella. I'll ask her to go for a walk. That mightn't be right at Samantha's, though. I could make a move with Samantha. She should be the one I try with. It could work out. But even as I think these things, I know it's false bravado.

I drink a little more, then head home and stuff my stash under the bed. It'll have to survive there while I get ready. Then, after my shower, as I'm just finishing pulling on a pair of pants, Mum knocks on the door and comes in.

'Mum!'

She laughs at my embarrassment. 'Are you going out again?'

'I'm going to a party.'

'To another one?'

'My friend's having a party.'

'You need to eat something.'

'I ate something now.'

'What?'

'A hot dog.'

Mum doesn't push it. She goes back down the hallway and then I hear two things: the kitchen door slides open and Mum tells Dad that I've said I've eaten something. I hear Dad's *he-he-he* chuckle and he says something that I can't make out. But they'll be talking about me now, about me going out, about me drinking and coming home late. It annoys me that they discuss everything like I'm a kid – well, I am a kid, but a little kid.

I decide to change into another pair of jeans (scratchy), t-shirt (stifling), and a short jacket (unnecessary, but I'll need somewhere to hide the scotch later). It's stuffy in the bathroom and the night's humidity is sticky. Worse, I'm feeling that lethargy that seeps in when you stop drinking.

Mum's on the couch, Dad on his chair when I poke my head into the kitchen. They look so old and tired, Mum's face drawn. Steph moved out today – it hits me how frightening that must be for Mum, for her daughter to go out into the world, especially when Mum and Dad so obviously think Steph's ill-prepared and the world's so dangerous.

'I'm going,' I say.

'Don't be too late,' Mum says.

'Be careful!' Dad says. 'There's a lot of stupid people out there!'

I slide closed the kitchen door, grab my stuff from under my bed, then hurry out to meet Ash at the corner. I see him loping down the street in no hurry. He lights up a smoke when he gets close but has his gaze fixed on the bag containing the scotch and the Coke. He looks inside the bag.

'What the hell …?'

He pulls out the scotch bottle I've been drinking from – about a quarter of it is gone. I blink at it. I really didn't think I'd drunk that much.

'You already been drinking?' he asks. 'What's up?'

'Steph moved out today, so I felt restless and went and got the stuff,' I say. 'And you got some the last time, so it was my shout. We'll need more Coke.'

Ash grabs one of the remaining Cokes out of the bag, spills some out, and fills it with scotch.

'No problem,' he says.

43.

Samantha trembles when I kiss her cheek. Or it might just be me on shaky legs. Then Ash kisses her on the other cheek and I feel jealous – it's not that it's Ash, but just the way he's been with Deanne and Rachel. Who knows if there's been anybody else? Or if Samantha might fall for him?

'Happy birthday,' I say. 'From us.' I hand her our clumsily wrapped gift.

'Thanks,' Samantha says. 'I'm glad you could come. Both of you.'

The music – Rick Astley, singing one of the handful of hits that's always playing on the radio – in the garage blares so loud you expect to see the roof bouncing. The backyard has a downward slope, so I can imagine the tables and benches that have been set up sliding down the yard and piling into the fence. It won't happen. Of course it won't happen. But I see it anyway.

Ash and me take a seat at the vacant end of one table – opposite some of the geeks who excel in our computer class. On the next table sits Deanne talking to Mickey. Under the table, I can see his hand is on her thigh and they both drink from bottles of lemonade, although maybe there's something more in those bottles. You can't trust anybody these days.

At another table is Gabriella and Scott, close enough to suggest it's likely what'll happen tonight. Gabriella flicks her hair back once and sees me in the process. She holds her hand up but it's just an acknowledgement – nothing more familiar than that.

Ash gestures to another table, where Kat and Rachel sit, Kat stunning with her blonde hair tossed back, wearing this boob-tube thingy that looks like it's going to slide down at any moment and black leather pants.

'Notice anything?' Ash says.

'The tube thing she's wearing?'

'No.'

'The leather pants.'

'Nah.'

I lean to the side so I can make out that Kat's wearing stiletto heels. I point them out.

Ash shakes his head. 'No boyfriend.'

And, of course, he's right. We only ever see the boyfriend at social functions, so it's not hard to forget he exists.

'This could be my night,' Ash says.

Riley and Felicia come down the drive and share an exchange with Samantha. Felicia gives her a gift-wrapped box and Riley says something to her so they all laugh those polite, fake laughs you laugh when something not that funny's been said but you all want to show that you're in on it. The gift makes me think how Ash and me didn't ask Riley to get in on Samantha's gift, and he didn't include us in the gift he got with Felicia.

Samantha gestures Riley and Felicia to the yard and

the two come over, arm in arm. There's a point where they split, Felicia to head over to Kat and Rachel, and Riley to come to us and then they stop and grin at each other – grin with this sickening sweetness. They kiss and I wonder how they work out who gives in to who. But Riley's hand goes down onto Felicia's hip and urges her in our direction. Within moments, they're sitting opposite us.

'I was thinking–' Riley says.

'Congratulations,' Ash says.

'Ha ha. I was thinking we should do something for new year – also be like a farewell, since I won't be coming back to school next year.'

'It's such a cool idea,' Felicia says and kisses him on the cheek. 'It's the end of the decade, too!'

'Where?' I say. 'Your place?'

'We're selling up. Mum can't afford it since Dad left. I'm going, Ray's got his own place, so she's going to get something little for herself.'

'Where do you want to do this new year's thing then?' I ask.

'Soccer ground behind the school. It's summer, so it won't be cold. Bring your own drinks. It's not near any houses, so nobody will complain about the noise if we bring a stereo or whatever. What'd you think?'

Ash holds up his Coke to toast him.

Riley turns to Felicia. 'Should ask…' He points at Kat and Rachel.

Felicia starts to get up. Riley puts a hand on her thigh, so she sits back down.

'Call them over,' he says.

Felicia beckons them over. We shuffle across on the

benches. Kat sits next to Ash. Her perfume is its own environment. You can't identify what it is, it's that strong – not that Ash cares. Rachel sits on the other side of the table, next to Felicia. Riley outlines his new year's plan again.

'Sure,' Rachel says. 'I'm easy.'

'We know that,' Kat says, but she says it in such a jokey, offhand manner that all the mystique that surrounds her evaporates. Rachel's mouth drops open in mock horror while the rest of us laugh.

'Well?' Riley says.

'Sure,' Kat says. 'I'm in.'

Riley's idea spreads, going through not only friends, or friends of friends, but also people we don't even like, like Mickey and Lachlan, until everybody's either relaying they'll be there, or they come over to pat Riley on the back or tell him what a great idea it is.

I drink to keep everything numb, while Riley laps up the devotion. New dynamics form around me the way they always do at parties: Ash almost stops drinking as he chats with Kat, Kat laughing like she's one of us; on the next table, Scott now has his arm against Gabriella; Deanne sits between Mickey and Lachlan as the three of them scoff their lemonades. Everybody's with somebody. Again, I feel that isolation – it's not bad like it has been, but it's there, so I retreat and find my way to the bathroom.

The scotch is catching up to me and everything spins. I splash cold water on my face and know I've now drunk too much. Bile rises in my throat and I double over the toilet but nothing comes out. I wait there as nausea overcomes me. Nothing. I make retching sounds, trying trigger it. I've drunk enough times to know that if I'm going to vomit, I might as well get it out. Still nothing. The bottle of scotch – maybe still a quarter left – bounces in my pocket. I'll take a break. That's the best thing to do.

So I stumble out onto the veranda and prepare to face the rest of the night.

44

A hand falls on the middle of my back. 'You okay?'

Samantha. Beaming at me. The way Samantha does.

'I'm...tired,' I say. 'My sister moved out today and I was up early helping her pack and stuff.'

'Oh. Okay. Do you want to sit down?'

I follow her to one of the tables and we sit on a bench, facing one another. She's pretty tonight, Samantha – she always is, but she's wearing this red dress and her hair is all done up so it's blown back and wild. The gold bracelet I bought her is around her wrist.

'You think they've given us the essay for the Boland yet?' she asks.

I tell her what I told Gabriella – that reading the other essays, it's usually an essay where the writer can make a positive change on the future.

'Oh, that's a good idea,' Samantha says. 'I should read those, too. I wonder if it's Mr Baker's identity essay.'

'That's not really about change.'

'But it's about seeing who we are. Gabriella wrote this piece about how she's somebody who tries her hardest and even if she doesn't succeed, she can at least know she tried.'

That sounds simple but meaningful.

'I'm halfway through mine,' Samantha says. 'But I don't like it.'

Quiet between us. Bon Jovi's 'Lay Your Hands on Me' starts up in the garage. It occurs to me that she's expecting me to ask why she doesn't like it.

'You written yours?' she asks.

'I've tried to a few times but don't know what to say.'

'Why not?'

'I'm thinking about the way he wanted us to write it.'

'Lachlan wrote it exactly the way Mr Baker told us *not* to write it.'

I glance over at Lachlan, Deanne sandwiched between him and Mickey as they drink from their lemonade bottles. They're loud and animated and laugh lots, so I have no doubt now they're drunk. Lachlan scowls at me, maybe jealous I'm with Samantha. Under his table, he has his hand on Deanne's knee. Mickey has his hand on her other thigh.

'I want to do a good job,' I say.

'You write well. Well, it seems you do whenever you've had to read something in class.'

'I want to be a writer.'

Samantha blinks. 'Really?'

'Yeah.'

'You've never told me this.'

'I've never really told anybody. Except Ash. And Riley.'

They're on the next table, Ash still chatting with Kat, while Felicia sits on Riley's lap and they kiss, Riley's hand halfway up the inside of her thigh. Rachel's gone – who knows where? Maybe to dance. At the next table, Gabriella and Scott get up, hand in hand. I hope they're walking into the garage to dance, but instead they walk down the drive. They might be going to make out – or maybe they've gone to fuck. Either makes me sad and envious.

'What do you write?' Samantha asks.

'Short stories,' I say. 'About this character, this boy, Jean Razor.'

'That's a strange name.'

'I know. But it sounded good when I made him up.'

'What're the stories about?'

So I tell her about Jean Razor and the way the Grave Shadows murdered his parents, captured him, and brought him to the Crimson Tower because he has an ability to sidestep into parallel dimensions and they want to sacrifice him, leech that power and grow stronger once they've fed off it.

'Only he escapes,' I say, 'and learns how to jump into parallel dimensions.'

'What's in the parallel dimensions?'

'It's Earth, just an Earth where we've made different decisions – like on another Earth, instead of sitting here with me, you might be sitting here with Ash or Riley.'

'So, there are two Jean Razors whenever he goes to one of these Earths?'

'No, he steps into the Jean Razor there and gets to control him.'

'None of those other Jean Razors have this power?'

I shake my head. 'That's what makes him special.'

'Why does he have the power?'

'I haven't really worked that out yet.'

'What's he going to do with it?'

'He's going to overthrow the Crimson Tower.'

Now Samantha's sceptical. Out of the corner of my eye, I see Riley and Felicia get up. I expect they're going somewhere to get some privacy, but they go into the garage so they must want to dance – or Felicia must want to dance.

'I'm working on a bigger story,' I tell Samantha.

'Like a book?'

'Yeah. That's where I'm really working all this stuff out.'

'It sounds interesting.'

'You're probably not into science fiction.'

'Some of it's okay.'

Samantha rests her hand on my knee. Her attention flatters me. Besides Steph or Ash, I've never had anybody to talk to about my writing. Even Riley scoffs. So this is nice. As is the way Samantha looks at me so devotedly. I could lean over right now – and I do lean in a bit – to kiss her. Then I project a whole future: boyfriend-girlfriend, going out, hanging out, her reading my stuff, her helping me with this.

Why not?

I sit up.

The *why not* is because my motivation is I want her to save me and that's not fair on her. I see her sad, frustrated and crying when I fail to live up to whatever expectations she's built in her head. They'd have to be deluded – not because she's deluded, but because they're expectations about me. I couldn't disappoint her like that. Right now, I'm perfect to her and it's nice to be perfect somewhere.

'I'm gonna get a drink,' I say. 'Want something?'

'I'm okay.'

I fish out a coke from one of the drink barrels in the

garage. The music's slow now – Richard Marx's 'Right Here Waiting for You'. It's a beautiful ballad with tinkling piano. Felicia and Riley dance cheek-to-cheek, as do Mickey and Deanne. Mickey's all class, with his hands on Deanne's butt. Somebody brushes up behind me – Ash. He grabs his own Coke, but his gaze goes to Deanne.

'What's happening with you and Samantha?' he says.

'Just talking.'

'That all?'

'That's all. What about you and Kat?'

'She's nice.' Ash's eyes still haven't left Deanne.

The music stops and the dancers break – well, apart from Riley and Felicia; they stay stuck together. Mickey and Deanne leave the garage and walk down the drive. Kylie Minogue's 'Wouldn't Change a Thing' starts up.

Ash's nostrils flare. 'I hope she's okay,' he says.

I catch a glimpse of Mickey and Deanne disappearing into the night.

'Jealous?' I say.

'It's Mickey,' Ash says, as if that explains it all – and it does. Some guys are just dicks.

Ash pulls the scotch bottle from inside his pocket and fixes a mix with his Coke. I know I should stay off the alcohol a bit longer but Ash mixing is about all the convincing I need to do the same.

We go back out into the yard. Other kids have commandeered Samantha, so that's a relief I don't have to snub her or string her along. But Kat's also gone. A couple of other girls are there now – a striking redhead and a short, homely blonde. Of course, Ash introduces us and sidles over, so he's closer to them. I can now stay on the end of the bench and have them think I smell or something, or I can join them.

I join them.

'Cindy,' the blonde introduces herself.

'Nadia,' the redhead says.

Ash chats to them with his usual breeziness. Nadia's aloof but Cindy makes up for it with a friendliness like she's known us all her life, telling us that they're crashers and that they wish there was something to drink. Ash thrusts his Coke bottle at her. Cindy sips tentatively, grimaces, then takes a swig. Nadia is a lot more restrained, sipping at it like it's a latte.

'You want to dance?' Ash says, as Alice Cooper's 'Poison' begins in the garage.

'Sure.'

Him and Cindy disappear into the garage. I look at Nadia.

'I'm good, thanks,' she says.

'So…where'd you come from?'

'Hampton Park.'

'You walk here?'

'Yeah.'

'How'd you hear about a party down here?'

'My sister.'

And that's it. She doesn't want to talk – or it might just be me, so I let it go.

What's left of the night unwinds in a blur, everybody always moving, separating and regrouping into different clusters: Gabriella comes back alone and sits at a table with Rachel; Riley and Felicia walk out together; Samantha chats with her friends, but every now and again will look at me.

Everything's always shifting. I wonder how long the friendships that exist here will last, and how many of the relationships will endure.

Not many, if any.

Nothing's forever at this age, is it?

SUMMER

December 1989

45.

At home, I strip down and hear the scotch bottle clunk in my pocket when I throw my jacket to the floor. I pluck it out – still about a quarter left. I slip the bottle in the gap between the bookshelf and the corner of the room.

I sleep uninterrupted, although a lot of that has to do with how much I've had to drink. Sunday is horrible – three sedatives through the day and I try to sleep through how I feel. Part of it's hangover and I'm working out that *this* is always worse the day after I've been drinking. I'm tempted to drink again, although somewhere along the line, I'm going to have to face this. So I bear through it best as I can. Monday morning, the hangover is gone but I feel like I'm going to fly apart. The only thing that holds me together is knowing I'm going to see Dr Dimmock in three days. I can hold on until then – or at least, that's what I tell myself. I take my sedative the moment I wake up, stick another one in my pocket and struggle through my morning routine.

I set off early, thinking I'll have to wait for Ash but he's already at the corner, smoking a cigarette. He thrusts the packet at me. I take one without thinking. We walk to school, Ash with his head low, brooding. When we get to the bridge, we sit on the bank. I remember being here two days ago, drinking and thinking everything was fine. We light up another smoke.

'How'd you go with Samantha?' he says. 'You seemed to get into it.'

'She's nice, but I don't think there's anything there – not from my side.'

'Why?'

'We've talked about this before.'

'But I wonder: I see a girl and I think about where I can get with her.'

'No? Really? You?'

'Ha ha. You look at them like you're gonna have a relationship. So what don't you see in Samantha that stops you from trying?'

I lie back on the grass. The sedative has blunted the anxiety and, for a moment, I can fool myself that things might be normal again.

'I don't feel *it*,' I say.

'What's *it*?'

'What do you call it? Clickability? How well you click with somebody? That you can imagine being with them? That you lust for them – but not like you do, but that you actually want to be with them and be with them again.'

'My God.'

'You understand?'

'You're an old man.'

'That's what goes on in my head. Why're you asking?'

'That girl Cindy last night, I liked talking to her. I was thinking maybe I was feeling something more.'

'Maybe you're maturing.'

'That's a pretty mean thing to say.'

'Well, what?'

'Maybe I was drunker than usual.'

'So, you're trying to find out why it's an aberration?'

Ash chuckles. 'Who knows?'

'And Kat? She disappeared last night.'

'Obviously didn't trust herself around me.'

'Right.'

Kat, in these little denim shorts and a green singlet with the straps sliding down her shoulders, is the first person I see when we get to the courtyard. Deanne, over with her friends, wears a semi-transparent blouse and a little skirt. Riley and Felicia sit on one of the benches. Then Samantha's in front of me, rolling on her heels.

'Did you bring me your stories to read?' she says.

'Sorry,' I say. 'I forgot.'

She slumps. I want to promise her I'll bring them tomorrow but now I see the danger in that. She probably only offered to read them so there'd be a reason to have contact with me. That'd lead her on more and would hurt more when nothing comes of it. I wish this didn't have to be so complicated.

In first period, Mrs Grady hands back our Legal Studies essays about an alternative form of justice. Unlike Mr Baker, she goes haphazardly around the room as she returns them. Ash gets his back, with a 'B-'. Then Mrs Grady goes across the room, then comes back and hands me mine: 'B+', along with the comment, 'Very inventive but I'm not sure it's practical.' She floats back across the room, then comes back with Riley's – those pages in green ink I saw when I visited him that night. She smiles at him. 'Well done,' she tells him. She sets the essay down. 'A-' is scribbled across the top. Then she goes back around the room to finish returning the others.

Riley doesn't smile, doesn't beam, doesn't do anything – he sits back as if Mrs Grady had done nothing more than return a pen she'd borrowed from him.

Me and Ash gape at him.

'What?' he says.

'Good job,' I say.

'What did you write about?' Ash says.

Now Riley grins and opens his mouth like he's going to tell us, then says nothing. In the toilets at recess, we push him about it until he grows surly.

'I had an idea, okay?' he says. 'Why're you so surprised?'

'Didn't think you cared since you were going to the Navy,' Ash says.

'I wrote it before I decided that. If the Boland shit is decided on *that* essay, I'll win.'

He ignores that the Boland is also about grades across the year, attendance and attitude.

'Is that why you put the effort in?' Ash says.

'What do you think?'

Like I've said, Riley's smart but doesn't push himself. But Ash nearly takes him up on his challenge. I don't even think it's about the essay but because Ash is beginning to dislike aspects of who Riley is. But, finally, Ash decides not to pursue it.

'Cool – well done,' he says.

Riley's victory is short-lived. The next morning in English, Mr Baker hands back our book reports for *To Kill a Mockingbird* while collecting our book reports for *The*

Catcher in the Rye. The homework he returns to Ash has *B−* on it, to Riley a *D*, and mine has *C+*.

I frown at the grade. It's not good for my Boland chances. It was one of the harder pieces because of the stuff going on in my head. I found it hard to get into the book, so I could only write a report from my choppy understanding.

Mr Baker gives me this funny look as he takes my *Catcher* report, which is short and messy. I struggled to read the book and barely took anything in, so I don't have hopes for the report to get a good grade.

Riley thrusts his forward. It has a single short paragraph written on it. Mr Baker stops, puts his hands on his hips and glares at Riley. Riley slouches back in his chair like it's a recliner he expects to extend under him.

'Is this it?' Mr Baker asks.

'I guess.'

'I can't imagine you covered the book in any scope.'

'You're probably right.'

Everybody knows Riley won't be back next year, so can't be threatened with failing or expulsion. Mr Baker lets out an explosion of breath.

'You may need to work on your respect to authority where you're going,' he says.

'Fuck you.'

'Get out.'

Riley shrugs, packs his bag and leaves the classroom.

At recess, we try to hunt him down but he's disappeared. Stories get bandied about, the tamest that he's been expelled, the worst that he did a runner, but not before scratching *FAG* all over Mr Baker's car, this battered yellow Volkswagen van. Then a new story emerges that

Riley's assaulted Mr Baker and that generates momentum because nobody sees Mr Baker until Gabriella spots him in the library during the last period.

On the way home, Ash decides we should visit Riley after dinner. I almost find an excuse not to. I'm jittery again, so the first thing I do when I step in the door is grab a sedative, then lie on the bed and wait for it to take effect. Mum comes home not long after and fixes dinner. I struggle through it, then hurry over to Ash's place. You can hear his brothers screaming as they play. Ash is out the front door before the bell's finished its second chime.

We don't talk on the way to Riley's and there's an oddness in this, like we're only going to see Riley out of an obligation to the friendship we've shared, rather than because we're concerned. I don't have that same concern I did when we were worried about Riley being a no-show at school for a few days.

Not only does his front lawn have a *FOR SALE* sign on it, but there's a SOLD sticker stuck across the front of it. The light's on in the lounge but there's no car in the drive. Riley answers the door after two rings, cigarette hanging from his mouth, his eyes heavy, like we woke him from a nap.

'They were gonna suspend me,' he says, when we're in the lounge, 'but Mum came and told them I've been having trouble since Dad took off. They bought that.'

'What do you care?' Ash says. 'You're out of here next year.'

'That's what I thought.'

'What do you mean?'

'Mr Baker went and looked up the Navy – I need to have

passed this year with good marks in Maths and English. Maths isn't a problem but the fag's got me in English. He said he'd pass me if I tried hard for the rest of the year. Cunt.'

'That's only like five weeks,' I say.

Riley rolls his eyes. 'Trust you to defend him.'

The phone rings – Felicia – so Ash and me sit in the lounge while Riley takes the call in the kitchen. After about fifteen minutes – and after we've worked out Riley's in no rush to get back to us, if he's planning to get back to us at all – Ash goes into the kitchen to tell him we're leaving. We let ourselves out.

'You think at all about next year?' I say. 'Be just you and me.'

'Maybe that's the way it's meant to be,' Ash says.

46.

By Thursday, nobody's talking about Riley anymore. They're talking about Deanne sitting alone on a bench in the courtyard, crying. At recess, Riley joins us in the toilet for a cigarette and tells us what he's heard.

'That night at Samantha's party,' he says, drawing on his cigarette, 'she double-teamed Mickey *and* Lachlan.'

'No way,' Ash says.

'People look at her now, the way she's slutting it up. They're talking.'

'She's just dressing trendier,' I say.

'I'm just telling you what's being said.'

In our third period Social Studies, Deanne sits at the back of the classroom alone, eyes red. Kids whisper in one another's ears. Mickey and Lachlan – seated up front – snigger. I look at Deanne – her makeover subdued compared to what she had been wearing – and don't know what to believe.

When the bell rings to signal lunchtime, Ash leads us out of the classroom, then hangs by the door. I wait, unsure what he's doing. Riley stops behind me and folds his arms over his chest.

Mickey and Lachlan emerge from the classroom.

'Toilets,' Ash says. 'Now.'

'What's your problem?' Mickey says.

'You go there now or you'll find out,' Ash says.

Mickey and Lachlan frown at one another.

Riley takes a step forward. 'You don't want to find out, do you?' he says.

Only minutes later, we're in the toilets – Ash makes sure Mickey and Lachlan go in first, then stands between them and the door. Riley and me stand behind him. My heart thumps – I've seen Ash like this and know it has the potential to get ugly. Riley lights a cigarette. He doesn't care. This is all theatre for him.

'What's your problem?' Mickey says.

Ash glowers at him.

Mickey thrusts a hand into Ash's chest. 'I'm getting sick of your hero–'

Ash uppercuts him in the stomach. Mickey's breath explodes from his mouth and his legs give way. Lachlan jumps forward to grab Ash but Ash slings him into a toilet cubicle – we hear the clatter of him hitting the toilet.

'What's this shit you're spreading about Deanne?' Ash says.

He points a finger at the cubicle in which he threw Lachlan. We can't see what Lachlan's doing – we can only guess he's making ready to come out.

'Stay in there,' Ash says.

Mickey doubles over onto the floor. Ash kneels by him and yanks his face up.

'Why're you saying this shit about Deanne?' Ash says.

'I'm not saying anything.'

'Rumour's going around you two fucked her,' Ash says. 'Who else would start that?'

'It wasn't me, okay?' Mickey grows teary. 'We made out for a bit. She didn't want to go further. I didn't say shit!'

'He didn't,' Lachlan's voice echoes in the cubicle. '*We* didn't.'

Their fear is so obvious that it's hard to believe that they could be lying.

'Then who did?' Ash says.

'How the fuck do we know?'

Ash rises, confused – this hasn't gone to plan. This obviously isn't just about Deanne. This is about his mum and dad, and the stuff he doesn't tell me. He said his dad slapped her once. There must be more.

'Anybody asks you,' he says, 'anybody says anything to you, anybody congratulates you, anybody even looks at you, you put them straight. Got that?'

He doesn't wait for an answer. He spins and charges through me and Riley. Riley spits on the floor right before Mickey, then follows Ash out. I go out after them both.

Ash stays angry the whole day. When the final bell goes, we walk home wordlessly – well, until we get to the corner where we separate. He says a goodbye to me but I pull him up.

'You all right?' I say.

Then he does what I least expect: he laughs, like this has been the punchline to some big joke.

'I hate that sort of shit,' he says. 'I'll see ya.'

I walk home, tense, unsure if it's because of the way I'm feeling or because of what Ash has done. I dump my bag, then rush to the train station. On the ten-minute ride I decide it has nothing to do with Ash. This *is* Ash. I'm used to it. I'm nervous *while* it's happening, but then everything's back to normal because Ash resets to normal – well, normal as far as I know him.

I check in with the receptionist at the hospital and then sit in the waiting room. When Dr Dimmock calls me in, I tell him about how I've been feeling, and how it so quickly and unpredictably fluctuates.

'*When* do you feel at your best?' he asks.

'When I'm writing,' I say.

'Why do you think that is?' he asks.

'Because I lose myself in it, I guess.'

'Perhaps you want to bring in some of your stories.'

He writes me a new prescription for the sedatives and tells me to book another appointment for a fortnight.

And that's it.

I tell myself that Dr Dimmock's lack of concern is only because things *must* be okay. You're probably thinking that no doctor – especially a psychiatrist – would be so blasé. But that's Dr Dimmock. My illusion of movie psychiatrists and lying on couches and having miracle breakthroughs of some childhood trauma shatters.

Summer comes to bludgeon us into submission over the coming weeks. The days grow hot, so all you see at school are shorts and singlets and thongs and sandals, and the days stretch endlessly into muggy nights where it's impossible to get comfortable. But the heat also means the school year's ending.

Mickey and Lachlan grow subdued and cower like disciplined dogs whenever Ash is around. Ash grows in people's eyes – he's always been this force unto himself but he gets a lot of respect for what he's done. Unfortunately, that doesn't help Deanne. High school being high school, the rumours about Deanne not only go on for several weeks, but are embellished, until stories are going around about her and the football team. She grows quieter, and she dresses more like she used to – in plain, shapeless clothes.

Ash flirts with Kat, sometimes sitting with her at lunch. Samantha drifts away from me, maybe finally working out we're going nowhere. I barely see Gabriella. In classes, Mr Baker reminds us that our identity essays are due while Mr Tan commends us for our essays. I get an A+ for predicting computers will become smaller and spread into every bit of technology we know. I thought the essay was blah. Maybe I'm my own worst critic.

Steph comes over Sundays for lunch. The first time she does, she's tentative and doesn't say much. Mum and Dad prod her for information about living away from home, like they expect to find a weakness they can exploit.

'Who does the cooking?' Mum asks.

'We swap.'

'And the cleaning?' Dad asks.

'We haven't been there that long that everything's a mess.'

'Who takes the garbage out?'

'We swap all those sorts of things.'

Dad chuckles. 'Swap,' he says, like it's the most ridiculous thing he's heard.

'Don't forget Jim's wedding's only a few weeks away,' Mum says.

'I know,' Steph says.

'You're still bringing Todd?'

'I'll see.'

'What do you mean you'll see? They have to know for the reception—'

'You've already told them we've got one extra.'

'Are you going to come with us?' Mum says.

'I'll meet you there.'

'Meet us there?' Dad says. 'You should come with us.'

'So, I should drive back here so I can go with you? Why?'

'We should go as a family.'

'Forever?'

'Until you're married.'

Steph stiffens. Dad sees she's close to blowing. It's different from when she lived here – all she could do was storm out to her bungalow and how much of a moral victory was that? It's the bungalow Dad built for her. But now, she could get in her car and leave to the flat she's paying for herself.

'All right, all right,' he says.

Steph wolfs through her food. When she's done, she challenges me to a game of pool, and we retreat to the garage.

'You writing?' she asks.

'Some.'

'I started my course.'

'That's great.'

Although it doesn't sound great the way I say it. I don't mean to not be enthusiastic. It's just the way it comes out. Even Steph's disappointed. I try to fix it.

'What's it like?' I ask.

'I'm really enjoying it.'

And that's that.

The next Sunday, Dad's cutting the roast when Steph

tells him and Mum that she's working as a cashier.

'A cashier?' Mum says.

'You gave up a job selling furniture to work as a cashier?' Dad says. 'How much are you making?'

'It's only until I find something better,' Steph says.

'Something better,' Mum says. 'Something *better*. You gave up school, you gave up your other job, now this.'

'You go from one thing to the next to the next,' Dad says. Then his voice drops, because it's time to be serious. 'I worked thirty years cleaning because it was the only job I could get when we came here. I didn't like it. I wanted to do other things. But I did it so we could buy a house, we could pay bills and we could afford to get things for you and your brother.'

'I don't understand the point of what you're saying,' Steph says. 'That's what I'm doing – I'm working to pay my way.'

'Your way to *what*?' Dad says. 'You don't know what you're doing.'

Steph throws her hands up, gets out of her chair and leaves the house. It's not long before we hear her car start.

'You fool,' Mum says. 'You don't know what you're doing.'

'She needs to have a plan for her life.'

'You don't have to keep telling her.'

They start to argue, so I give up and go to my bedroom.

That week, when I see Dr Dimmock, I bring my journals – the A5 ones that have the short stories in them and the A4 one with my work in progress. He thumbs through them so quickly he can't be doing much more than scanning paragraphs. When he's done, he hands me back the books, nods his head, gives me a, 'Hmmm', and asks if I need a prescription.

And that's it.

I walk back to the train station, a little more confident in myself.

47.

They release the Boland longlist at school – and it *is* a long, with hundreds of names. Everybody I expect is on it: myself, Ash, Samantha, Deanne, Ethan, Gabriella – it also includes students from the other schools in our area.

It injects some excitement into a school year that's unravelling. Everybody's looking to the holidays, or what else they might be doing. Students who aren't longlisted relax. Those who are refocus on their schoolwork.

Ash invites people to a birthday-lunch-barbecue and pool party at his place, but does it so matter-of-factly. Riley, on the other hand, struts around – if anything, not being on the Boland longlist has made him more sullen – and makes sure everybody knows about his farewell/new year's party.

'It's gonna be huge,' he says in one of the few recesses he spends with us.

We're lounging on the aqueduct. The water from the creek is almost gone, leaving nothing but weeds and junk people have tossed in. It's sad to see what lies on the bottom, hidden for most of the year.

'That'll be the night,' Riley says.

'The night?' Ash asks.

'For Felicia and me.'

'This is going on longer than *Days of Our Lives*.'

'Hey, hey, hey.'

'Why don't you just marry her?'

'What's your problem?'

I feel that tension between them both, as well as Riley's surprise.

Ash shakes his head.

Riley lies back, hands folded under his head, cigarette poking up from his mouth. 'What about you and Kat?' he says. 'You talk to her enough now.'

Ash shrugs.

But later, when we're in the toilets smoking and Riley's back with Felicia, Ash tells me, 'I've been talking to that girl from Samantha's party – Cindy – and I've become confused. Cindy's funny. It's like us hanging out. Kat's hot, but there's not a lot else there. At least, between us, that is.'

'So, what're you gonna do?'

'Don't know.'

That night when I get home, Mum reminds me about Jim's wedding this Saturday. I remember Jim at Aunt Mena's funeral challenging me on what I was going to do with myself. After dinner, I take a walk and all I can think is that I haven't gone anywhere since that funeral. Everybody is moving forward – Steph with her place, her course, her job, Riley with Felicia and the Navy, even Ash, with all his relationships. All I'm doing is struggling to tread water, then bouncing off the bottom occasionally so I can break the surface and gasp for breath.

That Thursday, when I sit in the waiting room before seeing Dr Dimmock, all the symptoms are there: the tight chest, the shortness of breath, the panic and the manic thoughts that things aren't real, or that I might snap and grow violent. I try to talk myself through it and tell myself that there's no reason I should feel so bad – nothing's happened. But it doesn't work. Then the anxiety hits, a surge that rocks me and I'm sure somebody's come along and shoved me from the chair and that I'm on the floor but, no, here I am, still seated.

I tell myself I'll be okay and it settles to what I can only think of as manageable terror. But as it hits again, I think I should knock on Dr Dimmock's door, or go to reception and tell them it's urgent. But again, it settles to this background noise. Things become spotted around me. I develop the fear that I'm not here, that this waiting room isn't real. I'm somewhere else. This is a façade. I tell myself that's stupid but can't shake the thought.

The door opens and Dr Dimmock sees out a patient. I'm up before the patient is even out the doorway and brush past him to let myself in. Dr Dimmock stays at the door, looking at me like he's going to tell me I've been impolite or something and that I should I go out and come back in all over again. But then he closes the door and sits down in his chair.

Everything spills out then – I don't hold back on any of it. I list all the current symptoms, and then expand on them.

'A lot of the time I have thoughts that things aren't real,' I say. 'Like, even now, I can look at the wall behind you and wonder whether it's real. I know it is, but some part of my head keeps insisting it isn't. It's like I'm in a constant argument with myself.'

Dr Dimmock says nothing. And does nothing. His face doesn't change.

'Sometimes I worry I'm gonna hurt people,' I say. 'Like, my dad was carving the roast once, and I was scared I was gonna grab the knife and hurt somebody with it.'

'Do you think you'll hurt somebody?' Dr Dimmock asks.

'No, but it gets in my head. Other times, I worry that I'm gonna hear voices.'

'Have you heard voices?'

The question is a slap across my face. What I want Dr Dimmock to say is, *No, you won't hear voices – you don't have to worry about that.* Just the question confirms the possibility I might.

'No.'

Dr Dimmock nods and scribbles something down.

'What should I do if I do?'

'Don't listen to them.' Dr Dimmock leans back in his chair and his eyes narrow. 'Has anything changed since the last time I saw you?'

I think about it, then shake my head.

'Is there anything you're worried about?'

Jim. And him asking me at his wedding what I'm going to do. But am I really worried about that? There's the Boland: I've been longlisted. But that hasn't made me nervous.

'I don't think so,' I say. 'What's happening?'

'You're heading for a nervous breakdown.'

'*What?*'

I'll pause, because you'll be thinking, *There's no way a doctor would tell you that.* But that's exactly what he says, like he was telling me I had something stuck between my teeth. And surely he'd know, because he's a psychiatrist. He must've seen this happen countless times before.

Dr Dimmock sets his pen down. 'School is the only structure in your life. You entertain the notion of becoming a writer, dealing in the fantastic – this character who can shift between dimensions. Like the walls of his world aren't real to him. Do you see the connection? You live in a world that's fantasy. It's little wonder you have these feelings that things aren't real.'

'Why don't other writers feel this way?'

'Oh, they do. Lots of them do. You should stop writing. Put away writing. You need to ground yourself. Be practical.'

'I'm scared that once I leave this office everything's going to come apart.'

'Perhaps you'd like to take a respite in one of our hospitals?'

One of our hospitals can only mean a mental hospital. My only experience with them is what I see in movies – crazy people, mean staff, unfair treatment, nothing but despair. I want to believe that's not going to be the truth, but at this stage, the only thing I know is if I end up in a hospital and see the other patients there, I'm going to worry myself into something worse.

I shake my head.

'Are you certain?'

'I guess.'

Dr Dimmock writes out a prescription. 'I'm going to prescribe something different to help you cope,' he says. 'Forget the sedatives you've been on. One to three of these a day as needed.' He tears the prescription sheet out and hands it to me. 'But, for now, I want you to ground yourself. Forget about your writing. Put it away.'

'For *how* long?'

'Twelve months. At *least*. Just think about the here and *now*. I'll see you again in two weeks.'

I stagger from his office, trying to work it out – he tells me I'm heading for a nervous breakdown but I can wait two weeks for the next appointment? I hold onto that as reassurance. Maybe the nervous breakdown thing was a scare tactic. I mustn't be that bad, and he must be sure this prescription is going to take care of things.

There's not much of a queue at the reception, so I'm able to make the appointment straight away but while I'm sitting in the pharmacy, the anxiousness seethes.

They call my name and I take my pills. They come in a little brown bottle. I unscrew the cap, pull the cotton insulation aside and dump a pill onto my palm – it's small, white and glossy. This is my salvation now. I dry swallow it and walk from the hospital, waiting for a sense of peacefulness.

Only it never comes.

On the walk to the train station, on the train ride home, and then the walk home, everything's still raging in my head. I want to believe that this new pill works a different way – maybe it's not about peacefulness, like the sedative. I estimate that an hour's passed since taking it at the hospital and walking into my bedroom. There's no way it should take that long. The sedatives never did.

My A4 exercise book sits on the top of my bookshelf. I open it, trace my hand over the page and feel the ink on the paper. Under it is the leather journal Ash and Riley gave me, untouched but inviting. Could Dr Dimmock be right? I *do* live inside my head. I never thought I could get lost there.

I slam the cover shut and thrust the journals into my bookshelf.

Time to start fresh.

48.

Friday's worse at school. The sun's too hot on my face and the wind too sharp on my skin. I struggle through because that's what I've become good at. The new pill isn't doing a thing.

Throughout the day, we're called in to talk to Counsellor Hoffs. Riley goes during second period Maths with Mr Tan, but he's back within minutes, smirking because he knows what he's going to do. Ash is called in during third period Social Studies and doesn't come back for twenty minutes. He sits down, mumbling, 'What a waste of time.' Others are called during fourth period English, when Mr Baker reminds us our identity essay is due next week. I think I'm going to miss out for the day – and for this week – but I'm called late during fifth period Open Room.

'How've you been doing?' Counsellor Hoffs asks once we're seated.

'Okay, I guess.'

'You sure?'

I shrug sullenly.

'Your grades have grown inconsistent. I need to ask you if anything's been an issue. Home maybe?'

'My sister moved out.'

'How's that affected you?'

'It's quieter.'

'Does that bother you?'

'No.'

'Has there been anything else? Bullying at school maybe?'

'Nope.'

'Girlfriend troubles?'

'Uh uh.'

Then, tentatively: 'Drug use?'

I almost snort with laughter. Yes, there've been drugs – prescription drugs.

I shake my head.

'Does school bore you?' Counsellor Hoffs ask. 'Often, intelligent students find the work unchallenging, so it doesn't engage them.'

'Maybe sometimes, I guess.'

'What's the matter?'

She's not an idiot. She must've seen other students like me. I can't be the only one. And who knows what other teachers might've told her? For a moment, I'm sure I'll sob.

'If you want to talk, you can talk to me,' Counsellor Hoffs says.

But I can't. If I can't talk to friends, why would I talk to her? She's only doing this because it's her job, although I guess that's no different to Dr Dimmock. But at least Dr Dimmock isn't connected with the school.

'I'm okay,' I say. 'I'm tired and stuff.'

'All right.' Counsellor Hoffs opens a folder and slides some pamphlets across to me. 'These are from some of the universities that have writing programs. I thought it might help for you to see what's out there.'

I grab the pamphlets but don't look at them, like looking at them might make me crazy. 'Thanks.'

The bell rings to signal the end of school. I wait for Counsellor Hoffs to dismiss me. She smiles.

'Congratulations on your Boland longlisting,' she says.

'It's a big list,' I say.

'But you're on it.'

I think about how I wanted to focus on the Boland, to mean something, to have something to work towards that would carry me out of this. Does it still mean anything to me? I can't work out what's going on inside my head. I *want* it to mean something, though. I want it to save me.

'Are you sure there's nothing you want to talk about?' Counsellor Hoffs says.

I nod.

'Okay. But if you change your mind…'

'Thanks.'

I toss the pamphlets in the first bin I find outside.

When I get home, I lie on my bed and try a meditation. By the time Mum and Dad come home, things have settled – not a lot, but enough that when I trudge into the kitchen for dinner, I can go through the motions of eating the chicken wings Mum has fried. Dad eats opposite me and drinks from a beer. A beer would be good now. I wouldn't even care if it had some effect on the medication. Mum grabs a pot of boiled rice from the stove.

'We're going to your Aunt Toula's tonight,' Mum says. 'For Jim's wedding. Are you going to come?'

'Do I have to?' I say.

'You should come.'

'My head hurts. From…this. Do I have to go tomorrow?'

'Of course you have to go.' Mum plants the pot of rice on the kitchen table. 'What are people going to say if you're not there?'

'I don't feel good.'

'You're fine.'

Despite the hospital, despite the fortnightly appointments, she doesn't get this. It's not that she doesn't understand – I'm sure she would if I were her age, had her responsibilities and worries. Worse, they see me doing normal things – going to school, going out – and they think that means I'm fine.

'I would prefer not–'

'Tonight, you can stay home,' Mum says. 'But you do what you have to so you're all right to go tomorrow. Think about what people would say if you're not there.' She plonks spoonful after spoonful of rice onto my plate.

'What about Steph? Is she still going?'

'Yes. With Todd, I think.'

I know that can't be the case but say nothing.

'You don't tell anybody about what you're going through, all right?' Mum says, as she sits down.

'Like?'

'Anybody. They don't need to know.'

After dinner, Mum and Dad go to Jim's. I grab a key, lock up and take a walk. The evening is a pesky dusk that's timid and sleepy, although lots of people are out because the weather's warm.

I walk past Ash's, see the light on in the lounge and for a few seconds, I think about ringing his doorbell, although I don't know what we'd do. Just chat, *like normal*, but that's the last thing I want to do because there is no like normal anymore. So, I walk on, past Riley's. A red Subaru sits parked behind Riley's mum's car – I'm sure the Subaru's Riley's dad's car. So, his dad's over, although Riley mightn't be.

I keep going, end up close to Samantha's and wonder if that's random or if I'm hoping I might bump into her. I keep walking, taking side streets I never knew existed. Night falls and everybody's gone inside. I like the quiet. I wish it could be quiet all the time.

It's late when I get home. I've walked – a couple of hours maybe. Mum and Dad still aren't back. My legs are sore and tired, but in a good way, and out of habit I pull out my homework and spread it out onto my bed.

The noise in my head is now a dull throb. I curl up and an inescapable sadness fills me. I open my folder to English and look at the criteria for Mr Baker's identity essay. I don't even know if I should be writing this. Maybe I should put it away since it's creative. It's all irrelevant anyway because I don't know where to start. I've never known where to start since he gave us this stupid thing.

I push my pen to the page and scribble in big letters…

I don't know who I am.

49.

Mum knocks on the door in the morning and tells me I have to get ready for Jim's wedding, although we have plenty of time. I skip the new pill Dr Dimmock's given me and muddle through breakfast. After I shower, I'm all hot and sweaty, so have to duck back in. It's not going to be a comfortable day; the shirt I put on scratches my armpits and the tie chokes me.

Then I remember there's still what's left of the scotch that I took to Samantha's party. That's the salvation. Unfortunately, when I check the fridges – one in the kitchen and the one in the garage – there's no Coke. We do have some small bottles of Cream Soda. I take two, go back to my bedroom and make the first mix. The taste is different – tangy and sweet but wholly nice. I make the second mix, then stuff both bottles in the freezer until Mum tells me we're going. She doesn't ask when I drag out both bottles, now a slushy ice. I sip from the first on the drive up to Aunt Toula's house. By the time we get there, I've almost finished one bottle and feel a looseness I haven't for a while.

Aunt Toula greets us at the door and exchanges kisses with us. Lots of cousins are here, milling about. Tables are covered with food – leftovers from last night, and stuff that'll stay for the day. They have the air conditioning on, too, which keeps everything nicely chilled.

Jim comes out of a hallway, dressed in the slacks of his suit and a singlet. He does all the greetings and when he shakes my hand, he tries to crush it. He runs his other hand through my hair.

'Looking good,' he says, then points at me, as if to say, *We'll talk later*, or something like that.

We gather in the garage, where Jim takes a seat and his best man – a big, typically Greek guy with dark hair and a uni-brow – shrouds Jim in a cape, lathers his face and then shaves him, while everybody cheers and shouts encouragement, the way we might at a football game. The pre-wedding shave is a Greek tradition. It's meant to show Jim's last shave as a single man – I don't know why the best man does it, though. It's not like he was shaving Jim before – well, not as far as I know. Everybody flings money into the cape – Dad gives me a twenty to throw in. Once Jim's shaved and he's bundled all the money up in his cape, the best man helps Jim dress in his shirt, blazer, and bowtie.

On the drive to the church, I finish the first mix and stuff the other one in my pocket. We find a parking spot right at the back of the lot, Dad checking repeatedly that the car fits perfectly between the lines. Others are walking to the front of the church – uncles, aunts, cousins. Mum and Dad go and talk to Uncle Teddy and Aunt Nadia. Their kids are talking to other cousins. Everybody's in little groups, chatting and laughing. I stand off to one side, until Steph arrives with Olivia. Steph's in this modest royal blue dress with puffy shoulders, while Olivia's in this strapless red thing that shows off her cleavage and is tight at the hips. Any other day, I'd memorise the way she looks in it.

She tousles my hair. 'Getting shaggy. We'll have to cut it again soon.'

Mum looks our way and sees Olivia. Nothing registers on Mum's face but she'd be overjoyed there's no Todd. Other cousins come up to us – Uncle Teddy's daughters Alexis and Lydia and their brother Egan, who's my age.

'Hey, filth,' Egan says – he doesn't mean anything by it. I've hung around with Egan and his friends in the past – they throw around 'filth' like it's the equivalent of 'buddy'. But, now, it's the way I feel.

'Hey,' I say.

We hustle into the church and find seats. Sweat beads on my head. It's a while before the priest comes out and the ceremony begins. The anxiousness skyrockets. I focus on Jim and Nicola, Jim in a black suit with shiny lapels, the train of Nicola's wedding dress draping back into the aisle. Jim grins this big stupid grin, but I can't blame him. Nicola looks great and whatever else might happen, they have this moment.

I'm not going to lead you through the whole ceremony. When something takes a long time, people complain that it goes 'forever', but 'forever' could learn a thing or two from Greek weddings. The priest – and I pick now he's the same guy from Aunt Mena's funeral – fires off his typically quick and indecipherable Greek. At times we stand, then sit, then stand, and sit again, and make the sign of cross. Sweat trickles down my face. The armpits of my shirt chafe. I can't breathe in here. My lungs balloon but can't let go of the air. I shoot up and slip down the aisle and outside, then head around to the side of the church, where I light up a cigarette. It's not the best idea when I'm struggling for breath, but right now it seems reasonable enough.

'Hey?' Steph, coming around the corner. She frowns. 'You okay?'

'Yeah. Just hot in there.'

'You sure?'

I nod.

'Okay. Want to come back to my place for a bit? Get away from Mum and Dad. You can come with Olivia and me to the reception.'

'Sure. That sounds good. Thanks.'

Steph puts an arm around me and gives me a squeeze.

'You can go back in if you want. You'll miss it all,' I say.

Steph smiles. 'I'm okay out here.'

50

Mum scowls at us when everybody files out. As the limousine takes away Jim and Nicola to get photos done, everybody mills around. I lean against the corner of the church, on the edge of the crowd, and watch as Steph finds Olivia, then taps Mum on the shoulder as she's talking to Uncle Paul and Aunt Mary. I can't hear what Steph says but I see Mum's face flicker and she seeks me out. She smiles and nods and Steph and Olivia come back my way.

The drive back to their place is short and once there, I sink onto their new L-shaped sectional couch. They have a big TV and a fridge purring in the niche assigned for it in the kitchenette. Other things make it feel like home – bookshelves, tape racks and there's Steph's stereo. On the walls are pictures from their overseas trips – usually the two of them standing in front of some amazing backdrop, like the Eiffel Tower, the Statue of Liberty or Stonehenge.

I sit on the couch and sip from my mix – it's warm now, but it's keeping me balanced – as Steph goes into one of the bedrooms to change into some sweats. Then Olivia goes into the bedroom and changes. Steph sits on the couch and switches on the TV, drops the volume low and flicks through the channels.

'Sorry I haven't been able to take you to your appointments,' Steph says.

My gaze flits to Olivia, who's gathering washing and stuffing it into a basket.

'Olivia knows–'

'Why did you tell her? I ...' My voice trails away as Olivia goes into the laundry – just off the kitchenette – to stuff things into the washing machine. 'I don't want her thinking I'm a freak,' I say, all quiet.

'You're not a freak.'

The washing machine whirs. Olivia leaves the laundry and goes down the hall.

'Don't be like Mum and Dad,' Steph says. 'Like Mum especially, where everything's gotta be secret.'

I sit back and sip from my mix.

'Come on. Don't get angry.' Steph rests a hand on my shoulder. 'How's this doctor doing? Is he all right? We can find somebody else.'

'You're busy anyway.'

Steph leans back and puts her feet on the coffee table. 'I'm sorry I upset you.'

I know I'm being a prick but can't stop myself. *This* can't be me. When people know, that's how they'll see me. I sip from my scotch and feel the busting urge to piss. It's also a good excuse to escape the tension. Olivia comes back and sits on one of the chairs, a book in her hand – Stephen King's *Pet Sematary*.

'I've got to use your toilet,' I say.

Steph gestures. 'Down the hall, last door on your right.'

I leave my mix on the coffee table and drift down the hall. The first door is the bedroom: Steph's and Olivia's dresses lie on Steph's queen-sized bed – it's the same one she had in her bungalow. A big antique armoire stands in the corner, although there's also a built-in wall-closet. The next door is on the other side of the hallway to what should be the other bedroom, but the only thing in there is a desk with a sketch pad on it.

What I should be thinking now is that there's two women sharing this flat and only one bedroom, but that's wiped from my mind by the sight of the designs of dresses and other clothes stuck on the walls – they're not crap scribbles either. The lines are strong and sure, with flourishing curves and a texture that makes them three-dimensional. The quality of them intimidates me. This is creativity. I have such a long way to go with my writing. Two more doors await at the end of the hall – a bathroom, and on the other side a toilet.

Once I'm done, I go back to the lounge room. Steph's still on the couch, arms folded across her chest. Olivia's slouched in the other chair, wearing glasses that make her look business-like, reading her book. I sit next to Steph.

'That other room…' I say.

'The other room?' Steph sits up straight. 'Oh! *Oh*! I thought the door was closed.'

'Those your drawings?' I ask.

'What? Oh. Yeah.' Steph smiles shyly. 'What did you think?'

'They're awesome.'

'You really think that? You're not just saying that?'

'They are.'

'That's what I tell her,' Olivia says. 'I told you, Steph.'

'Why didn't you tell me?' I say.

'Because Mum and Dad make everything like this feel as if it's so stupid.'

'What about me?'

'I guess I started believing them.'

'She believes them all right,' Olivia says.

'So…' I say, because this is when it should be easy to say, *You have only one bedroom*. Things make a bit more sense – Steph's regular lack of boyfriends, Steph and Olivia going overseas together, Olivia finally dumping Mario, Steph and Olivia coming to this wedding together.

I think about the way Steph exclaimed when I brought up the other room – she didn't mean me to discover this. If the door had been closed, I would've assumed it *was* the other bedroom. She and Olivia exchange guilty looks. Olivia sits up and rests her book face-down in her lap. They're going to come clean. But I don't want them to because now it's the truest relationship I know – truer than Mum and Dad with all their shouting and all their qualifications, truer than the phoniness of Riley and Felicia, truer than whatever it is Ash does – and I've blundered in. They shouldn't have to justify it for me.

I pick up my drink. My plan is gulp it down, but then I think that would look like I'm shocked, so I sip at it. Sipping's smarter anyway. The drink has to keep me even and last until the reception, although the scotch has eased the dread.

'So…what?' Steph asks.

'I was longlisted for the Boland,' I say.

'That's awesome!'

Steph gets up, hugs me and kisses the top of my head. Then even Olivia gets up and hugs me. The heat rises in my face. This is unusual, being congratulated for something. I didn't even tell Mum and Dad because I knew their reaction would be underwhelming. When Steph and Olivia sit down, I'm eager to change the subject.

'So…you must be having fun at your course?' I say.

'It's fantastic,' Steph says. 'Learning so much and hanging with like-minded people. I wish I had done this earlier.'

'It's not like you're ancient,' Olivia says.

'No, of course not – I'm glad I found it. Well, actually, Olivia found it.'

Steph goes on, talking about the stuff they're doing. Olivia goes back to reading her book. It's nice sitting here and chatting, with no worries about what's being said. I could come clean here about everything. I could. But I don't, and instead just hold onto the feeling, wishing I could hold it forever.

51

We get to the reception around six, the lobby filled with guests, the buzz of their talk loud and vibrant. Whatever relaxation the scotch gave me is wearing off and a headache's developing above my right eye. I grab a beer from a waiter's tray as he passes. He stops and studies me.

'Are you eighteen?' he says.

'Don't I look eighteen?' I ask.

Mum and Dad chat with friends – Mum tells Steph and me that when she lived in Greece, her cousin had a neighbour who had a friend who had an aunt, and this is that aunt and her husband, which makes us…? This is being Greek. We're all connected somehow.

The reception is huge, the dance floor ringed with an imitation marble balustrade, the hardwood floor polished like an ice-skating rink. The band's set up in a corner on a stage, maybe half the length of the hall away from us – which is great. The first thing you do at a Greek wedding reception is check the proximity of the band. At the front is the bridal table, long enough to fit Jim, his new wife, their parents and their whole bridal party.

I'm not going to go through the whole reception. It's not that important – well, it is to Jim, Nicola and their families, but for me, it's something to get through. I tense, thinking at first that it's a reaction to being out here, worrying that something's going to go wrong – and there's an element of that. There's something else, though: Jim. He's going to come up to me and ask me what I'm going to do with myself. The question should slide off me. It shouldn't matter. It *shouldn't*. I can tell him *brain surgeon* or something that'll satisfy him. But he's intimidating because he has done exactly everything he's wanted to do. How do you compete with that? How do *I*? I can tell him about the Boland longlisting. That's something genuine, although he might scoff because it didn't help Steph – well, as far as he knows. And I've only been longlisted.

I get through the first couple of beers quickly because I need to find that looseness again. Then the emcee – this big young guy, maybe thirty, who's balding and has a big hook nose – introduces the bridal party from each set of parents to the groomsmen and bridesmaids, the page boy and flower girl, and finally Jim and Nicola, arm in arm and waving, a spotlight highlighting them as they make their way across the floor.

The night alternates between meals being brought out and chatter. First, the appetisers (a choice of fish or lasagne – yes, even though lasagne is Italian, it makes appearances at Greek functions). Then guests talk among themselves. The emcee invites Jim and Nicola to dance. Then the parents. Then couples from the bridal party. Then everybody's invited. Steph and Olivia look at each other and I wonder if they'll have the courage. They don't. Dinner follows – chicken or beef. Speeches are made. Greek dancing – everybody ringed in circles, arms on shoulders, a kick here and there, circles moving around and around.

Steph dances a few, then forces Olivia to. I drink until the beer's numbed my head, although the band's clarinet – a steady whining – drills a hole through. Other guests mingle. Different cousins sit with me at varying times to ask how I'm doing, how school is and whether Mum and Dad know I'm drinking: I tell them good, good, and that Mum and Dad are okay if I have one or two beers. With everybody I speak to, I tell them I'm on only my second beer. I know it's horrible, that I'm sixteen and I'm drinking like this, but it's the only thing getting me by. One thing in my favour is drinking has never made me an exhibitionist or anything, so it wouldn't look like I'm drunk. Then dessert comes out – chocolate mousse or ice cream – with coffee.

Jim and Nicola do the rounds of each table then, Jim sitting between Dad and Mum and putting an arm around each.

'Maybe Steph next,' Jim says.

'We can only hope,' Mum says.

'You got a special man in your life, Steph?' Jim asks.

'Not yet,' Steph says.

'What happened to that guy you were seeing – your mum told my mum you were seeing that Australian. Tom?'

'Todd.'

'You were going to bring him. What happened? Didn't work out, hey?'

'No.'

'How about you?' Jim asks me. 'You might be next.'

'I'm a while away, I think,' I say, heart thumping. He'll ask now. He won't care that Mum and Dad are here. He'll ask. He's Jim.

'That's right,' Jim says. 'Have fun at your age.' He gets

up. 'I should get going. Hope you're having a good night tonight.'

He moves onto the next table. That's it. Maybe later. Maybe he'll ask me in private.

He has chances, too. During one of my trips to the toilet, I'm standing up there on the urinal with him, side-by-side. But nothing. Later, on my way to the toilet again, he's coming in from the lobby. He points at me, as if to say, *Hey*, and that's it. A third time, on my way back from the toilet, he's going out to the lobby. He winks at me and makes a clicking sound. Another *hey* moment.

On that occasion, when I get back, Steph and Olivia sit at the table, close together, posing for a photographer who's been going around asking couples if they want their shots taken – getting the shot done is free, but if you want the picture, you pay for it. It's the closest Steph and Olivia look to being a couple for the whole reception.

I sit down next to Steph and pour myself another beer.

'You're drinking a lot,' she says.

'I know.'

'You *are* all right?'

I hold up my hands, as if to say, *Well, who knows anymore?*

The night finishes when everybody makes rings around the dance floor and Jim and Nicola – Nicola's now in a tan suit and Jim in a grey suit – go from person to person and everybody wishes them well. Kisses on cheeks are exchanged. Hugs. And handshakes, handshakes containing money.

'Here,' Dad says and thrusts twenty dollars each at me and then Steph, 'give this to Jim.' He takes out another twenty and thrusts it at Olivia, barking in his heavily accented English: 'You, too!' Olivia gapes at him until Steph explains what's going on.

I wait among the guests, feeling a shortness of breath, although I keep telling myself I'm going to be okay. Would Jim ask me here? He moves from person to person, exchanging only a few words. He's getting closer. I want to back out of there and hide in the toilets, the way I would at school. Jim has exchanges with Mum, with Dad, with Steph, with Olivia, and then with my Uncle Teddy to my right. Then he sidesteps back and claps a hand on my shoulder.

'You don't think I've forgotten you, do you?' he says.

'No…'

Jim grabs my hand and shakes it. The twenty slips into his palm. He deposits the money in his pocket, then moves on to Aunt Nadia. That's it.

I drop back a step, then another, until I'm leaning against the imitation marble balustrade. Jim and Nicola finish going around the circle and then take off. And I'm left without having to answer Jim. I feel a combination of relief and like I just got robbed.

On the drive home, I slump in the back seat and roll open the window so the cold night air runs across my face. I can't blame Jim for not asking me – it's his wedding, so he has a lot more things on his mind. *Important* things. I guess, in a way, his whole life starts here. But, still, I also can't help feeling like I'm forgotten.

And don't matter.

52.

I stay in bed the next morning until the need to use the toilet drives me out. My tongue is furry and my head clogged. Still, I take one of the new pills, fumble through breakfast and then go down into the garage and set up the pool table.

As I thrust my cue forward, the floor crumples beneath me. The splatter of the balls coincides with an explosion of fear that consumes me. The tremor in my arms crawls up into my back and sinks into my stomach until nausea rises and my head spins with a certainty that I'm going to pass out. My legs grow weak. This is it. This is where I've hit the point of no return. And it doesn't abate to where it's manageable, just keeps rolling over in waves.

I run into the house and slide open the kitchen door. 'Can we go to hospital?'

Mum's ironing on the bench that separates the kitchen from the dining room. Dad's on his chair, reading the paper. Both look up sharply.

'Why?' Mum comes over. 'What's wrong? What's the matter?'

'This…' I lift my hands to my head.

'It's all right,' Mum says.

'Can we go? *Please.*'

It's not long before we're repeating the trip we took last time – Dad driving and dropping us off outside, Mum going up to reception and me doubled over in a chair, my head in my hands. Now, there's nothing but chaotic thoughts and the certainty that this is the breakdown Dr Dimmock warned me about.

Dad shows up and paces. Mum tells him to wait by me and walks off. Some untouched fleck of my mind wells up with guilt over what I'm putting them through. I feel like a burden. And a failure. Is this what it'll be like for the rest of my life? Will I always be relying on Mum and Dad – and Steph – to save me?

I'm faulty. I wasn't built to function in this world.

Steph comes before too long and sits next to me. She puts an arm around me. 'What's wrong?' she says.

'I feel like I'm falling apart.'

Steph rubs my back. It's good to have somebody there I can talk to but again, I think about the inconvenience I must be. She must've been relaxing on a Sunday. That's where Mum disappeared to – to call Steph. So, Steph puts everything on hold to come see me.

'It'll be okay,' she says. 'You'll be all right.'

I can't believe that – not anymore. Things have been happening inside me that I haven't been able to stop. They've torn up the way I used to think and things that I used to do unthinkingly – like going to a party or a wedding – have become a war.

My name's called and I'm led into another of those little rooms. Steph comes with me, while Mum and Dad wait outside. I get a different doctor this time, a big woman with wavy hair tied back but for the fringe that hangs loose, my file in her hand. She introduces herself as Dr Carlisle and puts the file besides me so she can check my vitals – pulse, heartbeat, blood pressure. I tell her what happened but how that's only the tip of everything that's been going on. Steph puts her arm back around me. Dr Carlisle picks up my file and flicks through it.

'My brother's been coming here a while,' Steph says. 'I don't want to be walking out of here thinking he just has to tolerate this.'

'Of course not,' Dr Carlisle says. 'I don't want to prescribe anything over what's already going on. I'm going to give Dr Dimmock a call.'

Dr Carlisle pulls back the curtain to let Mum and Dad in, Mum's eyes misty.

'What's happening?' Mum says.

'She's going to call the doctor he sees,' Steph says.

'What do these doctors know?' Dad says.

Then it's quiet because nobody knows what there is to be said. I close my eyes. The thoughts are dimmer. It's tiredness. Or maybe resignation. That always seems the answer: escape in sleep. But I always wake up. That's reality. And reality is this. This always. This waiting for me. Sleep is better.

Dr Carlisle comes back through the curtain. 'Dr Dimmock is occupied with another patient at another hospital,' she says. 'But we've arranged for him to come in tomorrow at nine.'

'What's my brother supposed to do until then?' Steph says.

'Dr Dimmock said to take two of your sedatives and one of your new prescription.'

'And if that doesn't work?' Steph says.

'Then come back in here.' Dr Carlisle looks at me. 'You'll be okay. Trust me.'

53.

The pills do work. My mind grows quiet and drowsiness hits. I lie on the couch. Mum, Dad and Steph tiptoe around me. When they talk, it's in hushed whispers. Mum makes dinner – sandwiches – and I eat sitting up. Then we settle in front of the television and watch a movie like a normal family would.

At 10.30, I say goodnight to Steph, Mum and Dad and go to bed. I crawl in under the covers and it's not long before my mind wakes. It's just a single thought: that I might hear a voice. That hangs there, wavering. Then I worry that I might lose control. Other possibilities trickle in until my head's filled. It's a long time before I sleep but I sleep well and when I wake, I don't feel so bad.

I go out to the kitchen and find Steph's slept on the couch. The guilt fills me again. Mum's sitting at the kitchen table, sipping a coffee. No sign of Dad, so I can only guess he's gone to work. Steph stretches, yawns and sits up.

'Do you want something for breakfast?' Mum says.

'Sure,' Steph says.

We eat French toast quietly at the kitchen table. It's the most peaceful meal this kitchen's seen. After we're done, Steph showers, then I do. Then it's back off to the Western, Steph driving.

I expect we'll see Dr Dimmock in his little office, but instead we see him in a suite that overlooks the hospital gardens. Dr Dimmock sits on a leather couch. We sit on plush chairs opposite him, a glass table between us. All those weeks I was spiralling out of control, I got the little office, but you get luxury when you lose it.

Dr Dimmock keeps his focus on Mum, although his eyes occasionally flit to Steph. Mum's sad – you can see it on her face. There's no other way to describe it, nothing great or profound. *Sad*. But Steph scowls and has drawn herself up so she's at eye level with Dr Dimmock.

'What exactly is happening?' Steph asks. 'Or, more importantly, *why* is it happening?'

Dr Dimmock holds out his hands, as if to say he has no answers. 'It could be circumstantial, it could be hereditary, it could be organic,' he says. 'But we do have recourses.'

'Such as?' Steph's tone is hard.

Dr Dimmock levels one hand above two pill boxes that sit on the glass table that separates us. 'Antidepressants,' he says. He taps the taller box. 'We can start on a low dose – seventy-five milligrams. But this should help.'

'Should?' Steph says.

'Unfortunately, this isn't an exact science. Sometimes, it is a case of trial and error to find the right medication. But we've had good success with this, and people come to lead perfectly normal and functional lives. However, they have an accumulative effect, so don't expect an immediate response.'

'So, he has to keep taking them?'

'Three a night.'

'For how long?'

'Possibly the rest of his life. But let's worry about now.' Dr Dimmock taps the taller box. 'You may feel some start-up effects.'

'Like?' Steph says.

'Dizziness, dry mouth, even some anxiety.'

'So, the pills for the anxiety cause anxiety?'

'It can be maybe seven to fourteen days before you feel the benefits of these, although a month will give us a more accurate estimate of how your body is regulating the medication. I know this seems a long time. That's why we have these.' He picks up the flatter box. 'These are a sedative that will give you some peace in the short-term. I want you to take one three times a day. Then we can talk again Thursday-week.'

'Thursday-week?' I say.

'We can book you an appointment this Thursday if that'll make you comfortable, but we really would've seen no benefit from the antidepressants between now and then.' Dr Dimmock smiles. 'We're taking the right course.'

Steph drives us home and again, there's nothing but quiet. When she pulls into the drive, I get out of the car and run up into my bedroom to examine the medication. The antidepressants, called 'Sinequan', are capsules. The flatter box – the new sedatives, which are called 'Ativan' – has tiny pills. I pop one out of its foil and dry swallow it. Then I dump both boxes in my drawer just as there's a knock at the door. I expect Mum to come in, but there's the knock again.

'Come in,' I say.

It's Steph. She sits on the bed and puts an arm around me.

'How're you feeling?' she says.

'Embarrassed.'

'You don't need to be embarrassed.'

'Who else is doing this?'

'Everybody's got their own stuff. You mightn't see it. But they've got it.'

'Thanks.'

'Are you okay with this medication?'

'Is there a choice?'

'If you have any reservations, we'll find another doctor.'

'It's fine. It'll work out.'

Steph squeezes me to her. 'I'm going to go, but if you need me, you call me – straight away. Even if it's at work. I gave Mum the number.'

'She all right?'

'She'll be okay. Let's worry about you for now.'

But it's not long after Steph's gone that Mum comes into my bedroom, hugs me and cries over me. 'Don't worry,' she tells me. 'You'll be all right. You don't go to school this week if you don't feel good. You don't have to go for the rest of the year. Just be all right. Don't worry.'

I want to assure her but my voice chokes up. I hate that she's feeling like this.

'When I had Steph, I was sad for years,' Mum tells me. 'Your father had to help with everything. I was sad and couldn't stop worrying.'

Some things suddenly make sense – at least as far as Mum and her pills go. But the situations are different. I didn't have a baby. I didn't have a household to worry about. This has come from nowhere, with no reason that I can see.

'Don't worry,' Mum says, although the words are lost in her sobbing.

'I'm all right, Mum,' I say. 'I'll be okay.'

And I want to believe that. The peace I feel from the sedative, the Ativan, is so blissful that it washes over my whole body and leaves me euphoric.

At night, I take the first dose of Sinequan, expecting more of the same. But I become so dizzy I lie down. Then there's a throbbing in my head. Some of the weird thoughts come back. Then the anxiousness, although that's a result of having weird thoughts.

I get up, unsteady on my feet, and that makes me panic, too. Medication shouldn't affect my balance, should it? Once I take a few steps, I feel surer, although everything around me has that unreal sense that worries me more.

It doesn't feel safe to be awake, so I go to bed, curl up, and slip away into the comfort of the darkness.

54

I wake before six, but stay in bed, slipping in and out of sleep until the phone rings. Mum answers it and I can't make out what she's saying. I get up, my head crowded with too many thoughts, too many emotions, all of them bustling to take charge but only wedging themselves tighter. Grabbing an Ativan, I go into the kitchen just as Mum's hanging up the phone.

'Your friend Ash,' she says. 'He wanted to know if you were going to school today. I told him you were sick.'

I check the clock that hangs on the kitchen wall: 8.15. I could rush through breakfast and shower and get to school, but being away from the house is too scary right now. I take my Ativan and make breakfast. Within fifteen minutes, everything dissolves inside my head and then it's that calmness again. The day doesn't seem so daunting now.

Steph rings just after I get out of the shower. 'How're you feeling?' she asks.

'Okay.'

'So no issues with the medication?'

'I had a bit of dizziness from that antidepressant but I'm okay today.'

'Okay. Good. Maybe this is the thing, then.'

She says that like we have an option. It *has* to be the thing. What else is left? Dr Dimmock said that it can be trial and error with the medication but I don't have the energy for that either.

That night I get dizzier after the Sinequan. I go straight to bed and wake with a mild headache and disorientation, although that might be because my whole schedule is skewed. I'm now without everything I'd normally do. After I get out of bed, I mope through the day, then feel worse the next morning. Something new is opening in me – something cold and undeniable that keeps telling me there *is* nothing.

'I'm going back to school tomorrow,' I tell Mum during lunch.

'Are you sure?' she asks.

'I'll be okay.'

'You tell them you were sick,' Mum says. 'You don't tell them about this.'

I take a walk after lunch down to the shops, although I detour around the school. Ash's birthday is Saturday, so I should get him something. Then I see it: a silver flask. I buy it, then go to the liquor shop.

'Two...' I say, and then the words die because I'm not drinking, not like this. 'One flask of Johnny Walker.'

In one of the side streets on the walk home, I fill the silver flask and think about how this has been okay. I've gotten out. I've done a bit. I'm not the invalid I thought I'd be. But I still can't shake that emptiness. Something's missing. Is it my writing? Maybe it's my friendships. Or maybe the opportunities I've lost this year. Or maybe it's all of them, wrapped up and showing me that there's not a lot left for me out here other than living with this.

I'm short of breath by the time I get home and strange thoughts tumble around in my head. I take an Ativan and within fifteen minutes, things are peaceful again. But still, I'm not sure what I should be doing. I lie on my bed and lose myself to a sense of disembodiment that crashes down. The phone rings and Mum calls my name. I take it in the hallway.

'Hey, what's up with you?' It's Ash.

'Been sick.'

'With what? Herpes?'

'Gastro.'

'You okay?'

'I'll be at school tomorrow.'

'You're sure you're all right?'

'Yeah. I'll be fine.'

'Okay. Cool. Guess what!'

'What?'

'You're on the Boland shortlist.'

It takes me a moment to even remember what the Boland is – of course, the Fellowship. I smile. And then my smile grows because *I am* smiling – it's a glimmer of happiness that shines through this and tells me that I can *mean* something, that I can *be* something other than all this.

'From our school, it's you, Ethan, and Gabriella.'

Ethan was always likely to make it. Gabriella's a surprise – she's smart, I've always known that, but she's not recognised for it like…

'No Deanne?' I say.

'Uh uh.'

And then it also clicks to me that Ash obviously didn't make it.

'I'm sorry you didn't make the list,' I say.

It sounds awful – patronising. I don't mean it to sound like that.

Ash chuckles. 'It would've been a shock if I'd made it,' he says. 'I'm glad you did – you could win this!'

The excitement stays with me through the rest of the evening. But the nightly antidepressant does the same things, only worse again. I know that it doesn't last and my body's getting used to it but I scurry into bed because, again, the safest place to be is in the dark.

Come morning, I race through breakfast and hurry from the house. It's good to see Ash, standing on the corner waiting.

'You look like shit,' he says.

'Really?'

'How much the gastro knock you about?'

'A bit.'

We walk slowly to school. The sun beats down and already I'm sweaty. Other kids idle along, joke and laugh. They exist in the moment. That's all they worry about. That's all they should worry about at this age. I envy them, because now I'm different. It almost makes me cry.

'You want to keep going?' Ash asks when we get to the bank by the bridge.

I slump onto the grass and lie back. Ash offers me a cigarette. The first puff makes me so dizzy I almost toss it and I'm glad I'm lying down. I let most of the cigarette burn away, then take another puff. Now it tastes better.

Ash stands at the top of the aqueduct. All the water's gone, leaving the weeds and rubbish.

'You don't have to come to my birthday Saturday,' he says.

'What?' I sit up.

'If you're not feeling well.'

'I want to come.'

'I'm just saying, if you don't feel up to it, I'm okay if you don't come.'

He knows more's going on but he's not pushing it – the way I don't push him. It makes me think about the value of good friendships. It's not always about talking or sharing. Sometimes, it's just about being there for one another, even when the other person doesn't want to talk or share.

'I'll be there,' I tell him.

55.

The swell of kids in the courtyard welcomes me. They're so alive and oblivious. Samantha startles me, coming up from behind.

'Hey, you okay?' she says.

'Yeah. Recovering from some gastro.'

'Must've been bad.'

'It wasn't good.'

'Congratulations on the Boland shortlisting,' she says.

'Thanks.'

She's the first of many well-wishers – Ethan, Jake, and even Felicia congratulate me. This is good – no, *great*. This is being known for something other than being sick and absent. I search faces for Gabriella. We're in this together. But I can't spot her.

'Hey!' Riley comes out of the toilet, swaggering the way he does. He holds his fist up. I knock it. 'Well done,' he tells me.

The congratulations keep coming – even from the teachers, like Mr Tan in Computers, and Mrs Grady in Legal Studies. At recess, going to the canteen to grab a juice, Gabriella pulls me up. This is the closest I've been to her since Ethan's birthday. I smell her, sweet and welcoming, see the whiteness of her skin, feel how soft it could be and then I can only think about that missed chance in the bathroom.

'You all right?' she asks.

'Yeah.'

'You still look a little out there.'

'I'll find my way.'

'Good.'

She smiles but it lacks the usual spark. I can see now her eyes are a little red – she's been crying. And she looks tired. They're just little things I bet others wouldn't notice, but I've become an expert at identifying small signs.

'Are *you* okay?' I ask.

Gabriella's lips draw thin. 'Don't tell anybody?'

'Sure.'

'My parents are getting a divorce, so a lot of stuff's been going on.'

'I'm so sorry.'

'If you knew my parents, you'd know this is overdue.'

'You should meet my parents,' I say.

Now she does smile, genuinely. She's got a great smile, and she goes from looking like a sixteen-year-old girl to a mature young woman.

'Congratulations on your shortlisting,' I say.

'Congratulations on *your* shortlisting,' Gabriella says.

We're unsure of what to do – should we hug, should we kiss one another on the cheek, should we shake hands? It feels so good to talk to her, to connect and to be *normal* – or at least *normal* as it's recognised in high school.

'I've got to go,' Gabriella says. She jabs a thumb over her shoulder.

'Don't you have Social Studies third period?'

'I'm going home. I've got to help my mum.'

'Oh. Okay.'

'Nice talking to you.'

'You too.'

Third period is the best I've felt *ever*. The Boland shortlisting. Talking with Gabriella. I see a whole future untarnished by this. I can *do* anything. I can *be* anything. But come lunchtime, when Mr Baker pulls me up in the teacher's staff room, that good feeling frays.

'You were meant to hand in your identity essay yesterday,' he says.

'Oh. Sorry.'

'I take it you've been sick. If you can get it to me at your first opportunity ...'

I nod.

'Congratulations on the Boland shortlisting.'

When I get home, I go straight to my bedroom and look at that one line I wrote for the identity essay: *I don't know who I am.*

I put it aside and push my pen to paper and think about who I am. I write, but the essay comes out exactly as Mr Baker told us not to write it – as a dossier. I write about half a page on who I want to be, before I realise that's wrong, too. I scrunch up sheet after sheet after sheet.

This should be meaningful but I can't find any meaning in it. It shouldn't be this hard. I think about the way this has debilitated me, the way I've felt good one moment and horrible the next. I think about today with Gabriella, and then the times I've felt apart from everybody else. I think about wanting to write, about Ash saying that writing might be who I am but Dr Dimmock telling me to put my writing away.

And as these things scramble in my brain, I look more and more at that single line and know it sums me up in a way nothing else can. Given the Boland has shortlisted students, this identity piece can't be the essay they're using to judge the fellowship. I slip it back into my folder and put my folder in my bag.

The next morning, that uncertainty unravels into the typical agitation. Ash and me don't say much as we walk to school. I hope to see Gabriella but she's not here. I do see Deanne, sitting on one of the benches, staring at her feet. She's reverted to the way she used to dress, like she can reverse time to a date before all the innuendo about her. I think I should go over and talk to her, but Riley comes out of the toilet.

'Hey!' he says.

Ash casts a glance over his shoulder at Deanne too, but we end up joining Riley in the toilet. He takes out that cigarette case we bought him for his birthday and offers his cigarettes around. We light up, like we're sophisticates about to indulge in some weighty discussion.

'She's been out there all morning,' Riley says.

'That stupid shit somebody started–' Ash says.

'Stupid shit's being said all the time,' Riley says.

'Not like this,' Ash says.

Riley waves it away.

They're both right. Stupid shit *is* always being said. But Deanne was this shy little nerd who found popularity and then what she used to find that popularity – something as stupid as a makeover to look good – was used against her. Bizarrely, I think about what her identity essay would say.

When the bell goes and we hurry out, Ash calls to her just before she enters the classroom.

'Hey!'

Deanne turns.

'You okay?' he says.

Deanne's face grows contemplative. Then she nods. 'Yeah,' she says. A smile breaks out – she looks now like an amalgam of the nerd and the vamp. 'Thanks for what you did.'

Ash frowns.

'To Mickey and Lachlan,' Deanne says.

'It was nothing.'

'Thanks anyway.' Deanne heads into class.

The day tumbles onwards, and my attention turns to two things: seeing if Gabriella shows up (she doesn't) and avoiding Mr Baker so I don't have to personally hand over my identity essay.

Come the end of the day, I tell Ash to hang on, creep into the staffroom, and slip my one-sentence identity essay on Mr Baker's desk.

56

Saturday, I sleep in as much as I can so there's less day to face. I finally get up around eleven, have breakfast and shower, then go stand on the back veranda. It's a gorgeous day. Ash couldn't have written a better day for his birthday: clear skies, with this clean heat that's neither suffocating nor sweltering – perfect to sit by the pool and have a drink or two. I debate it: I can skip the Ativan and drink, or take the Ativan. It's a testament to my fear of what's lurking under the medication that I don't want to risk it, so I take the Ativan, and decide I'll bring an extra one with me, just in case.

After dressing in a pair of shorts, a t-shirt and sandals, I grab Ash's gift and walk to his place. Several cars are parked in the drive, including Riley's mum's car. I ring the doorbell; Ash answers it straight away, then leads me out back.

'Riley's mum's here?' I say.

'She's not the only one.'

We go out through the back door, where Ash's dad is handling the barbecue – one of those big outdoor grills, as well as a couple of the little round tabletop ones. Riley's mum, Ethan's mum (in these little shorts that are probably suited more to somebody like Kat, as well as a bikini top) and some bronzed-skin guy (who I think might be Jake Fichera's dad) set up tables with bread, rolls, salads, and drinks (but nothing alcoholic).

'Dad invited them to help,' Ash says.

'Where's your mum?'

'Working until tonight.'

'Oh, I almost forgot.' I shove my gift into Ash's hands.

He tears it open and stuffs the flask in his pocket. 'Thanks,' he says. 'This'll come in handy. Not going to be easy to drink with the oldies here.'

Ash's pool fills the backyard, a rectangle with bulbous ends and a Jacuzzi. Riley and Felicia lounge in the Jacuzzi, while Ethan and Jake sit at one end of the pool, feet dangling in the water. Ash's brothers are bouncing around in the water with a ball. Riley holds up his hand to acknowledge me. I wave back and sit on one of the banana lounges. Ash sits on the one next to me and sneaks drinks from his flask.

'Would be better beer weather,' he says.

'I'm not drinking. I figure I better take it easy after this week.'

Over the next hour, nearly everybody else shows up. Gabriella's stunning in a pink bikini but it's Kat who turns heads. She wears a string lime bikini that even has Ash's dad and Mr Fichera gaping at her and Mrs Seger and Mrs May shaking their heads. Kat dives into the water, knifing into it without a splash, then rears up in the middle of the pool, tossing her hair back.

The last person to show up is Deanne. She's wearing a filmy white shirt and denim cut-offs. She looks around, spots Ash and smiles. It's such a big, real smile that I think she must be coming through the stuff she's been dealing with.

'Happy birthday!" she says.

She kisses Ash on the cheek and hugs him.

'Help yourself to anything,' Ash says.

She finds a banana lounge and strips down to a yellow one-piece. Then she dives into the pool and splashes around with the other girls.

'She looks better,' Ash says with genuine delight.

'Yeah.'

I look around and realise who's missing. 'So…no Cindy?'

'Catching up with Cindy tonight,' Ash says.

'Kat during the day and Cindy at night? That's why this is an afternoon thing.'

Ash grins.

Food's served so I grab myself a plate, deciding on a couple of sausages and a steak. I go back to my banana lounge, missing the attention I was getting yesterday. It's not long before Samantha – picking at a salad – sits next to me.

'Feeling better?' she says.

'Yeah.'

We eat, but I can hear her mind ticking over, trying to find conversation starters.

'What happened with your stories?' she says. 'I thought you were going to let me read some.'

'I stopped writing.'

'Why?'

'I needed a break.'

'A break from what?' Ash says, plonking himself down on the lounge on the other side of me.

'My writing.'

'You're not writing?' Ash says.

'No.'

'Why not?'

'I thought I needed a break.'

'You're about to become a superstar with the Boland!'

I don't think so. But I recognise that's Mum and Dad talking.

'I'll see,' I say.

The afternoon goes on, everybody swimming or sunning themselves. Ash ends up in the jacuzzi with Kat, sitting close enough to her that I know, under the water, he has his hand on her leg. People leave me alone, probably because they think I'm still recovering, or it might be that I seem sullen and unapproachable. Then it occurs to me that it's me not making the effort. But the thought of engaging people fires off streamers of panic.

The parents clean up the remnants of lunch. Mr Fichera and Mrs Seger sit nearby and drink beers. I'd think Riley would be embarrassed to have his mum here, but he's oblivious of her. The heat grows until it's a bubble in the yard. I finger the Ativan inside my pocket, then get up and go inside.

I go to the bathroom but the door's locked. A familiar girl's voice hollers that it's occupied, so I walk down the hallway. I've been to Ash's so often, I know it as well as my own place and there's another bathroom as part of his parents' bedroom. But as I walk down the hallway, the sounds of stifled grunts slow me.

The bedroom door is slightly ajar. Mrs May lies face-down on the bed, complexion red, vein in her temple pulsing and her hands knotted into the covers. Pillows under her crotch prop up her butt. The hands that claw into her waist are tanned and worn. The flesh of her butt bounces as a set of tanned hips, the looseness of the stomach just beginning to hang low, thrust into her. There's no rhythm; it's a hard thrust in, then a slow withdrawal, then a hard thrust in – the way a bowstring might be pulled back to fire an arrow. Now I glimpse the man: Ash's father – of course it would be. His face is sweaty, jaw clenched.

I rush down the hallway and stop at the screen door as the sun flashes into my eyes. A toilet flushes and another door opens.

'Hey.'

It's Gabriella. This would be a fantasy for any guy my age. And just from a physical point of view, she's stunning, but she's been in the toilet and I imagine I can smell that on her. I tell myself that's stupid, that I can't smell anything. I don't even know what she was doing in there.

'You okay?' Gabriella says. She rests a hand on my arm. She's nice and warm.

'Yeah,' I say.

She waits, expecting me to say something – there's so much I could say to her, like why I deserted her that night, why I haven't chased her up, why I've been so fucking weird. It's not just Ash. Others are noticing, aren't they? That's why I'm alone here.

'You coming out?' Gabriella says, already heading for the door.

'In a minute.'

She nods and goes out and I use the toilet, dreading I'm going to smell something that I'll forever associate with Gabriella, but there's nothing. I flush, wash my hands and duck into the kitchen. I berate myself for letting her go like that.

In the kitchen, I pour a glass of water, take my Ativan and stare out the window. Everybody's having such a good time. Their laughter and cheers as Ethan bombs into the pool are a language I can no longer understand.

One certainty wells up inside me.

I don't belong here.

57

It's hard going back out there, seeing Ash in the Jacuzzi with Kat, Ethan in the pool splashing Rachel, while their parents are inside doing what they're doing.

I sit on the banana lounge, thinking I should make an excuse and leave. Ash told me I didn't have to come if I was sick. He'd understand. And I convince myself that this is justifiable. But it's not long before the Ativan breathes its magic and there's only that peacefulness again.

Deanne climbs out of the pool and stands over me. 'Why don't you come in?'

'I will in a bit,' I say.

She sits on the banana lounge next to me and throws her wet hair over her head. 'Did I congratulate you for getting shortlisted for the Boland?'

I think about it but can't remember – there were so many people that day, although I'd sound arrogant if I said that.

'I don't think I did,' she says. 'I was going through some stuff.'

'The rumours,' I say. 'I'm sorry you had to go through that shit.'

'It doesn't matter,' Deanne says, with astonishing

resolve. 'It's done. People aren't still talking about it, are they?'

'No.'

'It ruined my chances with the Boland,' Deanne says. 'I set myself to win it. I knew exactly what I had to do, who I'd ask for as a mentor and what I'd do with the money. But then those rumours went around and I couldn't focus.'

'I know what that's like.'

'I missed four assignments – got two Ds and two Fs. My parents were *so* disappointed. They said I was too interested in being popular. But until the rumours, I was doing all my work.'

That sadness creeps back into Deanne's face and I wonder if her newfound happiness is a mask. She jumps to her feet, spins and dives into the pool, splashing Gabriella, Ethan and a group of others.

Gabriella waves at me. 'Come in!' she says.

I strip off my t-shirt and jump into the water. It's cold and startling. There's lots of splashing, lots of laughing, but now the Ativan works against me. It's not doing anything wrong. It's doing exactly what it's meant to be doing. But it's unnatural to be *so* calm – not when everybody's so alive.

Gabriella jumps on my back and tries to dunk me. I feel her breasts push against me, her naked skin on my own. Her legs wrap around my hips. Then I tumble into the water and gasp for breath. She floats off me and I come back to the surface, shaking the water from my eyes.

Mrs May comes out the back door, maybe looking no different to before, but I imagine seeing the lilt in her walk, and that her hair's been dishevelled and patted into place. She sits at the table with Mrs Seger and Mr Fichera. Mr

Fichera passes her a beer and she takes a long drink, a satisfied look on her face.

Mr Handley comes out the back door. He swaggers up to the table, grabs his own beer and drinks. He and Mrs May exchange a look. It probably means nothing else to anybody, but I see the slyness in it, the secret they share, and their enjoyment that it is *their* secret.

'Want to go into the jacuzzi?' Gabriella says.

'Sorry?' I blink at her.

'The jacuzzi?'

'Sure.'

Riley and Felicia haven't budged from the jacuzzi, Felicia's long legs draped over Riley's lap. Ash and Kat sit opposite them, close together, but relaxed, Ash's arm behind her on the rim of the jacuzzi but also curled around her back.

'How're you feeling?' Riley says. It's the first words he's spoken to me the whole afternoon.

'Good.'

There's a sense of everything clicking into place, like everything that has been wrong this year realigns and now things are complete – Riley with Felicia, Ash with Kat, me with Gabriella. We could go out together, hang out, triple date or whatever.

'You finish that identity essay?' Gabriella says.

I open my mouth to lie, because I've become so good at lying and that's when everything breaks apart again.

'I nailed that fucking thing,' Riley says. 'Wrote about how I always felt I had a greater purpose, that I was tied to the service of my country and protection of my family and friends – shit mostly but that fag Baker will lap it up.'

'Mr Baker's okay,' Gabriella says.

'They shouldn't let fags like him teach. I'm young and impressionable.'

'You're probably a worse influence on him.'

Felicia kisses his cheek. 'You got that right.'

Others jump into the jacuzzi until it gets overcrowded and Mr Handley hovers over us with a camera and embarrasses Ash by taking pictures.

'Dad, easy,' Ash says.

'This is forever.'

Mr Handley keeps snapping away until Ash gets out of the jacuzzi and flops onto a banana lounge. That's the trigger for other kids to climb out of the jacuzzi. Most of them jump back into the pool but I get out and sit next to Ash.

'You all right?' I say.

'Yeah. Just embarrassing.'

'That's what parents are for.'

'If I ever have kids, I'm never embarrassing them.'

Around seven, people start leaving, at first just one here and there, but then in clumps. Kat gives Ash a kiss full on the lips before she goes; Samantha and her friends go, but not before she gives me a sidelong glance; then Gabriella; Mrs May, Ethan, and a whole group go together; and the same happens when Mr Fichera and Jake go. Finally, it's me, Riley and Felicia, although Riley's mum stands up and jingles her keys.

Crickets chirp as evening takes hold, the warmth of the day dwindling into a peculiar melancholy, like everything's saying goodbye.

'You want a lift home?' Mrs Seger asks Riley. She arches

her brows at Mr Handley. '*Home*. For another couple of weeks at least. Then it's a two-bedroom flat, until this one joins the Navy.'

'Separation isn't easy,' Mr Handley says. 'You on civil terms with your husband?'

'He's trying to be. I'm still finding it a little hard. It's not every day your husband leaves you for another man.'

Everything becomes quiet – Ash is in the process of having a drink, but the can stops halfway to his mouth; Felicia's pulling her shorts up over her leg, but she stops mid-thigh; Mr Handley is setting down his beer on the table, but then holds it aloft. Just the crickets now, much too loud – almost like they're jeering.

Riley's eyes flash angrily. 'Mum!'

Now, even the crickets shut up. Ash looks at me, like he's thinking of saying something stupid to try break the tension. Felicia giggles.

Riley glowers at her, then pulls on his t-shirt and storms out. Ash is up first, and then I follow. We catch Riley just as he's banged open the front door.

'Don't worry about it,' Ash says.

'Don't worry about it? *Don't worry about it?*' Riley says. 'My dad's a fag. He's been seeing this other guy for five years on the side.'

'Is it Mr Baker?' Ash says.

'That's not funny! None of this is fucking funny!'

'Easy – just trying to cheer you up,' Ash says, although I'm not sure that's entirely true. I think with the way we've grown apart, Ash enjoyed sticking it to Riley – at least a little.

'I saw them once, you know?' Riley's voice almost

breaks. 'Start of the year. I saw them leaving a café. They hugged each other. I asked Dad about it. He told me the guy was an old school friend he hadn't seen in years. But I *knew*.'

I wonder if that's why Riley's been so antagonistic towards Mr Baker, and why he's constantly trying to prove himself by having sex with Felicia.

'So what if he's gay?' I say.

Riley tosses his head back and sighs, like I don't get it at all.

Felicia totters out, arms held wide. 'I'm sorry.'

She hugs Riley, although I don't know if she's sorry about his dad or about chuckling. Her face is turned to us when she rests it on Riley's shoulder, and her lips are curled up, like she's still trying to contain herself.

Mrs Seger comes out. 'Come on, you two.' She looks at me. 'Do you want a lift home?'

'I'll walk. Thanks.'

So that's what I do, enjoying the coolness of the evening and that I've been able to have a day out with friends, that I've done it without drinking.

When I get home, I see Mum lying on the couch, Dad lounging on his chair with his legs over the armrest and think maybe they're not so bad.

58.

Monday, I get up but don't go to school because I don't want to face everybody from Ash's party, everybody happy, going on with their lives, oblivious and hopeful. All that's now foreign. I'm also not sure what to say to Ash about his dad – do I tell him or not?

Ash calls Monday after school to see how I am. 'What's going on?' he says. 'You sick again?'

'Didn't feel great today,' I say.

'You coming tomorrow?'

'Probably.'

Silence. He can tell I don't want to talk.

'Don't forget the Boland's announced Wednesday,' he says.

It's the one spark that remains, although now that it's so close, I worry about the attention that comes with it. The announcement itself is nothing major – the candidates are called into the principal's office and told if they won or not. But then, for the winner, there are interviews with the local paper, a presentation by the council, photos – I remember it all from when Steph won it. That makes me think about when I was shortlisted and how everybody congratulated me. That made me feel good. I hang onto that.

The nightly antidepressant brings almost no side effects

and when I sleep, I sleep soundly, although I'm awake by 6.00. I go through my morning routine and meet Ash at the corner.

'Feeling better today?' he asks.

'Yeah. I guess. How'd you go Saturday night with Cindy?'

'Cindy's nice, but I don't want a girlfriend. She's gonna be serious. Last thing I want to do is end up like Riley and Felicia. And I think I can nail Kat.'

'That's classy.'

'I'm being honest.'

'Maybe Kat wants a boyfriend too. She had that other prat of a boyfriend long enough.'

'Yeah. That's true.'

We don't say much more until we get to the bank by the bridge, where we sit and light up cigarettes.

'How're things with your parents?' I say.

Ash turns sharply. 'Why?'

'Curious.'

'Curious?'

'I was just asking.'

'You saw something, didn't you?'

'Like what?'

'You were weird at my birthday. You've been weird a lot lately. But you went even weirder at one point. Gabriella asked me what was with you – said she saw you inside, like you didn't know you were in there. What did you see? Or hear?'

'Really–'

'You know, the three of us have drifted apart this year. With Riley, it's because of *who* he's becoming. With you…'

Ash shrugs. 'I know there's something you haven't been telling me. I'm not an idiot. So don't treat me like an idiot over this.'

'Your dad and Mrs May were having sex.'

Ash takes a deep breath and lets it out in a slow sigh.

'You're not shocked?'

'She's not the first. Fuck. I've never seen anything. But, sometimes, I'll come home and some woman will be there.'

'Who?'

'It's not always the same one. He'll say they're over to borrow something. Or to help him with something – with his tax, with his accounting, whatever. With his cock, more likely.'

'Does your mum know?'

'She knows he cheats. Then they'll fight. That's one of the reasons *why* they fight – well, there's lots of reasons, like his drinking and shit, but that's the *big* reason they fight. He'll promise not to do it again. He holds out for a while. Then it's the same shit. I think Mum stays with him for Tom because he's still so little.' Ash sniffs, then runs his wrist across his nose. 'It's not gonna last.' His voice breaks. 'What's the point of staying in shit? I don't get it.' He picks at the grass on the bank. 'What if I turn out like him?' he says suddenly.

'Why would you turn out like him?'

'Maybe I'm him already, the way I've been going – Rachel to Deanne to Cindy and Kat. Maybe I'll hit women like he does.'

He told me he saw his dad slap his mum – but that was when Ash was eight. The way he talks now, it must've happened again. Is that why he's so protective of girls like Deanne? It shows he *is* different.

'Look at the way you stood up for Deanne,' I say. 'You're not your dad.'

He drags his knees to his chest, his shoulders sunken, looking small, and I can see he's shaking – not a lot, but enough for me to notice it. Who knows the stuff he doesn't tell me and for the same reason I haven't told him about my stuff. Nobody wants to confess their vulnerabilities. Everybody just looks at it as being weak.

'You've got a choice, haven't you?' I say. 'You don't have to be like him.'

'But maybe it's nature. Maybe that's all there is to it.'

I think of Mum telling me how she got down and anxious after giving birth to Steph. Is *this* nature but evolved into something else for me?

Ash shoots to his feet.

'You all right?' I ask, getting up behind him.

'We're gonna be late,' he says.

He starts for school but what he's said makes me think whether there really is a choice in anything, or if things go the way they're meant to be.

59

When we get to the courtyard, we see Rachel and some of the other girls crying. Riley – instead of being in the toilets – is sitting on a bench holding Felicia. He waves us over.

'What's going on?' Ash says.

'It's going around that Deanne killed herself,' Riley says.

'What?' I almost bark it out.

Ash sinks onto the bench.

'Is it a rumour or is it for real?' I ask.

'Helen Rusevski–' Felicia says.

'Who?' Ash asks.

'She's a couple of years below us – she plays with my sister,' Felicia says. 'Anyway, Helen lives across the street from Deanne. Helen said an ambulance came yesterday evening. They carried Deanne out on a stretcher. There was blood everywhere and her wrists were bandaged up.'

'But was she…?' I can't finish the sentence.

'Helen said Deanne was all white and her eyes were closed…'

I see Deanne like I'm floating above her: she lays naked in the tub, the water bloody, her wrists poised on the rim and bleeding, her face going from pained to restful as her life ebbs away.

'Did she leave a note or something?' I say.

Riley shrugs. Felicia's crying too much to answer.

'I was talking to her at Ash's – she was telling me how those rumours screwed her with the Boland because she couldn't concentrate on her work.'

'It's a fucking nothing prize,' Riley says. 'Who cares? You're gonna fucking kill yourself over that shit?' Then, as if realising what he's said, he looks at me and adds, 'No offense. Just why would you kill yourself over that?'

The bell rings, so we mill into our classes and sit down. We have Legal Studies first up but there's no sign of Mrs Grady. Usually, when a teacher isn't around everybody would chatter. A lot of the girls are still crying – even Mickey is misty-eyed.

Mrs Grady comes in, striding with purpose to the front of the class. She takes a deep breath and places her hands on her hips.

'There's a story going around that Deanne Vega has taken her own life,' Mrs Grady says. 'Deanne *did* attempt to take her own life but her parents found her in time. She's in a stable condition and expected to make a full recovery.'

Lots of people break out into relieved smiles. But all I can think about is Mrs Grady's words: *Full recovery*. Something drove Deanne to this. Maybe it wasn't missing out on the Boland. It might've been a collection of things. While she might make a full *physical* recovery, who knows if they can fix the stuff going on in her head?

'I'm sure a lot of you are friends with Deanne,' Mrs Grady says, 'and you might want to visit her or call her but for the time being, let's give her family a bit of space. However, if anybody would like to talk further about this, feel free to talk to any of us, or make an appointment with Counsellor Hoffs.'

First period is scattered. It's great Deanne's alive, but she still tried to take her own life – that's not easy to digest. My mind goes back to Aunt Mena's funeral. At this age, who even thinks about death? Besides me? Me, Ash, Riley never talk about it, unless it's in some stupid, whimsical way, like when Riley said if he died before us, he'd come back to visit us.

Mr McCready is philosophical about it in second period Social Studies, and he puts the whole class aside to talk about what could motivate somebody to attempt to take their own life.

'We all have bad times in life,' he says. 'That's guaranteed. When these…' His eyes dart up to the ceiling as he searches for a word. 'When these *shit* feelings linger, they can develop into depression. This isn't just feeling sad. This isn't feeling down for a little bit. This is a prolonged melancholy. Has anybody ever felt like that?'

He searches the room. Nobody moves – it's like everybody freezes so it's not even mistaken that they might've experienced something like that.

'It's nothing to be ashamed of,' Mr McCready says.

Still, nobody moves. My face is on fire. I'm sure people can see it in me. A small part of me wants to throw up both hands. But I can only imagine what people would say and think. That's my mum talking. It's also high school – just like the rumours about Deanne. Even though they weren't true, even though Ash tried to stop them, they kept going. And growing.

'Deanne seemed happy,' Ash says.

Every set of eyes falls on Ash.

'I had my birthday on Saturday,' Ash says. 'Deanne was there. She seemed happy, didn't she?'

'Yeah,' I say. 'Happier than I'd seen her for a while.'

'Sometimes when people decide they're going to take their lives, their mood changes,' Mr McCready says. 'Making that decision takes the pressure off them. They feel like they no longer have to keep battling.' He sighs. 'My uncle took his own life ten years ago. So, I can speak from experience. Just know, help's available if you need it.'

By third period, everybody is talked out. At lunch time, Gabriella shows up with a big novelty *Thinking of You* card. She brings it up to where Ash and me sit on the bench and hands it to us, along with a black marker.

'I thought this would be good,' Gabriella says.

Ash opens the card – a lot of the kids have already signed it. Most of them have left inane stuff, like, *Get well soon,* and then signed their names. Riley and Felicia have signed it together: *Stay tough!* I want to scribble it out. Several of the girls, like Rachel and Kat, have left sweeter messages: *If you ever need to talk, call me!* and, *You're stronger than you think.*

It's a nice sentiment, but cheap, like it's a quick and easy way for everybody to get closure on what happened. Now it's all wrapped up and everybody can move on. How true will any of these people stay to what they've written? I bet it's only a handful.

You're a fighter!!! Ash writes. *Keep fighting!!!!!*

He hands me the marker. I have no idea what to write. I try to think about what I would like somebody to write to me, and finally scribble in my awful left hand, *You're not alone!* I hope the message has the double meaning, that Deanne understands that there's somebody else like her out there and that anybody else will think it's a message of community.

By the end of the school day, nearly everybody's processed what's happened. Deanne's okay. That's what people hold onto, rather than explore *what* drove her to try what she did. Nobody wants to get into the ugliness because it's not a comfortable place to be. Only Ash stays pensive.

He doesn't talk much on the way home. When we get to the corner where we separate, he stops and thrusts his hand out. I frown.

'Good luck with the Boland tomorrow,' he says.

'Oh.' I shake his hand. 'Thanks.'

He walks off, takes maybe five paces, then stops. 'Hey?'

I look at him.

'Don't worry about what Riley said about the Boland – you know, about it not mattering. You know Riley.'

'Yeah. *Yeah.*'

I go home and feel some apprehension, although I'm unsure what it's from. Is it the Boland? Given everything that's gone on, I can't believe I've made it this far. But here I am – a chance to win it. I see everybody thrilled – they'd be the opposite of the way they felt about what happened with Deanne.

I open my drawer and take out an Ativan, dry swallowing it. Mr McCready said there's help available if it's needed, but I've done nothing but get help this year to try and find a way to deal with this. I've had my good periods, but it's deprived me of things like focusing on my schoolwork, writing, having fun, and even doing something romantically with Gabriella.

I wonder about the treatment Deanne will get. Will they give her pills? Will they keep her in hospital? Who will be her doctors? Will they do anything? You can have a busted television or something that's beyond fixing. Is that the same with people? All these thoughts make me dizzy. I lie on my bed and stare up at the ceiling, thinking this is the position that Aunt Mena will lie in forever.

Here one day, gone the next.

That's when I recognise what scares me: it's Deanne's attempt at taking her own life. I don't know what pushed her, but that doesn't even seem important now. At one stage, she was battling through life. And then, she'd decided the battle was done.

Is it that simple?

Is it that easy?

Or is it automatic and something that you become a party to?

60

I wake earlier than usual, nervously excited about the Boland being announced. It's nice to be worried about *something*.

While I'm in the kitchen making breakfast, the phone rings – Steph. 'Good luck today!' she tells me.

'Thanks.'

'Just remember, it's not the be-all end-all.'

I thank her, hang up and race through breakfast, imagining my name being called, imagining what I would say and imagining everybody loving it. It's all absurd fantasy. I'd never be so relaxed.

Ash is already waiting at the corner when I walk up. 'Nervous?' he asks.

'Always,' I say.

We walk to school, stopping at the bridge as usual. He offers me a cigarette, but I don't take one. We sit there while he smokes, then head into the school. Everything that's happened with Deanne is forgotten. Gabriella's friends gather around her, buzzing excitedly, while Ethan and his friends casually kick a football around the courtyard. The thought that darts into my mind now is that none of us might win – it might be some kid from another school.

The bell goes and we file into Maths when the intercom

blares over the loudspeakers, calling Gabriella, Ethan and me to the principal's office.

We make the trip together. Counsellor Hoffs waits for us by the principal's door and ushers us in to where three chairs are waiting. She comes in, closes the door and stands behind us.

Principal Vance is a short man with a short moustache and although he's always smiling, you get the feeling it's a face he puts on for his students. His office is immaculate, with a big mahogany desk, his degrees on the wall and a bookshelf behind him that's home to expensive model aeroplanes.

'I'm sure the three of you are nervous,' he says, 'and I don't want to drag this on any longer than it has to be. The winner of the Boland Fellowship is from our school.'

I tense up.

'Two of you are going to be disappointed,' Counsellor Hoffs pipes in from behind us. She comes around to sit on the corner of the principal's desk. 'But keep in mind that it's an honour to have gotten this far.'

'Yes,' Principal Vance says, but I can hear in his tone he doesn't believe that. 'Congratulations, Gabriella.'

Gabriella shrieks, leaps to her feet and lifts her hands to her mouth. My mouth drops open. Ethan – to his credit – is immediately up and hugs Gabriella.

'Congratulations, Gabriella!' he says. 'You deserve it.'

I get up and hug Gabriella, too. 'Congratulations,' I say, with none of the enthusiasm of Ethan. I *do* feel it – I'm happy for Gabriella. But it's hard to be happy and disappointed at the same time, especially given the way I was relying on winning this. So, I say it again: 'Congratulations!'

'The Boland Fellowship essay this year was an assignment from social studies,' Principal Vance says. 'The question was how we can improve the world. The Fellowship committee loved your essay, Gabriella.'

Principal Vance and Counsellor Hoffs congratulate Gabriella and tell her she'll be awarded her certificate and prize money in the new year and the local paper will set-up a date to interview her. Ethan and me mill around like it hasn't suddenly become awkward for us to exist in this room.

When they finally dismiss us, we march back to class as Principal Vance announces over the intercom Gabriella's win. Everybody applauds Gabriella when we return to the classroom. Her friends get up and hug her. Ethan and me sidle away to our own chairs.

Ash leans over to me. 'Bad luck,' he says, clapping me on the back.

I don't want it to, and I don't mean it to, but the loss obliterates whatever resistance I've had to everything going on. The edginess and sadness flood in. I tell myself it's okay, it's okay, it's okay, this isn't the end of everything – as Deanne must've looked at it – and as Counsellor Hoffs said, it's great to get this far. I smile and try to stay upbeat over the next two periods, but it's just the latest face I put on.

'Fuck it,' Riley says at lunchtime, when we're sitting on the slope of the aqueduct, smoking. 'Like I said, it's *nothing*.'

'It would've been nice to win,' Ash says.

'We're dealing with reality, right?' Riley says.

'You don't have to be a prick about it,' Ash says.

'Like I keep telling you, it's a stupid prize designed to make us work harder.'

'If it means nothing to you, why'd you put so much effort into your Legal Studies essay?'

'You two ran around like you were special when you got on the longlist.'

'We did not,' Ash says.

'Sure – I saw it. I was nobody, right? Just your dumb friend.'

'Neither of us ever thought that,' I say.

'Be honest.'

'I've thought sometimes you don't try.'

'I don't try. I'm dumb. *Whatever*.'

I want to point out that those are two different things, but he doesn't give me a chance to get a word in.

'I wanted to show you both, I could've been up there with you,' he says. 'You didn't have to look down on me. But I didn't put in the effort because it's bullshit. I'm smart enough to know that. You two weren't.'

'Well, you've got everything worked out, right?' Ash says. 'Navy next year.'

'Yeah.' Riley flicks his cigarette into the creek and gets up. 'Maybe you two should learn from me.'

I focused on the Boland to get through this. But now with it done, all that remains is a yawning emptiness that welcomes me with a sense of hopelessness. During fourth period Art class, all I can think about is what comes next. No school, no homework, no writing, just me and Mum and Dad at home. What do I work toward?

In fifth-period English, Mr Baker hands back our identity essays. When he gets to our back row, I feel that familiar shortness of breath. He hands Ash his back (with a B+), and then Riley's (with a B), but he gives me nothing more than a glance. Then he returns to his desk and talks about how pleased he was with the quality of the essays. When the bell goes, I get up to join everybody as they tumble out the door, and I think I'm free, but he calls my name.

'I'd like to speak to you,' he says.

He gestures me to my seat, closes the door and grabs something from his desk – my essay. Of course, my essay. He lays it down in front of me, then leans on the backrest of a chair in the next row of tables.

'Would you like to explain this?'

I stare down at that single sentence: *I don't know who I am*. Then I look up at him. Shrug. 'I tried to do this, I tried to work out something good, and then…' I shrug again.

Mr Baker crosses his legs. 'The faculty has noticed you've been quieter lately. You're often ducking out to the toilets and the quality of your schoolwork has become spasmodic. Something obviously is affecting you and given what happened with Deanne, we're concerned. Do you want to talk?'

'I just…I…'

If this was another teacher, I might hold on. But I've always liked Mr Baker. His classes are never boring and I know he likes the creative side of my work. He's always been encouraging. And because it's Mr Baker, this is when whatever restraint has held everything back breaks under the weight of carrying this for so long.

I ramble about the early symptoms, about seeing all these different doctors, about going to the hospital and now about taking pills – it's a rough account. I don't go into all the details because I'm scared he'll think I'm crazy. My eyes grow teary and I keep wiping at them with my wrist. Several times my voice chokes up.

'It's okay,' Mr Baker tells me.

'It doesn't feel okay.'

'I've been on medication for anxiety – several times.'

'Really?'

'There were days I didn't want to get out of bed, let alone face the world. I had strange thoughts – bizarre thoughts. I think everybody does. We just attach greater attention to them because we become so hyper-analytical and that scares us. I don't want to downplay what you're going through, but things *do* get better. You need to believe in that. Medication and counselling helped me find balance. You *will* see it. Trust me.'

'Thanks.'

Mr Baker straightens up in his chair and smiles. 'Do you want me to call somebody? Counsellor Hoffs? Your parents? A friend?'

'I'm all right.'

'Are you sure?'

I nod.

Mr Baker taps my essay. 'Don't worry about this. In a way, it's brilliant. You have a lot of potential. That's probably not something you want to hear. But I see it in your work, particularly in your creative work.'

I brush the sleeve of my t-shirt across my eyes, thank him, and leave the room.

61.

On Thursday after school, I catch the train to the Western Hospital. The hospital is quiet with the holidays so close, like even sickness and injury have decided to take a break. There's nobody in the waiting room, so when Dr Dimmock's door opens and his patient leaves, I'm immediately up and on my way in.

'How're you feeling?' he asks, once the door is closed and we're seated. 'Any more anxiety or panic attacks?'

'No, they've settled.'

'Excellent.' Dr Dimmock opens my file and scribbles in it. 'And side-effects from the medication?'

I tell him about the start-up symptoms but how they've disappeared. He nods and smiles and writes down his indecipherable notes.

'You'll find you'll be able to lessen the dosage of the Ativan. Instead of taking three a day, try taking them only as necessary – but only ever as much as three a day.'

'I still feel…weird.'

'Weird how?'

'Flat. Very down.'

'Long-standing anxiety can develop into depression. We could look at increasing the Sinequan. However, I'd

342

prefer we get you settled on this dose. You appear much more stable.'

'I guess.'

'What else are you thinking? Is there anything else you want to talk about?'

'I want to be better than this.'

'This is a healing process. If you'd broken an arm or a leg, you wouldn't heal instantaneously. It takes time and rehabilitation. But we're on the right track. I want you to make an appointment for a month's time.'

'A month?'

'I won't be here over Christmas and in the week leading to New Year and I'll be away the first two weeks of next year.'

'A month?' I say again.

Dr Dimmock nods and takes out his prescription pad. 'I'll be sure to leave you with enough medication.' He tears out the prescription sheet and gives it to me. 'I think we'll find that by then you'll be on top of this.'

I march numbly from his office, but then the anger surges. I have no control of what's going on inside my head, but I'm meant to put it on hold to accommodate Dr Dimmock's schedule? I don't care that it's Christmas or New Year. I don't care that he thinks I'll be on top of it. I mean nothing to him. I'm a file. That's it.

Screw the appointment. I don't make it at the reception. And I don't worry about getting the prescription, although I do shove the prescription itself into my pocket. I can get it at any chemist. But I don't want to need it. I don't want this anymore.

I walk to the station and as the train approaches, I

get up from the bench where I'm sitting. I could jump in front of the train right now – hit the tracks just as the train arrives. Even slowing down to make the stop at the station, it's still going fast enough to squash me. And that'd be it. No more of this.

The train pulls up and I get on but the thought stays with me and others jump in. I should panic, the way I did when things didn't seem real, but now there's only resignation, and I wonder if that's it, if that's how easy you slip from self-preservation to ambivalence. I should go straight back to the hospital to tell Dr Dimmock this is what I'm thinking.

But I stay on the train and then hurry home. Mum and Dad don't ask me how I went, like there's a bandage that's been put on the wound and it's best left alone. But after a wordless dinner, Steph calls and asks for me.

'How did you go?' she asks.

'With my appointment?'

'With the Boland!'

'Oh. I didn't win.'

Steph's quiet, absorbing that. 'Remember what I told you,' she says finally, her tone even. 'The important thing I drew from it was proving I could commit to something. It didn't help me identify what I wanted to do. You *know* what you want to do. Right?'

Only I don't know if she says 'right' or 'write'. But neither matters now given I'm not writing.

'You okay?' Steph asks.

'Yeah.'

'Sure?'

'Yep.'

'Okay, what about your appointment?'

'He's happy with the way I'm responding to the pills. He wants me to take the Ativan less, if I can.'

'That's good. What about you? Are you feeling all right?'

I don't want to panic her. Telling Ash would be embarrassing, but telling Steph means that she'll worry about me and I don't want her to worry about me. I don't want to be that burden anymore.

'I think the antidepressants are still taking effect,' I say.

'Dr Dimmock did say it would be about four weeks before you really felt the benefit of the antidepressants.'

'I know.'

'We're coming over Sunday for lunch – Olivia was wondering if you want your hair cut?'

'Sure.'

'Okay. See you Sunday.'

The next day is the last day of school and at lunch, Riley suggests we go to the aqueduct one last time, so he, Ash, and I sit there smoking, although it doesn't feel like it used to.

'So, what happens with you and Felicia while you're in the Navy?' Ash says.

'I'll get leave. It's not prison.'

'And she's gonna wait around for you? You know, you're sixteen.'

'So?'

'So…it used to be all about how you were trying to fuck her, now it's like you're an old married couple. Have you had sex?'

'Look–'

'Have you?'

'No. But I will. Before the year's out.'

'You've been saying the same thing so long...'

Riley grins. 'We'll see, okay?'

'It's not even that important,' Ash says.

'I don't need you to make excuses for me.'

'They're not excuses – I'm just saying.'

'New Year's, okay? *New Year's.*'

I wish my life could be as petty as obsessing about fucking somebody.

62.

On Sunday, Steph, and Olivia come over, Olivia with her hairstylist kit. After lunch, she takes me down into the garage, sits me on a chair and covers me in the cape, then cuts my hair.

'How's your writing going?' she asks. 'I hope you don't mind – your sister showed me some of your stories.'

This is something else that keeps happening – writing keeps hitting me at a time I'm not meant to be writing. I grunt noncommittally.

'I read a lot of fantasy and stuff,' Olivia goes on. 'I really enjoyed yours.'

Flattery's always pleasing but right now, it only makes me yearn for something I'm not meant to have.

'I'm taking a break from it,' I say.

'Why?'

'The doctor told me to.'

'Why?'

'He doesn't think it's good for me.'

'I don't think it's good for you to not be doing something you enjoy – you do enjoy it, don't you?'

'Yeah.'

At night, I lie on my bed and flick through the blank pages of my leather journal. If I wrote again, what would happen? But it seems so pointless – not because of what Dr Dimmock said. I'm putting less faith in Dr Dimmock given the way our appointments have unfolded. It's just the way of everything.

So, I mope around the house, play some pool when I can force myself to do it, and take my long walks. I don't speak to Riley and only speak to Ash every now and again; he's now busy juggling Cindy and Kat. I whittle away the Ativan and get the occasional shortness of breath or muscle cramps, but nothing worse comes of it.

A lot of the time I think of Deanne and wonder what her thoughts were after she cut her wrists. Did she regret what she'd done? Did she call out to her parents? Is that how they found her? Or, as the life ebbed from her, did she welcome the darkness, knowing she wouldn't have to keep dealing with everything? If that's the case, how does she feel now she's still alive? Is she caught in some endless loop of being neither alive nor dead? That scares me most of all, that you can be trapped in your own personal hell.

For Christmas, Mum and Dad have a barbecue and have Steph and Olivia over. I think Mum suspects there's something more between them because they're so often together, but she says nothing and Steph doesn't push it. Once lunch is done, Steph and Olivia go next door for dinner and all we hear for the rest of the afternoon is laughter and fun.

We go into the final week of the year and there's that sense of anticipation and excitement. One year is ending – not just a year, but a decade. Surely that should signal something better. Surely.

Ash calls me on the Friday before New Year's and

says Riley's suggested they go down to the shops to buy something to drink for the party. I meet Ash at the corner and then we walk to Riley's place. He meets us outside, smoking.

'This is it.' Riley claps his hands together. 'The last hurrah. We're moving into Mum's new place first week of the New Year.'

We talk about little stuff – Ash about Kat and Cindy, Riley about Felicia, about school and what it'll be like next year without Riley. It feels good to make that small talk that's always come so effortlessly to us and captures the way we used to be before *this*.

'So, what're we getting?' Riley says when we get to the liquor store.

'Scotch is good,' Ash says.

Riley looks at me.

'Nothing.'

'What do you mean nothing?' Riley says.

'I'm not drinking.'

'So, you don't want nothing?'

'No thanks.'

Riley tugs on Ash's sleeve and goes into the liquor store. They come out a few minutes later with two bottles of scotch and a bottle of gin. We then go down to the supermarket, buy some big bottles of Coke, Riley gets some little ones and then he buys – with a great show to make sure Ash and me see it – a box of condoms.

'Just preparing,' he says.

We walk back and detour to the creek so we can sit on the aqueduct. Riley takes out three of the little bottles of Coke and pours a bit out from two of them. I stop him when he goes for the third.

'Okay, what the fuck's going on?' he says.

'What do you mean?'

'Not drinking at Ash's birthday, all those days off school, all those times you run off to the toilet during class, or to the library during the breaks.'

I look to Ash. He holds his hands up.

'I haven't said anything,' he says.

'I'm not fucking stupid,' Riley says. 'Just about everybody knows there's something happening. Felicia's noticed it and she's an idiot. So…what? You know about my dad. We're friends, aren't we?'

I can hear Ash's head ticking over because he'd want to explode about the way Riley selectively chooses when we're friends and when we're not. And it's not like he told us about his dad. We found that out by accident. But I tell them now; I tell them all of it. It comes out emotionless – not because it needs to, not because I want to share but because I don't care. Ash absorbs it all and his face doesn't change. Riley gapes.

'I'm sorry,' he says.

'He's not dead,' Ash says. 'You should've told us.'

'I was embarrassed. You keep things to yourself.' I turn to Riley. 'So, do you. It's the way things are.'

They drink quietly and we smoke until Riley says he's going to have to meet Felicia, so we walk him home and leave everything with him.

'Try to cheer up,' he tells me, before he goes inside.

I'm not sure what to say to that.

'Don't worry about him,' Ash says on the walk home. 'You don't…you don't feel like Deanne did, do you?'

'Sometimes. Sometimes I think about what she must've been thinking.'

'So do I. I think about it a lot – like the week before she tried, I asked her at school if she was okay. She said she was. And that seemed enough. But maybe I should've talked privately with her.'

'She might've seemed okay if you did.'

'She might've.' Ash takes a deep breath. 'You know, I get like that sometimes – down, dark, you know…?'

'Really?'

'Not as bad as you've been having it, but sometimes I get really down. I think it's, you know, watching my mum and dad. Hey, you want to talk to my mum?'

'What for?'

'She's a psychiatric nurse. She'll know stuff. I don't like this Dr Dimmock. You're saying he doesn't do much when you see him, then he loads you up with pills, then he tells you to stop writing, then, what? He's away for holidays? Fuck me.'

Ash's mum is in the kitchen, preparing dinner. His brothers are in the lounge screaming and playing. Ash tells his mum what I've told him and she listens initially while cutting and seasoning steaks, but then puts it aside and sits me down at the kitchen table and sends Ash out with the instruction to keep his brothers out of here while she talks to me.

She takes my hands and looks at me with big grey eyes that I can only imagine have seen so much stuff in her job.

'Some of these doctors, they're very reliant on

medication as their primary treatment,' she tells me. 'They throw pills at you. And if they don't work, they throw others at you.'

'So, I should stop them?'

'It's not that, because they have their place. But I want you to understand what you're going through. Everything you've told me – and I mean *everything* – is common to anxiety disorders. You don't feel like things *aren't* real because you enjoy writing; you feel it because it's a depersonalisation common to anxiety. Fears of going crazy – that's common. Same with these other thoughts. I know this is horrible but don't brood alone thinking you're going to end up in a psych ward. It doesn't happen – at least not the way that you're fearing."

'I just feel so broken,' I say. 'Like… *why*…?'

My voice wavers. She clenches my hands and smiles.

'A lot of people think you can only become anxious or depressed if something big happens in your life, or you have so much going on that it overwhelms you.'

I nod.

'Sometimes this just happens. It's no different to, say, becoming diabetic. We don't question it. It just happens. There's nothing wrong with you. It's life. We do the best with what we're given – that's all we can ever do. But you *will* be all right. Do you believe me?'

I want to, I want to be free of this, I want life to be the way it was before, but it all feels impossible – something so wrecked and ruined that it'll never be put back together the same way again. But she doesn't want to hear that; she wants to believe in something that might as well be magic.

I nod but know that's just another lie.

63.

As I drift off to an uneasy sleep, I try to hold onto the encouragement I've had lately. There's been bits of it from everywhere – Mr Baker, Olivia and Ash's mum. I know it should mean something but it's hard to believe in any of it.

On New Year's Eve, I wake at 6.00am but stay in bed and weave in and out of sleep. Just before lunch, I get up to face the day, trudge down the hall but instead of going into the kitchen, I walk out onto the veranda. It's murky outside – a plain, boring grey, like this day is no more special than any other. Yet this is it, this is the end of the year, the end of the decade.

This is the end of things.

I keep myself busy by playing pool, reading and prowling around my leather journal, until Ash calls and tells me to meet him at 7 pm. I eat and shower and tell Mum and Dad I'm going out – they warn me to be careful, because there are lots of idiots out for New Year's, like werewolves who come out for full moons – and then go to meet Ash at the corner.

'How're you feeling?' he says.

'I'm okay.'

We don't talk much as we walk down to Meadow Soccer Ground. The clouds are scattering. On the horizon, city buildings rise into a gorgeous golden evening that's tinged with crimson, like the year is trying to hold onto a certain beauty but is quietly bleeding and expiring.

Ash and me sit against one set of the goals and wait for people to show up. Riley and Felicia are first, each with an arm around the other's waist and Riley carrying all the drinks. He sets them down by Ash. Felicia looks at me and smiles and I know Riley's told her about my stuff and, instinctively, I know he's told her about my stuff so she's not focusing on his stuff.

Others show up as night falls, shadows like spectres coming to remind me what I'm not a part of. Ethan brings a stereo, which he sets down and tunes to a radio station which is doing a countdown to the New Year. He also brings two six-packs of beer. Everybody brings drinks and I get jealous that I don't even know if I can drink anymore on medication. I should check it. But it's annoying. Something I never would've once thought about now needs an examination.

A breeze sweeps across the ground and we stumble around in darkness, realising this hasn't been thought out too well. But then one of the light towers blinks on. Ethan comes out of the club room jingling keys.

'I did tell you all about my part-time job here, didn't I?' he says.

Kids cheer and now there's a real party atmosphere. I smell the alcohol, feel the radio vibrate, as it booms out music too loud so that the songs are distorted, and sense the energy as kids take up dancing. Gabriella spots me and comes over. She sits next to me, warm and soft.

'Hey,' she says.

'Hey.'

We're quiet. She keeps trying and I never know how to respond. And now it's like she's giving me a chance but only if I take the initiative.

'What did you write for the Boland?' I say. 'The essay about improving the world.'

'I wrote I couldn't wave a wand and improve the world,' Gabriella says, 'and all I could do was try improve myself and be the best person I could. I said if enough of us could do that, maybe we could start a chain reaction of change – us, those around us and the world.'

'That's clever.'

'You're not just saying that?'

'No. It is.'

Gabriella's face softens. In a movie, this is when the guy and the girl would lean in towards one another and kiss. I wish I was better at this.

'I'm not coming back next year,' Gabriella says.

'What?'

'Mum and Dad want me to transfer to this exclusive girls' college.'

'You're gonna do it?'

'I think, yeah. Because of the divorce, they're selling up, buying their own places. But they already had this planned before. Now with the Boland, they want to make sure I go to the best school.'

'That's…a shame.'

'Why?'

Felicia's smug little look haunts me. If I tell Gabriella the truth, I couldn't handle if she responded the same. *She won't, she won't, she' won't*, I tell myself. She's not Felicia.

But I'm still scared of putting it out there. Anyway, this isn't a love story. I'm not going to be saved by some cool girl. That's not her job. And those things do only happen in stories.

'I'm sorry,' I say.

Gabriella waits for more. She sighs and rises. 'Okay. I get the idea.'

She moves off. Felicia intercepts her and whispers in her ear. Gabriella looks back at me – not condemningly or anything like that. So that's good. But Felicia chuckles. Riley throws an arm around her waist and the two slip away. Felicia's probably told everybody – well, if Riley hasn't already, because I see now that that's Riley: he'd use it to make himself the centre of attention. I'm sure now that he started the rumours about Deanne. That's his style.

I know what's going to happen now – how many parties have I been to this year? I'm going to taper away into a shadow because I don't belong here. I belong to the darkness.

I pick faces out in the crowd: Ash and Kat, although Ash glances at me like I'm a dog who might stray away; Gabriella now dancing with her friends; Samantha with her friends; Lachlan and Mickey drinking a beer each; Ethan and Jake dancing with some of the sportier girls; I don't even know some of the faces. But they're a big ball of happy.

I get up and drift away. Fireworks pop – it's not New Year yet. I can tell that from the radio. Just premature poppers. Maybe I'll walk the streets. Only I hear a yelp, and then a cry of, 'Stop it!' I know the voice: Felicia.

Riley and her are silhouettes under the struts of the

scoreboard. They wrestle – well that's what it looks like. But it becomes clear Felicia's trying to break away from him. And then that her skirt is bundled up around her hips and her underwear halfway down her buttocks. She shrieks. Everything inside me balls into a single focus.

'Hey!' I say.

Riley and Felicia stop wrestling. I step forward and can just see Riley's face. He glowers at me. 'Can we have some privacy?' he says.

Felicia tries to wrench her hands free from him. 'I don't want privacy!'

'You fucking owe me!'

'I don't owe you shit. Let go!'

'Riley, let her go,' I say.

'Keep walking,' Riley tells him.

'Let her go.'

'This is none of your business.'

I hold my ground, my arms trembling.

'Fuck off!' Riley says.

'I'm not going anywhere until you let her go.'

'Or what? *What?* You weak, fucking cunt. What're you going do?'

I step forward, although my legs might be made of marble. Felicia breaks free and yanks her skirt down. Riley takes a few steps towards me. Now my heart's racing and there's an irony that at least I know *why*. I almost laugh at the stupidity of it all.

Riley stops in front of me and puts his hands on his hips.

'What the fuck is this?'

Ash is behind me – I smell the scotch first and then he brushes past me.

'It's fucking nothing, okay?' Riley says.

Other kids form an arc around us. Felicia runs to her friends and huddles with them. Riley's getting nervous, taking one step forward, then another back, knowing he's now losing face in front of everybody. He steps up to Ash and shoves him in the chest.

Ash sways but keeps his footing.

'So, this is what it's gonna come down to?' Riley says. 'You and me.'

Ash still doesn't say anything.

'Fuck you! Fuck you both!'

Riley tries to burst right between Ash and me, but Ash props his shoulder, not giving Riley any room. Riley pinballs off him, steadies and keeps going. Everybody parts for him so he can walk through, not looking back.

'You okay?' Ash says.

I nod.

'What about you?' Ash asks Felicia.

Felicia nods furiously. 'Thanks.' She puts a hand on my shoulder and says in a tone that's the most genuine tone she's ever used with me, 'Thanks.'

'Come on!' Ash says. 'Let's get back to it.' He shoos at them with his hands. 'You coming?'

'Just give me a minute, huh?'

'You sure?'

'Yeah.'

I stand there as everybody walks back into the spotlit area.

64.

It's the emptiness that gets me, expanding from the pit of my belly. My racing heart winds down until I'm sure it's still, although I know that should be impossible. The music from the radio fades and then it's just me.

Alone.

I climb the struts of the scoreboard, the wood coarse against my hands and reminding me that I'm still here, somewhere. The rickety trapdoor on the underside of the scoreboard squeals as I shove it open and I haul myself up into webs of blackness, although there's no roof, so the stars twinkle invitingly above me. I twirl as I reach for them, until I feel handholds in one of the walls and yank myself up bit by bit, scampering onto the top, crouching until I've balanced and then straightening, arms outstretched.

The wind whips me and gets into my clothes, cold fingers that prod and poke me and taunt me, as if to tell me I don't belong here. I have no idea how high I am from the soccer ground – ten or fifteen metres maybe? Hardly dramatic, but I'm terrible with heights. I totter around until I'm facing the creek. Meadow unfolds before me – an array of rooftops and streets that sprawl out to the city, the buildings just dots of lights.

Now total stillness overcomes me. Not the druggy

stillness, which is nice in its way, but a form of surrender, of resignation, after everything I've gone through. I want to hold onto it but know it won't last. The only real peace I've found through this is sleep, so maybe that's what I need, only a sleep I won't be getting up from. Like Ash said, a sleep without dreams. That'll be the end to this. And people will talk about me and remember me. That's the only time I'll have meaning with them – the only time I'll have meaning from my life.

Again, the wind buffets me, catching my outstretched arms until I'm sure it'll lift me. If I stepped off now, I could fly. I could soar away. It's like those other times I've thought that, but what jumps into my mind now is that moment I do step off, I'll disprove that I can fly and then there's nothing but the plummet.

The creek looms below me, although I can't make anything out in the darkness, but I'm sure it'd add another twenty feet to the drop. This is the best way. Deanne got it wrong, using a method that was slow. This can be quick.

I think of how jumping into it is like Aunt Mena's coffin being lowered into her grave. *Who will mourn for me?* That's what I thought that day. That's what I wondered.

I see people crowded around my grave: Mum and Dad and Steph and Olivia, Mr Baker, Ash would be there, probably even Riley, Samantha definitely, maybe Gabriella, my cousin Jim with his big head and new wife – the people pop in one by one until it goes from an intimate gathering to a crowd.

Fireworks pop over the city – a kaleidoscope fury that explodes across the sky. A single shriek behind me rises into a chorus of cries and then a roar as everybody welcomes the New Year. That emptiness, that apathy, shatters. I find it's just me, struggling to keep steady on top of a rickety old scoreboard.

I overbalance and in that instant I'm sure I'm going to fall, everything physical becomes slow motion, while all my thoughts race to hyper speed.

Why did *this* hit me? Nothing extraordinary's happened. It's not like there was a murder at school. There hasn't been some life-threatening illness. There are no vampires. There's nothing but what you'd expect from a normal school year – the sort of school year that schools everywhere are having.

And, in thinking that, it makes me realise how potent *this* is, because it doesn't need any of those things. It doesn't need some huge trigger. It doesn't need circumstances. It doesn't need the stuff you'd see in movies or in books.

This can just happen.

I remember thinking I was faulty. And that had given birth to this. Or this had come along and broken me and made me defective. But they're both simplifications – personalisation of this into something else, when the truth is much, much simpler.

I am this.

This is me.

And that's what this year has been about: *me*.

I think about all those everyday things I would miss doing, like hanging with Ash, playing pool with Steph and my unfinished, handwritten book that I was so enjoying. So many different experiences explode through my mind with the beauty and conflagration of the fireworks.

I think about the moment in the bathroom with

Gabriella during Ethan's birthday – unrealised maybe, but magic, nonetheless. Just like the times I looked for her at school, just like the moments I relished being with her. There have been similar times: hanging with Ash; or that first haircut with Olivia; or writing – moments that will always be timeless, which are worth holding onto, worth treasuring and aspiring to.

Like Gabriella wrote in her essay, there are no magic wands – not in real life. Everything is hard work. Getting anywhere is hard work. And it can be shit and painful and ugly but it's the only way to make the journey.

I might scoff at Jim but he's pushed himself to get where he is. There's a courage in that – a truth that makes it worthwhile. I recognise that now – even though I missed the Boland, I could only get that far because I did push myself. It's better than what Riley did, giving up, showing only that he had the potential but doing so little with it because he preferred to sneer at anything good.

And there's Gabriella – she must've had so much to juggle, dealing with her parents' divorce, but doing the schoolwork she needed to so she was a chance for the Boland. I think about the day we learned that Deanne had tried to take her own life. Gabriella went and got the big card and went around and got us all to sign it. Even with all the shit she had going on, she could still think about somebody else.

The wind swirls and I'm sure it nudges me just that inch I need to give me a chance to regain my balance. Everything snaps back into normal speed. I clamber down inside the scoreboard, carefully finding handholds and footholds, then jump the rest of the way to the floor. The planks of the scoreboard floor boom as I land. I find my way out, and climb the rest of the way down, then walk back onto the soccer ground.

Everybody's grouped together, wishing each other happy New Year. Ash greets me with a high handshake, Samantha hugs me and kisses me on the cheek and then Gabriella hugs me too but then grabs my face between both hands and kisses me full on the lips. Bodies jostle around me until I'm in the middle of everybody and everybody's celebrating the boundless promise of something new, of something unexplored, of what could be.

And that's when I realise something.

It's not so bad being here.

ACKNOWLEDGEMENTS

I've written lots of stories over my life in various formats – novels, prose, screenplays – but nothing has meant more to me than *This*.

I grew up with mental health challenges throughout the 1980s, a time when our awareness of such conditions and avenues for treatment were limited. Stigma surrounded mental health. You didn't speak to anybody, and hid everything as best as you could.

Lots of what happens in *This* is drawn from my own teenage life – so if there's anything that seems unrealistic, no, it actually happened. (A psychiatrist *did* once tell me directly I was heading for a nervous breakdown.) Attitudes were different. Treatment? Without a frame of reference, I don't really know.

Ultimately, I tried to keep everything as genuine as possible. Often, mental health issues are represented as a charming quirk in fiction, or it becomes emblematic – it becomes *who* the person is, which is unfair. People are a lot more complicated than that and shouldn't be defined by something they're going through.

A big thank you to Blaise van Hecke, who believed in this story and really found a fascinating charm in it; to Kim Lock, who is always so open and insightful, and whose suggestions are always so accurate; Bel Woods, for her understanding of the YA market and how the story fit; Tom O'Connell, who offered valuable feedback from a personal perspective; Phillip Tsafkopoulos and Arna Delle-vegini their insight; Sally Bird, for her understanding and support; my writing group of Blaise van Hecke (again), Jasmine Powell, Beau Hillier, and Gina Boothroyd; my dear friend Steve Tosevski, who lived through and survived the 1980s with me; and my family for their unending support.

Thank you to the Katharine Susannah Prichard Fellowship. *This* was selected in 2020, and I spent two weeks over in Western Australia obsessively reworking the story as the world around me (and everybody) went into pandemic mode. I got to live in a bubble before the bubble was imposed, and it gave me the space to find the core of the story.

Finally, the *hugest* thank you to Anna Solding and Gillian Hagenus and MidnightSun Publishing for taking a chance on *This*, as well as for their thoughtful editing. Thanks, Anna and Gillian, for getting behind the story, challenging me where I needed it, and cleaning up the mistakes I left behind.

And a thank you to everybody who's supported my writing journey, and responsible for making my writing a reality.

I wrote the first draft in 2016, and here it is seven years later. Its journey is instructive in a way – it shows that no matter how difficult everything gets, no matter how impossibly our challenges try to contain us, that we can find a way through to something better.

ABOUT THE AUTHOR

Lazaros Zigomanis is an author, screenwriter, and filmmaker. He's had four novels published, and his short stories and articles have appeared in various print and digital journals. He has also had screenplays optioned, and a raft of screenplays have placed in numerous competitions and awards.